The sum of all my parts

The once beautiful and vivacious Mariam, now old, is leading a quiet life in a Vellore suburb, where the highlight of her day is teaching crochet to four young women. While Nimra finds crocheting an escape from an oppressive household, Arifa, a busy housewife, seeks solace in the calm it affords. Cheerful Amreen, who longs for a child, attends for the camaraderie and gossip. For subdued Shaista, crochet allows her to retreat to a simpler past—devoid of a forced marriage and early pregnancy.

As Mariam reminisces about her life—the choices she made, the man she loved and the granddaughter who is lost to her—she resonates uniquely with each of the women, emboldening them to break free from their binding domestic problems. Mariam convinces them to recreate an elaborate crochet bedspread she hopes to present to her granddaughter at her wedding.

How does Mariam view her past through her cataractic vision? Despite her Western upbringing, why is Mariam's granddaughter unable to reconcile with her grandmother's past? How do the other four women reorganise their lives? Exquisitely outlining human folly, heartbreak and triumph of the spirit, *The Sum of All My Parts* is a gripping tale.

The sum of all my parts

ANDALEEB WAJID

AMARYLLIS

AMARYLLIS
An imprint of Manjul Publishing House Pvt. Ltd.
• 7/32, Ansari Road, Daryaganj, New Delhi 110 002
Website: www.manjulindia.com
Registered Office:
10, Nishat Colony, Bhopal 462 003 – India

ISBN 978-93-87383-81-4

This edition first published in 2018

Cover Design by DRAWATER by MISHTA ROY

Printed and bound in India by Thomson Press (India) Ltd.

For Amma, my grandmother,
and her love for crochet.

Part One

chapter 1

Vellore - 2011

Mariam rubbed her papery-dry thumb against her index finger, mimicking the motion of a prayer bead on its way down to meet the others in the tasbih. She glanced at the old Ajanta clock on the yellowing wall, her eyes willing the hands to move faster. The only sound in the room was that of the ceiling fan as it spun around in lazy circles, barely dispelling the heat.

She moved the pallu of her sari aside to let that semblance of a breeze from the fan cool her sweating neck, and then fanned herself with the pallu. As the sweat evaporated leaving her skin cold and clammy, she got up slowly, her back refusing to cooperate with the immediacy that her mind expected.

The girls would be coming soon. She stood up, a little unsteady and disoriented, walked the few short steps to the Godrej almirah in the corner, and turned its rusty handle down. The door opened with a loud creak and Mariam winced as she allowed the musty memories to sneak out, one mote at a time.

And yet, even though everything came flooding back to her as it did every single day, she focused on removing the plastic bag that was kept at her eye level. The bag finally slid out, it's thick, eroded, squarish, plastic handles creating a sensation of pin pricks along her lined fingers.

She shook it gently, as if by doing so she could dislodge all the memories along with the dust. The old grandfather clock in the hall outside chimed four times. Mariam sat on her bed and inhaled deeply the air that spoke of her loneliness before the others came, bringing with them their various scents. Jasmine-scented hair oil, mehendi-ed palms, Pond's Dreamflower talcum powder, sweat on some days and fresh soap on others.

Mariam positioned herself on the bed and sat more comfortably as she pulled out the sheets that everyone would be passing around. She glared at one corner, certain that it was an oil spot. One of the girls must have been scratching her head while reading the instructions! Shaking her head, she looked up with relief as the doorbell buzzed with its distinctive shriek. Deepa unfolded herself from the mat where she had been dozing in the hall, and went to swing open the door with her usual insolence.

Half an hour earlier

The urgency in Arifa's actions was so frenzied that it looked almost comical—whether it was in the way she pushed spoon after spoon of mashed rice mixed with the day's curry into her two-year-old son's mouth, or the hurried manner she served lunch to her mother-in-law before sitting down herself to eat desperate, quick mouthfuls of tepid rice covered in hot curry. Then she sat cross-legged and rocked her son, her knees moving so fast that Armaan, used to a slow drowsy rhythm, refused to fall asleep.

'Hurry up! Sleep, Armaan! I have to... ' she bit her lower lip stopping herself just in time. Armaan would never sleep if he learnt that she stole away while he slept, so she continued the rocking motion, throwing desperate glances at the clock in her room and at her son's alert face. All that hurry, and for nothing, she sighed as she slowed down the rocking. She couldn't help it—the need to be on time, every single day, was like a challenge that she gave herself. She couldn't figure out why she wasn't laidback like the other women she knew or why she couldn't dawdle and let everything happen on its own steam.

She ruffled Armaan's hair absently and rubbed his forehead with the tips of her fingers. He pushed her fingers away once, but then allowed her to massage his head. For all of one minute, the frenzy inside Arifa came to a standstill as she observed her baby, who was growing up into a toddler. She noted the way his eyelashes swept up in an arch, and she smiled as she followed the line of his nose with her eyes, at the slight dip in his chin. She wondered at the marvellous way in which he resembled his father and how that thought made her feel wistful and angry at the same time. She noticed how his eyes finally closed in an almost magical way as sleep claimed him. She slowed down the rocking motion and finally stopped it completely, sure that he was fast asleep.

Gently, she lifted his sleep-heavy body, arranged his head on the pillow and covered him with a light sheet. Then, once again urgency returned to her actions. She glanced at the clock. It was ten minutes to four and it was imperative that she be there on the dot. If the others came late, it wasn't her problem. *She* had to be on time.

She splashed cold water on her face, scrubbed it hard with soap and then patted it dry. Standing before her small dressing table, she unbraided her thick plait in brisk movements that made it look as if she were breaking a loaf of bread into hundreds of pieces. She used a generous amount of jasmine-scented oil to make sure there were no tangles in her hair as she combed it vigorously and redid a braid.

Finally, she picked up her bag, checked to see if everything was there, wore her burkha, and wrapped the scarf around her head, making sure there was enough left to cover her face on the road.

In the adjacent room, her mother-in-law was getting ready for her afternoon nap. Arifa popped in quickly and said goodbye before crossing the sunny courtyard, a common feature in old Vellore homes, opened the heavy door and stepped outside.

Earlier that day

There was a picture of Jayalalitha on the Tamil newspaper that was slowly being covered with dried mehendi grounds. Nimra rubbed her hands together, wincing a bit as she pulled away at the mehendi that seemed reluctant to leave her palms. Finally, with a last brush of her hands, she stood up, lifted the paper carefully and held it at the edges to ensure that the mehendi grounds lay at the centre in a line.

'Boo!'

Nimra dropped the paper, startled and dismayed to see the mehendi all over the mosaic floor where it would inevitably get under everybody's chappals and leave rust-coloured streaks when they went to the bathroom. She turned to her twelve-year-old sister Saira and shook her head, anger radiating from every pore.

'Get a broom and sweep this mess, right now!' she told her. Saira stuck out her tongue and shook her head.

'*You* dropped it. *You* sweep it up,' and saying so, she ran away to her room gleefully, her pigtails swinging behind her back.

Ever since the beginning of summer, Saira had become impossible. At first, Nimra ignored her antics but as the days went on and nobody noticed how atrocious Saira's behaviour was, Nimra took the matter to her father.

The outcome of that had startled her into silence. Her father decided they would give Saira her own room, a concept unheard of in her house. Until then, Saira and she had tossed and turned on two corners of a lumpy-mattress-covered bed while one of the maids had slept on the hard floor, cocooned under a scratchy blanket. There hadn't been anything like a personal room. But there was now.

Nimra had looked at her father, wishing she could communicate to him as easily as Saira did. In the days before Saira, when her mother had been alive, Nimra used to clamber onto his lap, slide down his chequered lungi until she could swing in the cradle between his ankles. Was it the same Abba? Was it the same *her*? As she yanked the broom out from its corner and swept up the scattered mehendi, she paused to scan the length of her arms and her palms.

She was immune to this beauty now. The fragrance of

henna was no longer inviting, ensconced with special secrets. It was something she resented.

'What happened?'

Nimra looked up at the woman standing at the door of the kitchen and shook her head. No use complaining about Saira to her. She wouldn't believe any of it.

'Nothing,' she muttered as she deposited the mehendi grounds and newspaper in the dustbin and walked away to the room that she now slept in. Once inside, she threw open the cupboard door and rummaged behind her clothes until she found the plastic bag. This wasn't *her* room. It was where she slept and where her clothes were kept, but through some unspoken arrangement, she was unable to brand it or brandish it as hers.

She sat at the edge of the bed, glad that Saira didn't know how much these outings meant to her. She pulled out the white lace doily and placed it on the bed, her heart filling with the simple joy of looking at something beautiful, magnified, because *she* had created it. She traced the edges slowly, watching the contrast of her hennaed hands over the white yarn; the slight roughness sparked a memory, one that she'd been trying to smother unsuccessfully. For once she gave in, closing her eyes as she drew her thumb across the woven yarn. But the sensation had evaporated, and she would need more than a mere touch to evoke it.

chapter 2

'Can we at least increase the fan speed?' Arifa asked, looking up at the slow-moving blades in increasing frustration and back at the slim steel needle she held in her hands. Why did she have to sweat so much? As always, her palms had started perspiring first, leaving damp blotches on the yarn and making the long needle slip from her grip. She placed the unfinished work in her lap and wiped her palms on her knees before picking it up again.

'It's on full speed,' Mariam responded, not looking at Arifa. Her eyes were drawn to the intricately woven circles that were emerging from the nimble fingers of these young women. To Mariam, the image was never clear enough, never bright, never sharp. For some time now, her eyes presented her with blurred images that lacked definition. It often felt as if one edge were bleeding into another. This was highly annoying for someone who had spent most of her life analysing the details of her existence.

'Bring it here,' she finally ordered Arifa who made a brisk 'tsk' sound as she looked up at Mariam.

'But, Amma, I'm almost done with this circle. Let me finish it first!' Arifa said as she bent her head back towards the doily.

'Sit here with me. I want to see how you do it,' Mariam replied, rocking slowly. Arifa bit the inside of her cheek and got up. She knew that Amma would turn it over and narrow her eyes at the messy tangle of threads and admonish her. Why on earth did the back of the doily have to be neat? Wasn't it enough that it looked pretty from the front?

She bunched her sari pleats together and got up, leaving them to swish down her knees as she walked towards Mariam. A quick glance at Nimra's handiwork showed that she was way ahead of everyone else and that irked her. The others, Amreen and Shaista, hadn't showed up today and Arifa knew that the lack of gossip had made today's session a bit dull and lifeless. Nimra hardly spoke to anyone, so naturally she always finished first.

Arifa sat down on the bed in a huff and thrust her unfinished doily towards Mariam who peered at its back first. She sighed and shook her head and handed it back to Arifa.

'Continue,' she said and Arifa bent her head towards the yarn, deftly wrapping yarn around the hook, pushing it in and pulling it out.

'Too tight,' Mariam muttered. 'You're holding it too tight. See, your stitches should be firm, not pulling at each other's throats for existence.'

What do you know? Arifa thought irreverently as she gazed at the old woman's bent head. Mariam looked at the doily myopically and shook her head; Arifa bit her lower lip.

'Redo this,' Mariam ordered and Arifa rolled her eyes.

'The whole thing?' she asked Mariam, feeling defiant. Mariam nodded.

'If you undo one section, the yarn is going to be frayed. Just snip it off here and tie a knot and start a new one.'

Nimra's head shot up in interest and Arifa subdued the urge to make a face at her. Really, she was being silly. She was at least ten years older than Nimra and the poor girl had done nothing to provoke her.

I'll show you, she yelled at no one in particular, in her mind, as she cut the yarn and rolled a fresh piece in her hands to make the slip knot.

'Easy, easy,' Mariam said, stilling the furiousness in Arifa's hands by pressing down on them with her own dry and frail ones.

'You know what you're doing, right?' she asked Arifa, who scowled a little and spoke through gritted teeth.

'Making a doily. Learning to crochet from you,' she spoke in curt syllables.

Mariam shook her head and smiled. 'Yes, yes, but the day that crochet needle becomes an extension of your finger and you let your mind relax is when you're going to finish learning.'

'Relax?' Arifa asked, the thought seeming to inspire horror in her.

'Why didn't your friends come today?' Mariam asked her instead, her eyes drawn towards the empty spaces on the mat where Amreen and Shaista usually sat.

'I don't know,' Arifa shrugged, feeling patronised, placated and angry all at the same time.

'But don't you people do that thing with your phones? Didn't you ask them?' Mariam asked, looking at Arifa with interest.

'SMS? I... didn't think of it,' Arifa replied, getting up from the bed. Mariam stopped her and she sat down again.

'Your problem is that your brain runs too fast. You need to slow down a bit,' Mariam advised gently and was surprised to see the near-hostile look that came into Arifa's eyes.

'Are you teaching us to crochet or something else?' Arifa asked Mariam and got up before she could reply.

Mariam didn't answer and watched her as she sat down next to Nimra in a huff and started the same in-and-out movements with her crochet needle and yarn, furious as ever as the chain emerged from her fingers.

'Nimra, come and show me what you've done,' Mariam said, deciding that it would be best to leave Arifa alone for some time.

Nimra looked at her uncertainly and got up, brushing her kameez with one hand. She sat at the edge of the bed, her head bent demurely. Mariam curbed the irritation she felt on seeing this assumed pose.

'You're not a bride at the moment, so you can sit straight,' she spoke the thought as soon as it formulated in her mind, regretting immediately when she saw the girl lift her head in surprise. There was a sense of betrayal in her eyes and Mariam rubbed her forehead absently.

'I meant,' she started slowly, 'just... just sit straighter. I think you've got used to sitting this way.'

Nimra didn't respond and instead handed her the doily she had been working on. Mariam took it in her hands and sighed. Two students, complete opposites. Would they be able to learn it in time?

Although she was inspecting the doily and inwardly grimacing at the loose stitches that defied shape or form, she glanced at Nimra every now and then. This one was a dreamer. Mariam closed her eyes and tried to go forty-five, no fifty years back, when she'd been twenty. By then she had already been married and had her first child. No, a few years further. When she'd been seventeen. Her throat dried up but her memories were intact. Mariam sat straighter and focused on the crochet lesson of the day.

'Where's the tension?' she asked Nimra. 'Why is everything so loose? And didn't I tell you not to proceed to the next row until I said it was okay?'

'I... I can't seem to hold it tightly enough for some reason,' Nimra spoke softly to her chin.

'Nimra, look at me,' Mariam said, infusing her voice with a little force. 'This won't do. What has happened to both of you today? Arifa is doing it too tightly, and you're doing it so loose!'

Nimra seemed upset at the criticism. 'But... isn't it pretty?' she asked Mariam, holding the doily by two edges.

'If you're looking at making a banian, maybe,' Mariam retorted and Nimra's face flushed. 'Where's the shape? It looks like the roti Deepa sometimes makes for me. Like the map of Hindustan.'

'Amma, why do you always say "Hindustan" and not India?' Arifa asked, looking up, all her resentment dissolving in the face of her curiosity and gratitude that Nimra was not getting any praise either.

'I've always... it's been... I don't know,' Mariam faltered. 'Here, hold it like this,' she swiftly changed the topic and held Nimra's hand firmly, showing her how to maintain tension in the stitches.

The hour was soon up and since Amreen and Shaista were not there, Arifa didn't linger when Mariam signalled that the day's class was done.

'Always in a hurry, that one,' Mariam murmured when Arifa

rushed out of the door, much like a speed post on its way to meet its eager recipient.

Nimra was collecting her things and Mariam didn't expect her to reply. But for some reason, she couldn't keep herself from asking.

'Before, or after?'

Nimra's eyes shot up again and she pressed straight, even teeth down on her lower lip as she answered, 'Before.'

chapter 3

Mariam pushed aside the curtain in the hall, and through a chink, saw Nimra walk away. She stared after her into the distance even though her slightly hunched burkha-clad figure had turned the corner and disappeared from view. She did this sometimes: stare at the air until it solidified before her rheumy eyes, molecule by molecule, and mocked her.

Biting her lower lip with her wobbly canine, she let the curtain fall back in place and out of habit, rotated and pushed the tooth back into the socket from which it had begun to dislodge. She didn't go back to her room. Years ago, she had read about plants that swallowed up insects whole and the concept had made her shudder. At times, she remembered that as she lay on her bed in her room. She fancied her room to be a giant plant, spewing digestive juices to erode her slowly, absorbing her essence until there was nothing left but her shrunken bones.

Mariam's house had been constructed to replicate their house in Vellore. Amid a growing number of garish bungalows, hers was the only house with a tiled roof, stuccoed walls, and red oxide flooring – a bunch of traditional clichés that her children had slowly learnt to resent. Even the sunny courtyard in the centre, made cheerful with a random array of potted plants, had failed to impress them.

When her daughter married and moved to Chennai, Mariam had never thought she'd see so little of her. But since Asma completely invested herself in her new family and life, she hardly ever looked back. Two years ago, she died of a prolonged fever. Her grandchildren were strangers and Mariam watched with resigned trepidation as her daughter's husband and children snipped off their connection with her, leaving only jagged edges and loneliness.

Deepa had gone to wash the tea cups after the girls had left and Mariam sat down in the empty hall that resonated with the silences of a once alive house. Sometimes at night, the silences crept upon her stealthily, as though homing in for a kill and she would get up gasping, her eyes quickly travelling to Deepa who slept on the floor. Mariam leaned back against the hard, wooden sofa and looked up at the intricately carved wooden ceiling interspersed with beams, until her neck ached.

Slowly, she got up and went to her room and returned the plastic bag to the almirah. Crouching a little, she hesitantly pulled out a bundle that had been wrapped in a once vibrant pink cotton sari from the shelf below. The colours had leached out leaving the cloth soft and fuzzy, but nestled within it was one of her most precious possessions.

Feeling foolish, she pulled it out and straightened up. Small popping sounds from her back made her wince but she ignored them and lifted the bundle to her cheek and rubbed it gently. She felt the contours of the contents with a light hand and debated whether she should open it. Finally, ignoring the arthritis that had turned her fingers into useless swollen appendages, she untied the knot at the top of the bundle, which led to various others at odd angles. Prising open tight knot after knot, she released the twenty-year-old fragrance into the air.

Later that night

The curtains were drawn and it almost tricked the senses into believing that the room was possibly cool because of the darkness that embraced it. But the air inside hung heavy and was stifling. Shaista curbed the urge to bite down on her knuckle and imagined herself heaving and taking in huge gulps of air. She kept her eyes tightly closed and forced herself to see an open field, the sharp icy tint of a blue sky, and if she focussed, she could inhale the aroma frantically released by the parched earth as it sucked in the raindrops.

But the illusion lasted for the nth of a second and before long, Shaista knew she was back inside her room, sleeping next to her husband of five months, her arms rigid, her body tensed, the back of her neck pooled with sweat, her eyes piercing the darkness to see the deeply shadowed ceiling.

He sniffled and turned and Shaista momentarily lost her control, panic cutting deep ridges within her throat. She sat up, breathing loudly, audibly, imagining herself clawing at the air.

'What?' he asked sleepily. Shaista shook her head, knowing he couldn't see her as she swung her feet down and desperately made her way towards the bathroom. The smell inside was not pleasant, despite being masked by phenyl, soaps and shampoo. She gagged and covered her mouth as something from inside threatened to spill over. She leaned towards the washbasin, her eyes registering mundane details like the grime settled deeply between the tiles, the drain flies that dozed near the mirror, her toothbrush next to his. She lifted her head a fraction to see her sweaty forehead and unbidden, an image swam before her eyes. She retched and vomited loudly, wishing it wouldn't wake up anyone, especially him. She ran water in the basin, wiped her mouth and splashed her face with the tepid water from the tap. Dabbing her face with the edge of her pallu, she stood for some more time in the bathroom, glad for the light but resigned to the fact that she must go back inside.

Stepping into the darkness that swallowed her, she skirted the bed and reached the small table near the door where she groped the air till her fingers connected with the jug of water. She sipped the water slowly, letting it slide down her scarred throat. A chink of light from outside had barely made its way inside the room and Shaista stared at it hungrily, imagining forms and shapes being defined in that weak zero-watt bulb outside.

She made her way back to the bed, knowing that he was probably awake but aware that he wouldn't do anything. She had lied to him the previous night that she had her period when in fact she was supposed to have had it two days ago. Her body was like clockwork, never late and yes, she knew what that meant. It terrified her completely, but for now, there was reprieve.

As she adjusted her body to the warmth of the bed, she thought about the class and what would have happened there. Crochet had been an excuse for her to get out of the house and now, two weeks later, she wished it wouldn't end as she logically knew it would. Her work reposed in her large shoulder bag, untouched for two days now. She had been so engrossed in it when she began that even her dreams comprised knots and shapes emerging from the cotton-wool-like mass that was her sub-conscious.

It had started as a friendly competition between the four of them, to see who would finish the doily first. She turned her head towards her sleeping husband, anger making a surprising entry among the gamut of emotions she was feeling at the moment, much like a magician's assistant—there one moment, poof the next! He couldn't possibly have meant what he said earlier.

She wondered who had finished making the doily first.

Much later that night

Images from the TV flickered quietly, shadows leaping across their bed, dancing, dissolving, disturbing. Amreen buried her face in the pillow, inhaling her own scents, and shut her eyes tightly. She finally let out a deep sigh and sat up. Her husband looked at her, surprised.

'What are you doing?' she asked him, feeling resigned and yet, the slightest bit indulgent.

'Movie,' he replied, smiling back at her boyishly, eyes back on the screen instantly.

'Without dialogues?' she asked him, edging a bit closer to him.

'Didn't want to wake you up,' he replied and she poked the side of his tummy, the little bit that jiggled slightly and *always* got tickled easily. He reacted as expected, jumping a little as though scalded by a hot iron.

'Amreen!' he admonished her in a loud whisper, eyes back to following the movie on the TV.

'I wasn't asleep in the first place,' she muttered. 'This light from the TV is too distracting. I feel like it's playing inside my head.'

'Hello?' she didn't nudge him again but rubbed her forehead as he continued watching the movie on mute.

She fell back on the bed and dramatically sighed. Installing a TV in the room had been the worst idea. She wished she could undo it, send back the TV that her parents had gifted her for her third anniversary, as though it could magically diminish the disappointment in her life. Amreen felt it keenly at times, the waves of unmet expectations that washed over her, finely tuned to a tiny little point until she wanted to turn to everyone and tell them to back off. This constant feeling of failure was eroding the edges of her marriage and she feared it would reach the strong pulsating core as well.

She turned around and wished she'd gone to the class today. But her husband's sister had come from her in-law's place for the day and there was so much work to be done that it hadn't seemed nice to leave everything and go away for her one hour of pleasure. In her mind's eye, she saw the crochet hook moving in and out hypnotically, crafting a legacy with yarn.

chapter 4

Two months later

Lips smacked together noisily as the aamchur—salt-encrusted dried mango pieces—were passed around and everyone picked up one to nibble at. Everyone except Mariam and Nimra. Mariam actually shivered when she saw the aamchur and shook her head, waved her hands as though by virtue of doing so she could physically push away those tantalising smells that had become so difficult to bear.

'This is so… so…' Shaista couldn't find words to describe the keen sense of pleasure she felt after relishing a piece of the dried mango. It tingled her scalp, and saliva pooled below her tongue and she ran over the tastes in her mouth, bringing alive the person she had buried deep inside, months ago when she came to Vellore for the first time. She refused to think that she was probably enjoying the sourness more because of her condition.

'Why aren't you having any?' Arifa asked Nimra as she sucked the tip of her piece noisily. They were all eating aamchur because of Shaista in the first place. They had been in the class for nearly twenty minutes when she looked up, sweat dotting her forehead, her chest feeling compressed as though it would turn inwards, panic marring her features. This feeling of claustrophobia had never occurred outside her bedroom until now.

'What is it?' Mariam asked, looking concerned. Instantly everyone had kept aside their work and crowded around Shaista until Mariam ordered Deepa to get some aamchur and a glass of water. Almost immediately, the feeling of terror vanished as Shaista drank the water and nibbled on the aamchur. The bottle in which Mariam had stored the dark, nearly black pieces, was soon passed around and everyone forgot about work, enjoying the taste of raw mango that had been sufficiently dulled by the sun and perked up with a generous dose of salt.

Nimra looked at Arifa uncomfortably. 'I... it's... it's not good for my skin,' she said. Arifa snorted, popping the piece inside her mouth and calmly chewing it even though it sent tingles up her jawline, making her wince.

'You unmarried girls have to take care of your skin and all. Thank god, I don't have to,' she said as she leaned forward to take one more piece before Deepa pulled back the bottle and twisted the cap around it.

'Arrey!' Arifa protested. Amreen giggled.

'Don't you know? *She* runs this house, not Amma?' she said as she carefully ate the last bit of aamchur piece she had.

Mariam looked around at the women and shook her head. 'If you girls have finished, then get back to your work now.'

Arifa looked at Mariam with the slightest hint of animosity before she picked up her piece and continued the round of treble stitches that Mariam had taught her some days back, twisting the yarn over the hook twice and concentrating on getting them right.

Everyone else had also picked up their work and continued, a little energised by the break, but no longer in the mood to work silently.

'How long have you lived in Vellore?' Amreen asked Shaista as she snipped an end with a pair of scissors, tied the end into a knot and tucked it within the fringe of the piece she was working on.

Shaista looked down and continued working, as though she hadn't heard her. Over her head, Amreen caught Arifa's glance and shrugged. The exchange was not missed by Mariam who watched the girls with her keen and observant eyes.

She reached a decision impulsively and cleared her throat, ignoring the frantic protests by the saner part of her brain. Everyone stopped and looked up.

'I… I want you all to help me with something,' she said and sensed the wariness that appeared in some eyes. They probably thought she needed money.

The skin around her eyes had thinned and she winced as she pressed her fingertips to her eyes. Her fingers were scarred and scratched her face instead of giving it relief. She got down from her perch on the bed and pushed aside their drooped shoulders with her knees as she walked towards the almirah.

Words were banal at times. They couldn't quite express what she wanted to tell them, although she suspected that she didn't really know what she wanted to say in the first place. It had been a nebulous idea that had solidified one warm afternoon two months back, after a phone call. At her age, it was hard to slot that call as life-changing. But it had made her realise how much she wanted to do this.

She felt their eyes on her back as she pulled out the bundle that she had replaced with care, back in its old spot. This time the knots were tied clumsily and she offered the bundle to Amreen, asking her to open them. Amreen did as she was told but before she could open the flaps of the sari, Mariam took it back from her and returned to her spot on the bed. 'Come here, all of you,' she said. She noted that Arifa and Amreen looked curious while Shaista looked bored, and Nimra, indifferent.

She pushed aside the flaps of the sari, pulled out the warm weight from within, and opened it carefully. Obviously, no one was impressed. Then, feeling like a magician, she threw open the crocheted bedspread with a flourish. Its folds draped and fell over the sides of her bed, dipping gently to the ground.

'What do you think?' she asked her students who were quiet.

'It's pretty,' Amreen offered. Annoyed, Mariam lifted a corner and sniffed it gently, inhaling the faint possibility of baby powder and the essence of a most beloved person. Her frown slipped away from her face as she reminisced quietly.

'What is this, Amma?' Arifa asked, crumpling the corner nearest her; Mariam felt rage leap within her, but she tried to control herself.

'Don't do that,' she spoke through clenched teeth as she tugged the bedspread away from her. She gathered it close to her bosom and hugged it, closing her eyes, wishing, wishing, wishing that she had made different choices in her life.

'This bed spread,' she started, loosening her grip on it and brushing away the wetness from her eyes, 'I made it for a very special person, many years ago. I need your help now to recreate it.' She skimmed her roughened hands over the pattern lovingly, finally shaking out the bedspread gently, bringing the top and bottom together to fold it.

Murmurs broke out instantly.

'What? Are you insane?' Amreen screeched and immediately lowered her voice. 'Sorry, but it could take years to finish it!'

'There are four of you. Each can do a corner,' Mariam said, prepared to tackle all forms of resistance.

'But we're not ready to take up something like this!' Arifa protested. Mariam looked at them all, their faces wary and hostile.

'What if you each do an individual project with me before we start this?' Mariam asked. 'Will you feel ready then?'

'What kind of project?' Shaista asked, her eyes running over the beautifully crafted stitches that seemed to populate the bedspread.

'Make something. Anything. To express yourself. To represent you,' Mariam said. Nimra looked up at her swiftly.

'Does this bedspread represent you?' Nimra asked in a quiet voice. Everyone fell silent.

'Aah,' Mariam nodded. 'That is a story I will tell when I have seen what each of you can make.'

'But we're just learning!' protested Arifa. 'How will we make anything good?'

'Who said anything about good?' retorted Mariam.

'And when do you want to do this?' Amreen asked.

'Sooner rather than later. I could die. So why take the chance?' Mariam said, rocking slowly, a smile on her face.

'Why?' Nimra asked. Mariam stared at her until she was a fuzzy blur in her eyes.

chapter 5

Nimra looked around the empty room, feeling uneasy. Her eyes scanned the spots where everyone usually sat, and although a part of her was glad that she didn't have to make small talk, she almost wished they were there. But Mariam had wanted to give individual attention to each of them as they started on their personal projects and she had suggested they come at different times.

Nimra was glad that her timings ensured that Saira was never at home when she left for her classes. Her father left for his shop at 10:30 every morning, so she helped in whatever way she could in the kitchen till 11:30, and then stole out. Nimra's house was in Sathuvacheri, a suburb of Vellore, with many leafy lanes and large bungalows that made it difficult to remember that you were living in Vellore. All the others, except Amreen, lived nearby. Amreen lived in Vellore town and was usually late for the class as a result.

Nimra looked up as Mariam hobbled in, a half-smile on her face. She indicated to Nimra that she should sit up with her on the bed. Nimra got up, a half-heartedly and rubbed the cold steel of the hook between her fingers.

'So, you have decided what you will make?' she asked Nimra.

Nimra nodded, and pulled out one of the pattern sheets which had a coloured picture on it. It was a pink and white doily with a pineapple motif, something easy and doable, which was why Nimra had liked it. She didn't feel the need to prove anything to anyone but was glad that at the end of the class, she would have created something out of mere air and yarn.

Mariam looked at it sceptically and held the page close to her face.

'Why don't you wear spectacles?' Nimra asked her before she could stop herself. It was no business of hers but the question had been asked already. Mariam looked up at her and smiled.

'Never needed them,' she said.

'But I know you can't see clearly,' Nimra murmured. Mariam didn't say anything.

'Okay, for this one, start with a choti of 10,' she said and Nimra nodded. Mariam spoke funny. Instead of chain, she called it choti, which meant braid in Urdu. Of course, the chain and the choti were one and the same. It was just that Nimra had got accustomed to reading the instructions on the pattern sheets in English, and she found Mariam's Urdu instructions a little unsettling. At times, she felt she could do without her once she learnt to decipher the English instructions, but it felt a bit disloyal.

'Where did you get these sheets?' Nimra asked, once again surprising herself with her inquisitiveness. The sheets were glossy and yellowed, a sign that they probably belonged to a foreign magazine that had been in circulation eons ago.

Mariam ignored her question and showed her how to follow the choti of 10 with a round of single crochet stitches. The tension in the stitches was not right. She was holding them too loose as usual.

'A little firm. Little more,' Mariam coaxed her.

Nimra tried to wrap the yarn around her finger tightly but when she had to pull the yarn into the hook, it loosened anyhow. She tugged it around her finger tightly once more, until it cut into her index finger almost painfully. Mariam shook her head.

'I don't know why you make it so much more difficult than it is,' she said.

'But, Amma, it's easy for you, I'm sure. You're an expert,' Nimra muttered.

'I wasn't always an expert,' Mariam countered with a smile. Nimra looked at her curiously. She had never really wondered about Mariam until now. Why did she live alone with Deepa? Didn't she have children? Or grandchildren?

Focusing on the stitches of the next round, Nimra realised they were complicated and she fumbled. Mariam held Nimra's hand with a firmness that belied her age, her dry hands chafing Nimra's as she showed her how to make sure her stitches were tight and even.

'So how did you become an expert?' Nimra asked her.

'I had a good teacher,' Mariam replied. They worked in silence for a while and Nimra realised she was beginning to enjoy it. Without the banter of the others, Arifa's competitive edge, Shaista's moody silences and Amreen's gossip, she realised she could focus better. When she had finished a couple of the rounds, she looked up and saw Mariam smiling at her.

'You know why I love crochet?' she asked.

Nimra shook her head as she tried to focus on the stitches once more.

'Crochet allows me to think my favourite thoughts while still creating something beautiful with my hands. That's why,'

Mariam grinned, leaning closer towards Nimra in a conspiratorial manner.

Nimra laughed a little uneasily.

'So, have any more people come to see you?' Mariam asked, and the smile that was forming on Nimra's face collapsed immediately. She shook her head.

'But they will,' she added in a quiet voice.

'It's part of life,' Mariam murmured almost apologetically. 'All of us have to go through it.'

'But so many times!' Nimra whispered, her crochet lying in her lap, forgotten.

'Something will change,' Mariam reassured her, wishing she could tell her words that were true. To her surprise, Nimra looked up, her eyes flashing.

'Maybe it already has,' she said.

'What do you mean?' Mariam asked, puzzled.

Nimra's throat was clogged as memories of the summer came rushing back. She hadn't told anyone about it. But she felt like she was on the verge of a precipice, and there was no option but to fall from its yawning height.

chapter 6

May 2011, Kuala Lumpur

There is a power in randomness that can jolt you awake and make you look around in furtive desperation. It was the same randomness that pulsed around Nimra every time she glanced at the shape of a head, the shadow on a jawline, or the way someone's hair curled at the nape crisply. The moment would pass and she could breathe, not sure why relief was trying to override disappointment in some absurd race in her veins.

Nimra looked down into her mug of milky tea, glad that her hijab covered her neck entirely and her fashion-conscious, Justin Bieber-obsessed cousins wouldn't have noticed the flush that had crept up. It had happened again just now when she saw someone pass by the café, where the three of them had been sitting, sipping tea and watching people.

In the distance, Nimra could spot the Petronas Towers glinting in the sunlight and she felt a familiar warm trickle of sweat run down her neck. If she could store this one moment, this single moment and flash-freeze it until it solidified into a gorgeous present that she could unwrap and inhale every time

Saira trod her down, she would have done so instantly. Lurking around her consciousness was the reason why she had initiated this morning stroll into the city with her cousins, who had been surprised and then delighted that timid Nimra was coming into her own, now that she was without her family.

Her days in Kuala Lumpur were blending into each other seamlessly, one tourist attraction after another, her cousins excited to show off their city to their countrified relative. In the end it was all a big muddle in her head. Only one thing stood out. Or rather one person.

A day after she had arrived in Kuala Lumpur with her uncle, her mother's brother, the family had gone out for dinner to a local restaurant. She had felt flushed with confusion and excitement that had rolled together into a constant churning in her stomach. For Nimra, it was culture shock of the extreme order—she had gaped at the miniskirt-wearing women along with the hijab-clad ones until her cousins had asked her to stop.

Her uncle Shahzad had moved to Malaysia around fifteen years ago when both his daughters were very young. After Nimra's mother died, he had felt an urge to restart his life elsewhere, while he could. He'd suppressed the occasional stab of guilt he felt about leaving Nimra without any relatives on her mother's side and had quietly parcelled his life, snipping away at corners and reminders until it was a neat package, and relocated to Malaysia.

He'd heard that Nimra's father remarried and the guilt loomed large over him, though he remembered his niece in every namaz, praying for her happiness. He often wondered how she had turned out and when he visited them years later, he'd been crushed by disappointment that she was nothing like his sister. Nowhere as beautiful, garrulous, and full of life. Nimra was pretty in a quiet sort of way. Only a slow awareness of her over time made one realise that she was her mother's daughter, in a few ways at least. Every year he had asked Nimra's father to allow her to visit them in Malaysia, but the trip had never materialised.

Saira's mother, the proverbial second wife and stepmother who fit inside every snug cliché he could think of, had been the reason why Nimra's life had changed for the worse over the years. The only good thing had been that her father had let her continue her education even after her basic schooling, despite her stepmother's machinations to prevent it.

He'd heard from the occasional phone calls that Nimra had finished her graduation and would be getting married soon. So he used that as an excuse to take her to Malaysia for a brief vacation. Nimra already had a passport because her stepmother had hoped that if Nimra got a proposal from someone who lived abroad, they might need it to send her packing as soon as possible. However, it had taken a fair amount of cajoling and convincing to let them send Nimra with him for a few days.

The restaurant where her uncle had taken them on her second day in Malaysia was in the open—a concept that further boggled Nimra's mind. She saw families sitting around tables on the pavement, chatting, sipping water topped with ice cubes, eating and laughing. She felt a couple of contrasting emotions tugging at her chest—a sense of calm serenity that she, too, was one of them for a brief period of time, and thrill that she was on her own. She could allow her excitement and happiness to show without fear of it being wiped away, and she smiled widely at something her cousin had said.

'You should smile more often!' the girl said, leaning back in her chair and winking at her sister. Nimra felt a little awkward around them as she still didn't know them well enough. She looked at their mother who was talking quietly with her uncle. Nimra felt a momentary pang of sadness thinking about what her life would have been like if her mother had lived.

Just as she was about to look away from her aunt, a movement behind her head caught her attention and she stared. Behind them, two white women in miniskirts and halter neck tops were placing their orders but Nimra barely looked at the expanse of exposed flesh she still hadn't got used to seeing. Her eyes were on the man who was taking their orders. He was dressed entirely in black, the sleeves of his shirt rolled up haphazardly to reveal sinewy forearms. She could surmise that he was an Indian, but it was his demeanour that arrested her completely. Perhaps it was that quirky smile, as though he were amused at some personal joke he would only share with someone special. Or the way his eyes crinkled into slits when he nodded. It was probably just the composition of his features in its entirety that held her in thrall. She would never know. She had never seen anyone like him before.

She wondered if he would come and take their orders as well. A crazy mix of emotions swirled inside her stomach, as though it were an effervescent mass, sending out a pop every other second. She quickly glimpsed at her cousins to see if they had noticed him too. They, however, were discussing a couple of boys they had seen on the LRT, whose hairstyles had reminded Nimra of a wet rooster. Her hopes plummeted when she saw another man come to their table, and Shahzad mamu ordered for them all.

It took some fifteen minutes for the food to arrive, and by then Nimra had memorised the man's face, hardly realising that it was pointless to do so. But she was without her so-called family and being released from those shackles had set her on a free-fall course, one that she was only too willing to oblige. She didn't expect him to notice her, but he did sometime later, as he refilled the glasses of the women seated behind her aunt. She felt her face freeze and she looked down at the formica table quickly, feeling a heated flush spread down her neck. She felt a little lost without her burkha and she fingered the pleat of her dupatta, grateful for the hijab on her head. Her cousins had been aghast when she had pulled out her burkha from the suitcase and they insisted she wear just the hijab as almost all Muslim women in Malaysia did.

Throughout the meal, she kept her eyes trained on the plate of steaming noodles placed in front of her and hardly spoke except when spoken to. She didn't look up at anyone and her uncle sighed, wondering what had happened to make her so withdrawn and shy. Nimra ate slowly, wrapping the slick noodles on her fork, poking it around on the plate until it speared a piece of soy-coated chicken and then lifted it to her mouth. Although Nimra knew that her uncle's family was not scrutinising her, it felt as though she was giving a performance that everyone around her was keenly attuned to. Would they laugh at her if she faltered? Her avid concentration was solely to avoid eye contact with the man who was serving the table behind her now.

At one point of time he passed right behind her and Nimra sucked in a breath, pulling her stomach inside, when the fabric of his trousers made the barest contact with her back, through three solid stripes of metal on her chair. When they were done, her uncle paid and Nimra quickly memorised the name of the restaurant. Just in case. When they left she looked around quickly, heart plummeting when she couldn't spot him anywhere. He had probably gone inside the kitchen.

'Shall we go?' Arshiya suggested. Her sister Shireen nodded. Nimra was reluctant to get up though. Now, nearly a week later, Nimra was positive she wanted to see him once again before she left for India that Sunday. She barely had four days of sunshiny happiness left and she was desperate to dredge up whatever she could.

'What plans do you have?' Nimra asked Arshiya, unwilling to get up from her chair. The café where they were sitting was nowhere near the restaurant, but she had seen him sitting in the café at this very table a couple of times, as she and her uncle had walked to the Masjid Jamek station to catch the train that would take them home. And hope had been renewed.

'Since we're in the city, we might as well go shopping?' Shireen suggested. Nimra sighed. She had a limited budget and it had already been exhausted even though her uncle had pressed a wad of ringgit in her hand when she had arrived.

'KLCC?' she asked tiredly and the girls nodded. It was odd how *she* felt weary and jaded about all the designer shops that her cousins just couldn't stop gushing over in the mall located in the Petronas Towers. To Nimra, they were just a bunch of outrageously priced shoes and clothes.

At night, there were times when she would close her eyes and listen to the drone of the AC as it purred out cool air, or the soft snores of her cousins who slept with her. And she would think about him. In all her twenty years, she had never seen anyone like him but then she'd also lived a very sheltered existence. Nevertheless, she knew that nothing would come out of this infatuation and she was happy about it in a perverse sort of way. When she went back to Vellore, all this would be a dream and she would have to learn life anew and get ready for marriage to some stranger. But she was neither in her home now, nor was she married yet. She was in transit and it allowed her to hold on to a bleak measure of hope that she might see him again.

It was the same hope that made her say, 'Why don't the two of you carry on? I'll wait for you here?'

Arshiya looked surprised. 'Alone?' she asked, looking at her sister, surprised at this new development. They hadn't yet got around to figuring out their cousin, who had been so scared and nervous when she first arrived.

'It's just a station away,' Nimra protested, amazed at her own ability to get accustomed to the way of life in Malaysia with such ease. 'And I'm tired. Don't feel like shopping today.'

'But… you were the one who wanted to come to the city, right?' Shireen asked, fiddling in her purse for the right amount of change. They lived in Petaling Jaya, which was far from the main city but still approachable because of the trains.

'Yes, but I think I'll stay here a little longer,' Nimra repeated firmly, almost positive that he would turn up that day. She didn't want to miss him.

Shireen looked doubtful but Arshiya seemed okay with it almost instantly. 'She has a phone and our numbers are on it. She'll call us if she needs us!' she reasoned as she tugged her older sister's arm.

'Listen, Nimra, don't tell Abbu that we left you here. And don't talk to any strangers and stay right here. Don't go anywhere else or you'll get lost!' Shireen instructed her as she allowed herself to be led away.

There was a reckless, eerie excitement skidding around Nimra as she watched her cousins leave. It was soon replaced by anxiety that he wouldn't turn up before the girls returned. She ordered another cup of tea and sat back in her chair, prepared to wait. She was looking out into the distance with unseeing eyes, a little lost in her dream world when he walked right past her and sat down at the adjacent table.

She peered into the steaming cup, worried and excited at the same time. What was she doing here? This was crazy! She lifted her head a fraction and glanced his way and saw that he was staring at her.

chapter 7

Mariam looked at the unfinished work in Nimra's hand and tried not to let her surprise show. She had never expected such a frank acceptance or acknowledgement of infatuation from this quiet girl, but then it just reinforced her belief that people will act differently when they think that no one's watching them.

Nimra had continued crocheting while speaking. After finishing what she had needed to say, she looked down at the piece in her hands as if for the very first time. She looked up at Mariam, her eyes registering anxiety and shock that she had revealed so much. Almost immediately, she started packing all her paraphernalia in her bag with hurried, haphazard movements.

'Be careful,' Mariam warned her. 'You'll break the tip of your crochet hook if you push it into your bag.'

'I-I-I have to g-go,' Nimra stuttered, getting up with an unhappy expression on her face. Mariam reached out and held Nimra's hand.

'Nimra, wait,' she pleaded but Nimra wasn't listening. It was as if by recounting the events from several months ago, she had resurrected them before herself once again and the pain that had inevitably followed had erupted afresh. She swallowed and then shook her head and Mariam spoke quickly.

'I'll wait for you tomorrow at the same time,' she said as Nimra left, her movements no longer placid and laid back. Nimra didn't reply.

As Mariam pottered around her house that day, waiting for the next girl to arrive, she wondered what the girls would think of her life, generously littered with the right and wrong choices she had made.

When Amreen arrived, she seemed breathless and excited as she plopped down before Mariam. Mariam noted her slightly round and fair features, her hair escaping from her braid on the sides and her flushed face.

'What happened?' she asked, ignited by her old-woman curiosity.

Amreen was still breathing heavily. She panted a bit. She controlled her breathing deliberately and shook her head. But her face was still red and she seemed as though she was trying hard not to giggle.

Amreen shook her head and then finally burst out giggling. 'Sorry, Amma. Sorry. It's my husband. You know we live in Vellore, right? He was dropping me here on the scooter. And then when he turned the corner, he asked me to get down and he parked his scooter. And then he made me race him till your house.'

Mariam was silent but disbelieving. 'Race?' she asked, the word triggering a memory of running around barefoot on baked terraces when she had been ten. 'You raced with your husband?'

Amreen nodded and giggled some more. 'He lost,' she added and then wiped the sweat at the back of her neck. She yanked away her burkha scarf, and unbuttoned her burkha and stood under the fan for a moment, trying to cool down.

What kind of husband asks his wife to race him, and what kind of wife complies with that request, Mariam thought, a little amazed.

'Why?' she asked instead.

'I don't know,' Amreen replied, and gave a short laugh as she came back to sit near Mariam.

'And you just ran?' Mariam continued, still unable to comprehend it. Amreen shrugged. She was getting a little annoyed with Mariam's continuous line of questioning. The yarn in her bag had gotten entangled with something else and she unravelled it slowly, refusing to look up. She hadn't given even a single thought about how odd they would have looked, running next to each other on the road. But then she'd thought that they were not in Vellore per se, and no one would know.

'So, have you decided what you want to make?' Mariam asked her. Amreen shook her head.

'It's so confusing!' she lamented, her breathing finally back in check. A muscle pulled in her ankle and she rotated it, easing the kinks and sighing in relief.

'Confusing?' Mariam asked, riffling through her pattern sheets.

Amreen watched Mariam arrange and rearrange the sheets, misgiving rising inside her. She missed the others. What was the point of getting out of the house if she couldn't even gossip with her friends?

'Do you want to try your hand at a crochet doll?' Mariam asked and Amreen's head shot up.

A doll? She didn't say anything but continued staring at Mariam.

'I have this one pattern somewhere inside the cupboard, I think,' Mariam offered, getting up with a little difficulty. Amreen's eyes followed her. Mariam spent at least ten minutes searching for the pattern and finally pulled it out from a dusty drawer in her cupboard.

'It's been years since I made this. You'll have to rely heavily on the pattern rather than my help.'

Mariam squinted at the picture and then shook the sheet again to dislodge the dust settled in the creases. She handed it over to Amreen.

The faded picture in black and white was of a smiling doll, arms akimbo, legs slightly apart. From the assorted shades on the sheet, she could surmise that different colours were to be used. It looked like a friendly doll, one that you'd want to pick up, and Amreen fell in love with it almost instantly.

'Oh yes,' she breathed, 'You think I can make this one?'

Mariam took the sheet back and peered at it again. 'You'll need thicker yarn and different colours for it. But if you want, you can practice now.'

Amreen nodded and Mariam handed her the sheet. 'Can you read the instructions? They are too small for me.'

Amreen took the sheet from her sceptically. If Amma didn't know how to read from it, how would she be able to help? And there were so many terms in the pattern, and abbreviations that Amma had never taught them.

'Do you know what all these abbreviations mean?' she asked Mariam.

For a moment, Mariam sat still, remembering a time many years ago when she'd ignored the notes, merely relying on the pictures and something else.

'I-I know what they mean,' Mariam replied nodding, and Amreen edged closer. 'What does it say to begin with?'

'Ch 2', Amreen read out. 'That means two chains, right?' Mariam nodded, her mouth twisting sideways.

'Just two?' Amreen asked again. Mariam chuckled.

'Yes, ma. It takes just two.'

Unsure of what the old woman was laughing at, Amreen followed the instructions with Amma's help. Together, the two of them set about making the head of the doll. It was complicated and unnerving and Amreen felt lost, wondering if she would be able to pull it off. But every time she felt like giving up, the old woman would prod her on, using the picture and the instructions to decipher what needed to be done next.

At the end of the hour, Amreen's fingers hurt and her back felt prickly.

'I don't think you're happy with this,' Mariam observed. Amreen nodded.

'It's just that... I'm not enjoying it. Looks like too much hard work,' she shuddered.

Mariam laughed. 'And you hate hard work?'

'I try and avoid it as much as I can,' Amreen replied, a mischievous glint in her eyes.

'What is it with you girls running away from hard work?' Mariam commented in general, looking into the distance, her eyes unfocused.

Amreen cleared her throat. Mariam still looked lost, but she regained her composure soon enough.

'What happened?' Amreen asked. Mariam looked at her as though seeing her for the first time.

'Nothing. Nothing. Just got thinking about my life when I

was your age,' Mariam replied, indicating that Amreen should get back to work. But Amreen's curiosity was piqued.

'Why? What were you like?' she asked.

'Not that different from you actually,' Mariam responded, her smile slightly grim. What could she mean, Amreen wondered. What could she have in common with this old woman after all?

Amreen looked at the clock. Her husband would be back in another half an hour. She looked at the unfinished doll's head in her hand. It looked a bit creepy. Did she really want to make this? For a child she didn't have yet and probably wouldn't?

Her chest seemed to close in on her as she took a deep breath. She had to get this out, this tumult that was inside her, she had to tell someone before it corroded her. She didn't know why it had come upon her now. Why did she want to tell Mariam? Ignoring the warning in her head about not divulging all her feelings to Mariam, of all people, Amreen fixed her gaze on her crochet hook.

'What comes next?' she asked, her throat dry.

chapter 8

Sometimes, a question can gather dust. It gets weighed down by concerns and smiles until it's too heavy to be lugged around. When you finally turn it over like a rusty key trying to fit inside a lock, you find that it has ballooned into something you never expected. It becomes a ticking bomb in your hand. And while you know the answer, you will not say it because you fear that it will set it off.

It had started as a routine question by well-wishers at weddings, almost as soon as Amreen was married. She never answered but merely smiled, and to the person who asked the question, the answer could have been anything. But the number of people who asked the same question over and over again grew with each month her period happened, bang on time. She still smiled instead of answering, but the smile was different. To the asker of the question, it was understood that there was some problem and appropriate sympathetic noises were often made.

Now, after nearly three years, the questions had stopped but they lingered in the air, invisible, pulling her down, crushing and breaking her. It was only faith and her husband's love which kept her going.

There were times when she thought he was simple-minded

and perhaps a bit of a fool. But when it came to matters of business, he'd hardly ever faltered. So maybe he was an emotional fool, she thought, her heart hardening a little day by day.

Before she got married, she'd seen relationships between couples metamorphose without their knowledge when they became parents. As an outsider, she was able to see clearly how a crucial bone had been lifted from the skeleton that had been the marriage, and instead, replaced by a warm and cuddly little baby who held everything together whether it wanted to, or not.

There were times now when Amreen despaired if she would ever have the support of a little baby to patch up her marriage, despite it not needing any patching up. In the early months, she would get up, real panic seizing her throat, locking it so she couldn't even cry out. The panic was rooted in second-marriage theories, supported by many instances from filmdom where the hero was married off to a more fertile woman if his wife was unable to give him a child. She could never voice this fear aloud to her husband because her throat was physically blocked. And yet, she sensed his mother's eyes on her all the time.

He would comfort her to sleep on the rare instances that he woke up with her and she would go to sleep with his arm around her waist, his large, warm palm resting snugly upon her sari-exposed navel. And yet, in her mind she counted the days of her life she was wasting not being a mother.

His sister got married six months ago and she was pregnant already. The news was met with a great deal of joy by her mother-in-law, followed by a speculative glance towards her.

'At least now I will become a grandmother!' she had

exclaimed. Amreen looked away and pretended to be busy chopping onions in the kitchen while her heart thundered inside her chest, shrinking and expanding with what seemed like great force.

Every year, on her anniversary, her parents gave her some sort of gift, usually gold, and it made her uncomfortable because it felt as though her parents were trying to subdue those very questions. The first year when her mother gave her a pair of gold bangles, her mother-in-law had been impressed; but not enough to change her stance towards her.

When the morning of her second anniversary rolled in, Amreen was vaguely aware of her husband pressing kisses on the back of her neck and she turned around with a smile on her face. But as things progressed from there, her mental space was invaded by the vision of the necklace her mother had gifted her the previous day. They were concerned too, but instead of asking her those damned questions, they avoided the topic altogether. Except for that one time when her mother had awkwardly stuttered, asking if they were using some sort of birth control. If you only knew, Ammi, Amreen thought, her mind coming back to the here and the now as she ran a finger along her husband's brow, catching a drop of sweat before it fell on her face.

Now, a year later, they had gifted her the LCD TV and Amreen could sense the disapproval steam off from her mother-in-law. But there was nothing she could do other than watch her husband become entranced with this latest toy, glad that he could watch his favourite Tamil movies in the privacy of his room, late at night.

That was four months back. Her husband was still the same, any changes in him, only external. They still laughed when they were together but the TV had slowly and insidiously become the third presence in their lives, in their bedroom, in their marriage. And it was not the kind that she'd wanted.

chapter 9

There was a time when I would spend an *hour* taking care of my hair, Arifa thought as she ran the comb down her waist-length hair in urgent strokes. She slowed down her hand deliberately and tried to take a deep breath. And another. But it wasn't happening. In the past few years, the change had crept into her veins, the one that wanted everything to happen quickly. Now. *This* moment.

As she braided her hair with the same nimble movements, she glanced at her son who sat on his portable potty, grimacing.

'Armaan,' she muttered, flinging back her long braid where it touched the dip in her waist. 'Are you done yet?' He shook his head and continued grimacing.

In the chaos that was her world, the constant running around for everything, trying to fit the day in her plans, there were few precious moments that Arifa could savour. Of course, she had to fight off the urge to do something, but she took slow steps towards the corner of the bed where she had kept her craft bag.

What an odd class it had been today, she thought as she rummaged inside the bag and pulled out what she'd been working on. It was a few months since she'd joined the class but she had forgotten why or how she had started going there in the first place. Her mother-in-law had known Mariam for years, so it must have been something someone said, and the fact that Mariam lived just two lanes away from their home.

Arifa had decided to do a sofa back, the kind she'd seen gracing the homes in a magazine once. She explained the idea to Mariam who nodded knowingly and had showed her how to get started. Arifa thought that the whole idea of doing 'something to represent' themselves was a load of rubbish. The old woman is getting senile, she thought as she followed her instructions.

The sofa back that they were doing was made up of identical, lacy, round motifs all joined together in a complicated way, but it seemed very elegant. Arifa had no real plans for it. She thought of their rexine sofa at home, the one her husband had promised to replace with a fancier one soon, and realised that this too, once completed would have to be kept aside. Like so much of her life, this would be just one more thing to be pushed into the loft, for better days that were yet to come.

It was an easy project. The daunting part was making so many motifs, each one attached to the previous one.

'Ammi?' Armaan asked and Arifa dropped the lacy motifs back into her bag and went to him, taking him to the bathroom. Her timing was the same because she'd requested for it. Armaan took his afternoon nap at that time, and she didn't see why she should change her schedule for the whims of this eccentric old lady.

However, it had been disconcerting to see no one else there except Mariam. At first the silence had been welcome. No distractions at all, she thought, as she worked diligently. But she kept looking up at Mariam, as though for approval, and to her consternation, it seemed as though Mariam was lost in some thought. Shouldn't she be focussing on her, her student?

'Are you alright?' she asked her, hesitantly.

'Huh? Yes, I'm fine,' Mariam replied. 'Maybe you should all come back from tomorrow at the same time. These silences are weighing me down.'

Arifa was exasperated. Why couldn't the old woman make up her mind?

'Call us separately, call us together,' she mumbled. Mariam caught the end of her sentence and smiled.

'Humour an old lady, ma. I thought I would be able to work better with you one on one but I'm not really enjoying it,' she said. 'It's better if you all came back together from tomorrow. Tell the others also, okay?'

Arifa was personally affronted but she didn't say anything.

'How's your mother-in-law?' Mariam asked conversationally. Arifa rolled her eyes.

'She's perfectly fine,' she replied.

'I just asked, ma,' Mariam said but Arifa realised she wanted to talk.

'She has everything she needs. My husband takes care of it. He works in Dubai, you know,' she said. Mariam nodded, watching how Arifa had managed to get her yarn tangled once again. While she unravelled the knots, she started talking about how she missed her husband. Mariam was certainly taken aback. Arifa had seemed so self-sufficient, like she was beyond all the needs and cares of other women. Emotional needs, at least.

After untangling the yarn, she looped it over the hook twice and pulled it out, continuing much like an automaton as she resumed talking.

'I've been married for seven years now. He's been here for

all of two years,' she went on. 'Ever since he found that job in Dubai, it's like… it's like… his frenzy for making money is stronger than his love for us. Also, he has no idea how much I have to do to manage the house, even though it's only his mother, Armaan and me living there. I look at women like Amreen and Shaista and I think of how easy they have it. Do they ever have to worry about paying the electricity bill? Every small thing, right from the cable bill to the household items that we buy, I have to take care of. Agreed, he sends the money and he sends enough, more than enough. But what use is that when he is not here?

'You know the other day, Armaan was asking me what his father looks like. I had to hunt for a picture of him from our wedding album and show it to him. Do you know exactly how much time he spends with Armaan and me when he comes to India? If he's here for a month, he'll be with us for just ten days. The remaining time he takes his mother to see her relatives. There are times when I feel like just exploding from the tension. In fact, I don't know if it's a good or bad thing when he comes because… because much as I miss him, his arrival turns around the entire schedule of the house. The last time he was here was months ago. I don't know when he'll be coming again. He tells me that he'll get us a computer and set up an internet connection so we can talk to him more easily. He says we can see him as we talk to him. I don't believe it.

'And even then, I'm sure his mother won't let us talk in peace. See, I don't have anything against her, I like her and she's a good woman. But he's her only son, so it's like he's split between her and us and I'm not that good a person to feel sorry for her. I… I just feel like those abandoned women sometimes, who don't have anyone to take care of them and who have to take care of everyone else.

'Does he ever realise that I too need taking care of? If I fall sick, then that's it. The whole household gets disrupted. And my mother-in-law can't take care of Armaan, at least not like I do. Our neighbours Lakshmi and those people who live on the other side, you know them, na? Mehek and her family? They both have children who are Armaan's age and they've already enrolled them in school. When I asked him last week when he called if we should also enrol Armaan in a school, he said it's my wish. *My* wish? When is anything *my* wish? Why *should* it be my wish? Isn't Armaan his son too? Shouldn't he worry about Armaan as well?

'At least people pity those abandoned women and give them sympathy. I don't get sympathy or even a little acknowledgement for how I am managing this household all alone. They think it's all so easy because my husband lives abroad and earns for us. Let me tell you, it's not easy at all. It's like he's there and yet he's not there.'

Arifa looked up at Mariam who was listening to her without a sound.

'Water,' she said, her throat parched and lips cracked. Mariam nodded.

'Deepa, get water for Arifa!' she called out. Deepa was in a good mood for some reason, and she made tea as well.

Steam curled up from the hot ginger-infused tea and Arifa blew on the surface. Ripples undulated rhythmically and she sipped the tea tentatively. For the first time in days, months, she did not feel the charged momentum billow inside her. She could sit here peacefully for another ten minutes. There was no rush.

chapter 10

At five, the Asr azan sounded faintly in the air, carried over by the wind from the main road. Mariam got up, her knees creaking as she made her way to the bathroom for her wudu. Shaista was supposed to come now; Mariam wanted to finish reading namaz before she came.

She remembered the clear sound of the azan from her childhood in Vellore, pure as a ringing bell, and the deepest sense of peace that she would feel whenever she heard 'Allah o Akbar'. The azan here in Sathuvacheri was a subdued one, further diminished by the sounds of traffic from the highway.

She rotated a chair towards the qibla and read namaz, sitting down as she had done for the last ten years or so. Some minutes later, she rolled the prayer beads between her fingers, their smooth roundness seeming to be her only connection with herself and the external world.

She had never expected the girls to reveal so much about themselves to her, just because they were alone when they came. It made her uncomfortable, being the recipient of all these secrets, but it also made her realise that she had missed this human connection all these years, this need to unburden yourself to a willing listener. As she waited for Shaista to come,

Mariam wondered if Shaista, too, would tell her something about her life. Despite what outward appearances promised, Mariam knew that the girl wasn't happy.

Sometime later, Mariam noticed Shaista taking slow and hesitant steps towards the room, the curve of her belly slightly more prominent. She sat down next to Mariam and winced as she touched her lower back a little.

'Back pain?' Mariam asked Shaista, who nodded quietly.

Shaista hadn't decided what she wanted to make. She looked at the pattern sheets, confused and a little upset for some reason.

'What's the matter?' Mariam asked gently.

'I don't know. I don't think I will continue with your classes, Amma,' she declared, but Mariam could sense a pleading in her eyes, something that said just the opposite.

'Why? What happened?' Mariam asked, feeling a little uneasy.

'I... my husband doesn't like me going out of the house,' Shaista said, looking down at her lap. 'But he let me come here because I told him it was just for a few months. Now, with the baby... '

'I see,' Mariam rocked to and fro. 'But try and tell him, a couple of months more won't harm the baby or you.'

'Harm the baby?' Shaista looked up surprised. 'That's not why he doesn't want me to go. He...' She stopped because she seemed to have realised that she'd said more than she'd planned to.

'I will not be coming from tomorrow, if that's alright,' Shaista said, cracking the knuckles of her left hand with her right.

'I've told the others to come back together at the usual time tomorrow onwards,' Mariam said. 'Will that make a difference?'

Shaista looked at her, frustrated. She shook her head.

'Why?' Mariam persisted.

Shaista shut her eyes tightly and opened them looking exasperated. 'It's a long story.'

'Well, all the better then. I like listening to long stories,' Mariam said, crossing her arms.

'Amma, I… ' Shaista looked on the verge of tears for some reason and Mariam softened her stance.

'Look, just talk to me. Tell me what it is that you're going through. You'll feel better,' Mariam urged her. 'And you can start something new with the crochet also. Maybe something for the baby? Then he won't mind?'

Shaista looked up, her eyes flashing. 'If I *am* going to make something, it won't be for the baby.'

Mariam was startled. She'd never seen Shaista look so angry or passionate. 'I want to make something for myself,' Shaista added.

'How about a… a hairband?' Mariam asked finally. Shaista's face broke into an uncertain smile. Mariam tried to subdue the pang of unease that she felt as she picked up the yarn.

chapter 11

Shaista's fascination with light and switches went back a long way. Until she was about ten years old, her village didn't have electricity. Now, when she thought about those days, she wondered how they ever survived.

She was used to electricity now, even enough to take it for granted. But each day, at least twice a day, when power outages plunged Vellore into insipid heat and semi-darkness, she remembered the early years of her life. She was the only one who didn't miss the whirring of the fan or who could still manage to finish chopping onions in an unlit kitchen, but the moment the bulb reignited, she would mutter a prayer to Allah while wiping the sweat beading on her forehead with the edge of her pallu.

Adapting to married life was not difficult. At least during the day she continued as before, cooking, helping in the kitchen, cleaning the house, doing what she had always done back in her home. It was at night that she couldn't understand how everyone expected her to just sleep next to a man, even if it was her husband. Human contact had been avoided in her life till then, except for the time when she hugged, held and kissed a baby or a younger cousin who would have come to visit.

She and her sister had slept in the hall, each having their own mattresses and pillows and bed sheets to cover them. And they rarely ever touched. It had been a measure of independence that she had taken for granted. At the time of getting married, she'd been aware that a little more than touching would be involved. But she'd never dreamed that she would be expected to lie in the darkness while a man loomed over her, almost every night.

She tried to like him, this man, her husband, with whom she had to live for the rest of her life. But in the thrumming darkness where she could barely make out his features, she abhorred this change that marriage brought. During the day, it seemed like he was another man altogether. It would seem as though her life was now a set of intersecting circles, the first one as a bahu and the second one as a wife. He expected her to fill his glass of water, even if it was half empty, while he ate. He flicked angry glances at her if she so much as ignored an empty section of his plate and daydreamed about the fields in her village. He barely talked to her, at day or at night, all the slots of conversation in his life being filled by his mother and his sister.

Shaista was not confused. She knew what she wanted and it was not this. This burgeoning in her belly, the reason why she had to wear her sari petticoats looser, this heaving inside her chest where an empty space seemed to be growing larger just as her womb enlarged with his child. Yes, it was his child. She was merely the vessel. She could not bring herself to feel anything for the foetus in her body as yet because she was too busy resenting the way it had changed her life. She could no longer abide certain smells, she needed to visit the bathroom at least twice every night, her feet seemed swollen sometimes, and she cried softly at night at this loss of control over her own body.

To the outside world her life appeared wonderful. She was married, she was already pregnant and her husband was well-to-do, having his own home and business. He was also reasonably good-looking. But even after so many months of marriage, he was essentially a stranger who slept with her.

Most importantly, his love of complete darkness at night was something she could never get accustomed to. On her first night as a married woman, he had sat before her and looked at her face properly for the first time. Maybe she was not what he had expected because he got up a little abruptly and switched off the light, plunging the room into darkness. She sensed him lying down next to her. Without uttering a single word, he reached for her hand and drew her towards him.

Feelings like hate and love were not a part of her emotional vocabulary, but even then she knew that what she felt for him was neither. There was a tiny space filled with fear and anger that inhabited that part of her heart where she ought to have felt something for her husband. These feelings were often rounded off with a generous dose of disgust. But again, these were not feelings that she acknowledged to herself.

The crochet classes that she started going for were like a bright spot in the sky, a place from where the sun beamed down abundantly upon her from behind the shapeless cotton clouds of her existence. The whiteness of the yarn, as she nimbly spun magic with her fingers, completed her wants and longings. It was the only time she knew contentment. But despite his apparent lack of interest in her, her husband noticed the change in her when she came back from each class. She didn't know that it was part suspicion and part jealousy that made him resent the time she was away and the reason why he wanted her to stop going.

Help came from unexpected quarters when her mother-in-law stood up for her, telling her that she should continue. She was not concerned about whether her mother-in-law had ulterior motives because she was only too happy to go back to that one hour of her life every day, where she was the creator of things beautiful.

chapter 12

Nimra winced every time she thought of how she had described the man she had seen in Malaysia to Mariam. The one she had become infatuated with. She had wondered if she could possibly quit the classes, but the prospect of having nothing to look forward to was unpleasant. The mehendi on her palms was again new, and she tried to avoid looking at it. The only time she was successful was when she was crocheting because then she looked at what was in her hands, and not what her hands looked like.

Since the time she had returned from Malaysia, her stepmother had escalated her efforts for the 'Get Nimra married' project. The first time Nimra had been 'shown' to some people, her stepmother had asked a neighbour's daughter to come over and apply mehendi on Nimra's hands, in order to make her look like a bride.

'With her wheatish complexion, it's going to be so difficult to get her a good match,' she was often heard complaining, but Nimra didn't care. She was living inside a bubble where happiness was transient and memories fleeting.

People came, they saw her, they made her stand so they could measure her height against some of their own people, they made her lift her head, lower it, they lifted her thick braid and murmured their approval. But every single time, they went and just didn't come back. Her stepmother was sure there was something about Nimra that was keeping good matches away, and she kept conveying the same to her, over and over again, until Nimra, too, began to believe it. She had now lost count of the number of times the neighbour's daughter had come and applied mehendi on her palms. Each squeeze of the cone and each delicate line that transformed into a dazzling pattern had become something akin to a tightening noose.

Yet, yesterday when she poured her heart out to Amma and told her about her Malaysia trip, there had been relief and remembered delight in equal measure. Both had led to mortification eventually and Nimra had come away from there, feeling slightly nauseous thinking about the whole episode.

When Nimra returned, Saira was home, watching TV. She was surprised to see her back from school so early and had to take a little time to rearrange her features into boredom. Saira caught the look but in yet another surprise for Nimra, she chose to ignore it. Instead, she was wincing for some reason.

Saira's mother came out from the kitchen with a glass of milk and a plate of almonds. Nimra went inside the room to keep her bag inside her cupboard and came outside to see Saira's mother wiping her forehead and murmuring something to her.

She felt something clench within her as a memory wafted in from the past—from a long time ago, of her mother's lap, comfort and security warming her from inside, something that she could now replicate up to a poor measure with a glass of hot Horlicks. She cleared her throat and wondered if she should ask what had happened but before she could formulate a question that would not be met with a sarcastic response, Saira spoke to her mother.

'Does it hurt like this every month?' she asked, grimacing and then lying down on the sofa, placing a cushion under her lower back. Nimra's eyes widened in understanding. She bit her lower lip, unsure of what to say. Finally, she looked at the clock. It was time for lunch and she had no idea if Saira's mother had made anything yet, busy as she seemed to be in coddling Saira.

Sighing, she ventured into the kitchen to make lunch and saw the half-hearted attempts of her stepmother, which she set out to redress. Sometime later, she walked back outside and saw that Saira had fallen asleep. Her mother was staring at the TV though not really watching it. Nimra sat down on an empty sofa, wondering why her stepmother looked so morose, as though Saira's first period was like the end of the world.

Maybe it was a combination of the situation and her mood, that made her uncharacteristically mellow as she looked at Nimra for the first time as an adult or equal. 'She was just a baby yesterday… and now… ' she trailed off. Nimra didn't know if she was expected to add anything to that. Your baby, my tormentor, she thought privately.

'In five years' time we have to get her married,' she continued, and Nimra looked down at the floor. 'Then she will belong to another family and will be gone.'

Words, at times, can be sharp and poky, puncturing our throat as we try and swallow them down. For Nimra, it seemed as though the edges had been rubbed out a little in her stepmother's tone, but even then, they were difficult to accept. She looked around the house where she had lived all her life and knew with a sense of finality of how her life would be after she gets married. Her mind played out scenes from the future of when she and Saira would return to their parents' place after marriage, which made the pokiness come right back, mellow mood be damned.

'At least six families have come and seen you so far. What is the problem? Why isn't anyone liking you?' her stepmother addressed the question to her and Nimra felt a sinking feeling in her stomach, a clutching and unclutching quite like the cramps that Saira was experiencing. She didn't know why people kept rejecting her because until now she hadn't given any thought to it. She'd in fact been glad. But there was a shift in the situation now. Although Saira was still a child, her mother had started thinking about her wedding already. It would be best if Nimra exited now, when her father was still interested in getting her married. A new home, new people, and a new life wouldn't be all that bad. Seconds later her mind presented her with the image of Rocky, and she swallowed, thinking of how she had babbled in front of Mariam.

chapter 13

May 2011, Kuala Lumpur

To a casual passerby it would seem as though the dusky girl sitting by herself, nursing a mug of tea, and the young man seated nearby had nothing to do with each other. But if you stood around long enough and scrutinised their actions, you would have been a little surprised.

It was a game of sorts where Nimra would look up at him and then swiftly look away, then return her gaze slowly. By then he would be looking elsewhere ostensibly and she would lower her eyes back to the mug, whose contents had cooled already. Then she would look up again in a few seconds and he would be staring at her again.

Thoughts crowded in her head, jostling to be heard first but she firmly pushed them back, especially the ones that were shouting out to be careful and to *think* about what she was doing. While she was earnestly ignoring the thoughts, he had decided to take the initiative. Before she knew it, he was standing at her table, an eyebrow raised at the empty chair. She nodded quickly, strangling the caution-bearing thoughts as she looked up at him.

'Alone here?' he asked. Nimra sought to understand the quality of his voice, almost forgetting what she was being asked.

She nodded and then shook her head, feeling her face flush. 'My cousins are at KLCC. They will be back soon,' she replied softly.

They sat that way in companionable silence, back to playing the game of staring and looking away—from close quarters now. Suddenly he leaned forward and the pretence slipped.

'What's your name?' he asked and Nimra looked up, surprised at the elementary question. To her, the last fifteen minutes had seemed like a much longer and very intimate time. As though she had already poured out her heart to him and searched within his eyes for everything she could find there.

'Nimra,' she spoke, finally gathering the courage to rest her eyes on his wildly expressive face.

'Never heard that name before,' he remarked. 'My name is Rocky,' and saying so, he offered his hand to her. Nimra looked at the neatly cut squarish nails, at the hair sprinkled on the top of his tanned hand, and his long, tapering fingers. And as if in slow motion, she took the offered hand. His grasp was firm and dry but she broke the contact almost immediately.

'Actually, it's Rahman but people here call me Rocky,' he leaned forward conspiratorially. Nimra sat back, startled at his proximity and how it seemed to open up something in her. She crossed her arms, trying to physically diminish the effect he was having on her. It seemed as though his very presence was exposing her in some visceral manner.

The stilted conversation continued, interspersed with long stretches of silence. At one point, Nimra looked at her watch and was startled. They had been sitting there for less than thirty minutes, but to her it seemed like hours. She looked around uneasily and he noticed her movements with interest.

'You got to go somewhere?' he asked casually, pushing back the chair at an odd angle as he plunged his hands inside his pocket to extract money. Before Nimra could reply, he was already walking towards the cash counter to pay for his tea. Nimra watched his springy step through blurry eyes; at the moment her mind was like a sponge that wanted to absorb every single movement he made.

Get up and leave before he comes back, a voice urged her. Nimra realised that the silence in her head had once again given way to thoughts that piped up and down relentlessly. A part of her was ready to get up and leave but a larger and more stubborn side compelled her to stay where she was. 'What will you do if he just waves at you and goes on his way?' the voice urged her once again and Nimra felt startled at that possibility.

She watched him come back towards her and dreaded what he would do, when he stopped near her table and asked, 'Want to come for a walk?'

'A walk!' her mind protested once again.

'Where?' she asked instead.

'Just around the square,' he said, waving his hands expansively.

Nimra made a spot decision. She picked up her mobile phone and texted to her cousins, 'Going for short walk nearby. Be back soon. Call me when you get back.'

She looked up and her face flushed when she realised she hadn't really responded to his query. 'Y-yes, I'll come for a walk,' she managed to mutter, her voice trembling a little. She looked down at the cellphone in her hand and hit 'Send'.

Feeling extremely conscious of herself, Nimra walked beside him as they left the café, and ambled through the market. Nimra was already familiar with the markets where people sold toys, bags, shoes, clothes and of course, the quintessential hijabs. She'd been immensely saddened by the sight of old people selling random things like boxes of ear buds and hairpins, trying to put together a living for themselves. Today, however, it seemed as though the rest of the world was out of focus and Rocky was the only person who stood out, crystal clear with bright edges as he walked beside her energetically, talking about his life in Malaysia.

She tried to keep pace with him, tried not to look at him too much, and then tried to take her eyes off him as well, but failed spectacularly each time. He noticed that she was panting with the effort of walking as fast as him and he slowed down and smiled. To counteract the effect of his smile, she asked him suddenly, 'Where do you live?'

The expression on his face faltered for a moment and he chose not to answer that question, deliberately conversing with an old woman who was selling sparkly brooches that she'd seen women pin on their hijabs. He picked up one dazzling brooch in the shape of a butterfly, with pink and white stones, and bargained with the old woman good-naturedly. All the while, Nimra stood nearby, feeling mortified, wondering if he was buying it for her. Why would he buy *anything* for her, the voices protested. She realised she'd be even more mortified if he didn't give it to her and so she picked up one that was shaped like a shell, and haltingly asked the woman for the price.

He looked at what she held in her hands, a little surprised. Shrugging, he replaced the butterfly brooch, and watched as

Nimra paid for hers. A little embarrassed by the episode, Nimra walked away, dropping the brooch in her bag; he soon caught up with her.

'So how long are you in KL?' he asked, resting his hands in his pockets casually.

'A couple more days,' she replied softly. He didn't say anything for some time, and they walked in silence, all the while some unspoken but tenuous bridge building between them.

'I didn't come here to be a waiter, you know,' he said with a self-deprecating smile. Nimra didn't know how to respond so she continued walking.

'I wish I'd finished my graduation back in India but I was arrogant then about making money,' he spoke as they passed the square. In the distance, Nimra could see the café where they sat a while ago. She hoped her cousins hadn't returned yet. Also, she was a little dismayed at his words. She wanted him to remain mysterious to her, and not morph into a poor little boy who had made mistakes and was now suffering for them.

'I came here and worked as a salesman in a departmental store and then did a couple of other jobs till I found the waiter's job. But I'm not just a waiter any more. I'm the head waiter and I've been trying to save up some money so I can… '

He continued speaking, gesticulating elegantly but Nimra was swept away in a wave of sorrow, combined in equal measure by desire and a feeling of doom. She listened to the words but their meaning eluded her and she watched with dismay as the café neared.

'I have to go now,' she interrupted him gently. He stopped talking, and smiled sheepishly.

'Sorry, I get carried away when I start talking about my plans. I'm usually at this café till lunchtime so if you're in this part of town, I hope to see you again before you leave,' he said, flashing a friendly smile at her.

Nimra looked down at the pavement, feeling irrationally upset. She didn't know what she wanted anymore. When he came and sat down at her table, she'd been sure it was because he was interested in her but he was behaving as though meeting her had been just like catching up with a fellow Indian. She nodded and made to leave when he cleared his throat.

'I got this for you,' he spoke in a softer voice. She looked at his outstretched palm—the butterfly brooch was glinting warmly, beckoning her, opening her heart in ways she never thought possible.

chapter 14

For Mariam, these four women now held a special place in her heart. She was certainly old enough to see glimpses of herself in each of them, but none of them had her impetuousness, which wasn't a bad thing, she reminded herself.

It had taken a while for them to open up to each other and to her, and Mariam realised that listening to each of their stories had made her want to do something she hadn't done in a long time. Tell them her own story.

'Deepa!' she called out immediately, sitting up on the bed, feeling energised. 'Make tea for me!'

Deepa's mother had been one of the old retainers who had chosen to live with the family of their employers, forfeiting their own lives, wants and desires, and Deepa had been born in the old home in Vellore. Mariam had no idea that the skinny little baby would one day become so valuable to her existence. When Deepa was around nine or ten, Mariam had told Deepa's mother that she would take care of Deepa and ensure she got married to a good boy. Things, of course, were different now. Deepa's mother died and Mariam was alone and it was Deepa who was taking care of her, going about her daily tasks with quiet animosity.

When Deepa returned with the tea, she placed it on the edge of the bed and was about to leave when Mariam spoke. 'Sit,' she said. Having lived with Mariam's family all her life, Deepa was extremely proficient in Urdu, probably more than Tamil.

'Why?' she asked belligerently, but lingered anyway.

'I know you've heard all their stories too,' Mariam said slowly, picking up her cup of tea.

Deepa shifted a little guiltily and then sat down on the mat, her arms crossed over her bent knees. She sat in silence watching Mariam blow on her tea and sip it slowly.

'Didn't make any for yourself?' Mariam asked her after a moment. Deepa shook her head.

'So, what did you think?' Mariam probed. Deepa knew what she was referring to, so she shrugged.

'Their lives are so fascinating, no?' she asked again and Deepa made a face.

'You could have watched TV if you were so bored,' she said, and Mariam started laughing, some of the tea from the cup spilling on the bed.

'Watch it!' Deepa warned loudly, grumbling as she got a cloth to wipe the drops of tea that would become sticky if left to evaporate.

'But what did you think of them?' Mariam persisted, unwilling to let go of the topic. She felt a modicum of guilt for not telling the girls that Deepa understood Urdu perfectly, but it had never occurred to her.

After a moment of stony silence, Deepa sighed and spoke, 'I like that one… the one who went to Malaysia.'

Mariam nodded in understanding. Nimra's ache was palpable, her words re-igniting memories that had been buried so deep inside her that she had almost forgotten how it felt. As if.

Part Two

chapter 15

Vellore, 1955

The acrid smell of fresh paint hung heavily in every room. There was no escape, no matter where I went. It pervaded the kitchen as well, where my mother was rearranging everything on the shelves now that the painters had finished their job. But the most important fact was that the sharp, chemical odour was an olfactory reminder that I was getting engaged the following day.

I sniffed the air and ran to my refuge on the terrace, unhappiness having become second nature to me. The feeling of dismay centred somewhere deep inside my stomach and had now settled there heavily. With each day that brought the event closer, something compulsive was being drawn from within me, like a drop or two that had coalesced into a larger, tighter, more painful knot. I didn't know why. I should have been happy by all rights, though.

My sister had taken leave from her in-laws and had been staying with us since last week, helping Ammi with all the preparations. Since I couldn't quite figure out why I was feeling so melancholy, I took to playing with her children on the terrace, making sure they stayed out of everyone's way, especially the kitchen, where dishes, that would be sent to my future in-laws' home, were being laboriously prepared.

Even in the midst of a hot and sweaty game of running around the terrace, it would catch me unawares, this feeling of impending doom. Life as I knew it was about to end forever. There would be no running around on terraces after I become a married woman, and when I have children of my own... I stopped thinking about it then.

There was a small alcove on one corner of the terrace, a shady, often dusty and cobwebbed place where I would sit as a child, mostly because people often forgot to look there and it made a great hiding place. I wandered over that side, alone today as the children had gone back to their home and would return in the evening.

My sister lived in Vellore with her husband and his family, I couldn't imagine what it would have been like if she'd had to go somewhere else, like Madras or worse, Bangalore. It was good having her around nearby because she visited often, and the pain of losing her to another family had slowly ebbed. I blew half-heartedly on the layer of dust under the alcove and shut my eyes as dust motes spiralled up and settled down again. I wish I could explain why I was so miserable, but I didn't know the reason myself. I crouched under the alcove and settled down, letting the dust attach itself to my sari because I really couldn't care any more.

This was the only place even the painters had forgotten to visit. Thank God, I thought, leaning back against the warm, gritty wall, shutting my eyes to my future.

The day before my engagement passed slowly, each minute stretching out almost painfully into the next. As I was the bride, I wasn't allowed to help in any of the activities; so I watched the household get busy with the different dishes they were preparing. Finally bored, I went inside one of the rooms where Raheema bu sat, her eyes squinting as she crocheted another skull cap for one of the men in the family.

I sat down next to her and she looked at me, her smile nearly toothless but nevertheless endearing.

'Are you finally ready to learn?' she asked me. I resisted the urge to run away from there. Raheema bu was a relative, but in what capacity, I was unaware of. She'd just been around forever, hunched over her crochet and the numerous skull caps she made for the men of the house.

'I... ' I wondered how to tell her that I wasn't interested in the knots and yarn at all. In fact, I wasn't interested in anything. I sat next to her, watching as she expertly brought hook and yarn together. Although crocheting didn't interest me, I was nevertheless mesmerised. The hook flashed in and out repeatedly. As she turned the skull cap I noted that she had finished one more round.

'Who are you making this one for?' I asked, realising that it was a rather intricate design, chosen from the depths of her memory.

'Me, who else did you think?'

I looked up in surprise to see the looming figure of Aasim as he bent his head low and stepped inside the room. In an automated response, I made a face at him, stuck my tongue out and looked at him cockily, all within a span of ten seconds.

'As if!' I smirked, and edged closer to Raheema bu who

seemed thrilled to see Aasim, more than she'd been to see me. But then, that was a given. Aasim could charm any woman, whether she was eight years old or eighty. Any woman except me of course. I usually couldn't stand him for more than thirty seconds and would slip away whenever he visited because he annoyed me in every possible way. But today I didn't want to go because there really was nothing else to do. And I had come to the room first, hadn't I?

'Of course she's making it for me,' he grinned as he sat down cross-legged on the mat and leaned close towards Raheema bu to see her handiwork. Raheema bu tittered like a girl as she showed him the design and I realised that he was right. It *was* for him.

'Why do you need one? It's not like you read namaz regularly or anything!' I shot at him and he made a face at me.

'How would *you* know?' he asked, 'You're always inside the house.'

'But Abba tells me he never sees you in the mosque,' I countered triumphantly. His face fell for the barest of seconds before he recovered.

'He is usually right in the front and he doesn't see me because I'm at the back,' he replied, but some of his cockiness had gone.

Aasim and I had known each other for the last six or seven years, ever since my sister's wedding. He was my sister's husband's younger brother and during her wedding, he had bullied me incessantly, making me cry by telling me that my sister had become *his* bhabhi now.

He trailed along with her whenever she came to visit us and I realised with horror that it was true. You just couldn't seem to get rid of him no matter what! It was only when my sister came here for her first delivery that he didn't tag along, because she was here for all of forty days.

He did visit her often, trying to make it apparent to me that *he* and my sister were a unit and I didn't figure anywhere. Both of us were about the same age but there had been times when I wished I could just murder him. More than my sister's husband, it seemed as though Aasim was the one who had taken away my sister from me.

When my niece was born, he came home with his family and looked a little upset for some reason. I had already seen the baby, I had scoffed, but he didn't respond. He seemed ready to cry though, and refused to meet my sister who kept asking for him. He had run away to the terrace and I found him there in *my* alcove, his head hunched over his knees, his shoulders shaking.

'Go away!' he yelled when I hovered near him, my joy at his distress not as joyful as I thought it would be.

'But why are you upset?' I asked, wishing I could drag him away from my favourite spot. He had the most disturbing way of usurping my places and people.

He looked up then, tears running down his face freely, wiped his nose with the back of his sleeve and sniffled. Yuck, I thought. Boys. Disgusting!

He caught the look on my face and tried to control his tears but couldn't stop himself. Despite my reluctance to touch him, I gently placed a finger on his shoulder and poked a little.

'What happened?' I asked, unwilling to believe that my tormentor of the past ten months was reduced to a snivelling little boy.

'She won't love me anymore, will she?' he asked brokenly and although I was only ten, the import of his words sunk in immediately. His mother had died when he was five and he had obviously seen my sister as a replacement.

'She has a child of her own now,' he said, plucking at some lint on his sleeve. The crying had subsided but the tears continued and he got up from the alcove without a word, wiping his face with the same sleeve he had rubbed his nose against a while ago.

I looked at him leave, compassion blossoming in my heart to be immediately replaced by glee—yes, perhaps my sister wouldn't love him so much now.

Over the years, as my sister had two more children, he had transformed into a playful uncle for them but we never brought up that conversation on the terrace. He was definitely embarrassed at his show of weakness and I couldn't possibly remind him, saying, 'Remember the time you cried like a girl on my terrace?' I could actually. But I didn't.

I looked at him now as he said something to make Raheema bu giggle and marvelled at the changes in him. I didn't know when he had stopped being disgusting. His hair was longer than anyone else's and he had a broad forehead. My mother who was intensely fond of him would say infuriating things like, only intelligent people have such broad foreheads, and that would make him beam until I reminded him of his performance in school.

'Thank God I don't have a sister,' he would say. 'Imagine *living* with someone like you!' and he would pretend as though he were about to throw up or die of choking. I absently noted how he had started getting a stubble on his face and while that should have disgusted me further, it didn't. I wondered what it felt like, but in a passive way, and I sat up straighter when he looked at me. It seemed he had caught me staring at him. Again.

Of late, whenever he turned up with my sister, I would find myself staring at him, wondering how he could have grown so tall while I was still the same height. I had stopped playing with him years ago; well, since the time my mother made me wear a sari anyway. I had tried playing in the sari too, but I would trip on the pleats and fall and he would laugh at me. What's more, my mother would get furious, telling me that I was a grown up and shouldn't play with boys any longer. I remember him looking at me thoughtfully as I walked away, my head high in the air. I was a lady now.

Our little staring game had progressed each time he visited and I realised with dismay that I was the one who started it every time. The thing is, he never looked away whenever he spotted me looking at him. He would stare right back until I got uncomfortable and looked away. Raheema bu was unaware of the staring match that was underway as she crocheted on glibly, telling Aasim that she had never done such a complicated design for anyone else.

It seemed as though a number of intense feelings were being funnelled into me the longer he stared back. I pursed my lips, deciding to get up and leave. I didn't know what these feelings were and I didn't want to know. I knew his eyes followed me as I left the room in defeat, although just in time for my sister who caught my arm and made me sit down in the hall.

'It's your engagement tomorrow!' she said, sitting down beside me, tucking her sari under her knees. 'You need to put mehendi now.'

Reluctantly I put my hands forward, and she daubed them with the fresh, green mehendi paste that someone had ground on the sill-batta. Aware that Aasim was still in the adjacent room, I pretended not to care and with more interest than it warranted, I watched as Apa placed a circle of the green paste on each palm. Then she daubed it on my fingertips, covering my nails. As the mehendi dried, it cooled my skin, wrinkling and tightening it, almost like the knot in my chest.

Aasim came out of the room and went in the direction of the kitchen where I knew he would get to taste all the dishes that were being prepared for *my* engagement. The mere thought should have infuriated me, but it didn't.

'Aasim, come early tomorrow?' Apa said as she saw him come back towards the hall, his mouth full of mithai.

He chewed, swallowed, nodded and then said, 'Of course, Bhabhi! I'll do anything to get rid of her, as soon as possible.' He nodded again in my direction.

'Aasim!' Apa reprimanded him but it was diluted with her smile. 'Don't tease the poor thing so much!'

'But it's true!' he said as he pushed his feet into his shoes and made to leave.

The knot in my chest had somehow moved to my throat and I fought to swallow it. Pulling my hands away from Apa's I ran in the general direction of the bedrooms, feeling a perverse pleasure at the look of shock on Aasim's face. It was only when I sat down on a bed that I realised I had been crying.

chapter 16

There were many trees in the backyard of my house. Sometimes honeybees would build their hives on the branches of some of these, one sticky cell at a time, growing rapidly in size and shape, while the bees buzzed around relentlessly. Abba usually had to get a few men to take down the hives; during that time we were not allowed to come out of our rooms lest we get stung.

As I noticed the buzz in my house on the morning of my engagement, I was somehow reminded of the hives and of how my house resembled the interiors of those hives. There was a mad, scrambling rush to heat the water on the wood stove and many people had woken up early just to be able to take a bath. Thankfully, no one had disturbed me yet, as I lay in one of the rooms pretending to sleep all night and failing miserably.

My eyes were contracted into slits and I felt a grainy, scratchy feeling around them which I understood was because of lack of sleep. I had tossed and turned the whole night, feeling uneasy about something and irritated because I was unable to pin down what it was. During dinner last night, I had allowed my nani to feed me because there was still mehendi on my palms. Just as

I lowered my head to sip water from the glass in her hands, I noted that Aasim had come back for dinner.

'Look at the baby!' he snickered while I glowered at him.

'Who asked you to come back?' I said, shaking my head at the last morsel of food on the plate from which my nani was feeding me. My face felt hot as I realised how silly I must be looking in my cotton sari, mehendi on my palms, my hair flying about, and being fed by my grandmother.

'No one has to ask me to come to this house,' he countered as he sat down in front of me, cross-legged, and started eating. 'This is my house too.'

What I hated about Aasim not having his own mother was that every time Apa visited us, he promptly started coming here for his meals too. My mother treated him like the son she never had and thanks to him, I knew enough about how pesky siblings probably were, although I had never called him bhaiya.

'Arrey! Why are you eating the cold rotis?' Ammi said, pulling away his plate while he laughingly tried to pull it back.

'Why don't you just stand on the tawa and eat?' I asked him as he smirked at me because of the preferential treatment he got.

He laughed at that and in a suspended moment our mutual animosity was discarded, and oh no! I was staring at him again. At the way his eyes crinkled at the corners and his charming smile, despite the bottom row having a couple of uneven teeth. Before he could realise I was at it again, I got up and walked away, deciding not to come out again until I was a bride. I went to bed.

But sleep eluded me completely. I could hear him laughing easily as he sat outside, talking to someone. Probably another aunt he was trying to charm, I thought in a huff. But the sound of his laughter was drilling a small hole inside my chest, little by little, expanding it until it felt that my chest would cave in.

I couldn't understand what was happening, so I closed my eyes and tried to think about my engagement. My fiancé. My new family.

My fiancé lived in Vellore too, and his family had come to see me a month ago. He had two sisters who were already married. Since he was the only son, his family had wanted a pretty bride for him. They had been searching for a couple of months when common family members and friends had informed them about me. My parents hadn't started looking for a groom for me yet, but the moment they heard that his family was asking, they promptly agreed.

I didn't know what he looked like, how old he was, how tall or short. My father had seen him and so had Apa's husband, and they were satisfied. I wondered if Aasim, too, had gone to see him but I doubted it, because if he had, he would have definitely made fun of the whole situation.

The myriad thoughts kept me awake and I heard Aasim's laughter for a long time, even after he had left.

I grimaced under the weight of the jewellery that was being piled on me and was ready to burst into tears. The sari which had come from my in-laws' house was unusually heavy because the zari work on it was made of pure gold. I wasn't impressed. Everything hurt. My neck, my arms, my head and I didn't know how I was going to manage to pull off looking regal in all these contraptions. Turned out, I needn't have bothered.

Apa wetted the edge of the surma stick and dipped it in the

dark surma powder to outline my eyes, but it made my eyes tear up instantly. The mehendi on my palms was dark red, an affirmation of something I couldn't understand. I immediately banished all sad thoughts and instead focused on how pretty everything looked—right down to the petticoat I was wearing. The edges had been crocheted with white lace by Raheema bu and I felt special as I stepped into it, but that was before the sari had been wrapped around me.

Sweat trickled down my face and Apa thrust a handkerchief in my direction, asking me to wipe it off and keep my head and eyes lowered throughout the day. My neck was already hurting but I listened to her, glad in a way that Aasim wasn't here to see me looking demure and shy. Because I *wasn't* demure and shy and he knew it and he would have guffawed loudly, just to annoy me.

The engagement was being held in my house and I didn't know what was happening outside the room, except for the odd titbit of news. They were here—my mother-in-law and her daughters along with a contingent of people from her side. After the ceremony was finished and the guests had food, the boys from our family would go to their house and perform something similar for my fiancé.

My role was extremely passive—it was just to sit still and look pretty, which I managed although not with ease. My back ached from hunching over in the way my sister insisted I do, the moment she heard that they were here. Later on, I was taken outside where they made me sit on a chair and piled what seemed like ten kilos of mogra flowers on my head. Someone shoved a ring onto my finger, clasped a fat necklace around my neck and slid a bangle up my arm and thus, I was engaged.

I was led back inside the room where I had to sit with the ridiculous amount of flowers on my head, sweating and suffocating every single minute of it, while my family made sure the guests ate properly.

As the bride, I was supposed to merely exist. Not look up, down or outside the room despite all sorts of temptations that made me want to do the contrary. I edged slowly towards the window from where I could see the hall and I saw the women eating. A tall, lanky figure walked past the window and I shrank back in horror. I didn't want Aasim to see me like a walking flowerpot.

I stayed inside the room and when someone brought a plate of biryani for me to eat, I refused. All I wanted to do was to remove the flowers from my head, yank off the heavy sari, peel off the itchy blouse and wear my oldest pink cotton sari, the one that I wore in the peak of summer.

By the time it was all over, it was nearly five in the evening. The house had emptied considerably as all the men had gone for the ceremony to my fiancé's house. Except I didn't think they would have draped him with flowers. Not like this anyway.

Abba, however, hadn't gone because only the uncles and the cousins were supposed to go, which meant that Aasim would have gone too. A part of me was worried about what he would say when he got back. He would grossly exaggerate everything and I would have to simply listen.

I ventured outside and Abba looked at me, surprised. He clasped my hand. 'My little girl,' he said proudly, as though I had accomplished something wonderful.

'Can I remove these flowers?' I asked, and Abba blinked in surprise.

'Of course!' he replied and I almost ran back inside the room where I tugged at the flowers that had been tied around my head. The moment I got rid of the flowers, I sat down on the bed and cried. I don't know why the tears came but suddenly everything seemed overwhelming. Apa came to the room and I ran and hugged her tightly.

'Mariam, what happened?' she asked me gently. I shook my head, unable to stop the heaving sobs that emerged from me. She made me sit down and helped me remove all the jewellery, and then she unwound the sari from my body. With each kilo that was lifted, my body felt lighter but my heart grew heavier. Finally, I rummaged in the cupboard and although my veins felt like they were being shot with something sharp and acidic, I managed to pull out my favourite pink sari and draped it hurriedly.

'Mariam!' Apa called out but I shook my head and ignoring her, ran upstairs to the terrace where I crawled under my alcove and breathed for the first time that day.

chapter 17

Only one star had made its appearance in the sky and I looked at it, feeling apprehensive for some reason. Downstairs, everyone was busy with the after effects of the engagement—the cleaning up, the sitting down and recounting of the day. I was not really needed even though it was supposed to have been my day.

I didn't know when he came upstairs because my eyes were trained on the sky, watching out for more stars.

'Move a little,' he said.

'Why?' I asked him defensively. I wasn't ready to relinquish my space to him today. Aasim sighed, and then without saying another word, pushed my legs together and physically moved me further inside the alcove while he sat down next to me.

'You idiot! There must be spiders here!' I said, grappling in the near darkness and trying to crawl out.

'Just sit for some time, will you?' he insisted. I hung my head and sat back, realising that his leg was squeezed very close to mine. It was hot and stuffy inside and I couldn't breathe. I told him as such and he relented, moving a little outwards so I could see the sky again and was no longer tormented by the thought of spiders.

'Why are you here?' I asked him after a while of sitting in silence.

'You weren't downstairs,' he shrugged.

'So?'

He didn't reply. I looked at his profile, belatedly realising that I was doing the staring thing again. Before I could look away, he turned and it began again. Only this time, the staring was from extremely close quarters and it caused the skin on my arm to erupt in goose pimples.

'Why do you keep doing it?' he asked, breaking the spell. I looked down at my folded knees.

'I'm so sad, Aasim,' I said the first thing that came to my mind and he looked at me surprised.

'Why?' he asked, picking up my hand and inspecting it absently.

He hadn't touched me since we were kids when we had fought like cats and dogs. After that incident when I had fallen on the terrace, tripping on my own sari, we hadn't so much as brushed past each other. And now he was sitting so close to me and holding my hand. The feelings his touch evoked were inexplicable.

'Why are you sad?' he repeated, his voice seeming to come from a distance, breaking into my thoughts.

'I don't know,' I said, pulling my hand away, warmth flooding my face. 'It's been there for some time. I'm just very sad inside. Here,' I said, pointing to my chest.

His eyes travelled to my finger and then I realised how ludicrous I looked and quickly moved away my hand. His gaze found mine and I couldn't look away.

The air between us was charged and both of us hadn't a

clue of what was happening at the moment. In the farthest corner of my head, I knew that this was probably wrong. We shouldn't be sitting here like this.

'I saw you today,' he said, his words puncturing the silence, cleaving the unease between us.

'Was it before or after the flowers?' I asked in a dull voice, remembering how I had felt just a while back. Although there were so many different things I was feeling now, none of it was close to the despair I had felt downstairs.

'Before,' he said, the hint of a smile playing in his voice; I looked up and smiled back.

'And after,' he added, putting his head back and laughing. I made a face at him and pushed his arm but he caught my hand and yanked me forward. We were now sitting very close together. The initial feeling of slight discomfort and unease was being slowly but effectively drowned out under a cloud of unfamiliar sensations.

I could see his stubble. Curious, I raised my fingers to his cheek and touched him lightly. He let me explore his strong jaw and I rubbed my thumb around his chin but when my fingers traced the little indentation under his lower lip, his eyes darkened and he caught my hand.

I could actually feel my breath stop in my throat as he leaned in towards me, pulling me closer towards him until there was barely an inch between us.

'You're so beautiful,' he whispered, as though surprised by the fact. And then we were both yearning to move closer to each other as he kissed my forehead, my cheeks, the side of my neck and then he looked up at me, as though asking for my permission.

What was I doing, I wondered, excitement surging within. This was Aasim. The boy I hated, who annoyed me, who made sure I was always the butt of his jokes. He thought *I* was beautiful?

I closed my eyes and finally he kissed me on the lips, pulling me even closer. With barely a heartbeat between us, I kissed him back, not knowing what I was doing. I didn't know people kissed this way. I had never seen or even heard of anything like it. But it was so wonderful, this intimate connection between us, this final breaking down of barriers that had unspooled the knot inside my chest and set me free.

I clutched the back of his head, afraid he would move away, and we stayed there kissing, revelling in the gloriousness of this sudden discovery, until the sky was sprinkled with stars.

I groaned when he moved away, breathing heavily. He shook his head as though to clear it, and then shook it some more.

I looked at him, afraid that I had done something to anger him, but then he had been the one to invade my space, break down my walls and cause this tremulous ache.

I was afraid to talk because it would make everything normal, and this magical moment that was suspended in the stars would cease to exist.

'Aasim,' I finally ventured, wishing there was some way to communicate without the banality of speech. He took a deep breath and then he cupped my face in his hands and rubbed his lips against mine as though he couldn't help himself. He caught my lower lip with his teeth and then sucked it gently, but then he moved his face away.

Unable to look away from his face, I saw him rub his mouth with the back of his hand as though it could remove all traces of what had happened now and that singular action caused an eruption inside me. How dare he?

I surprised him by launching myself at him, kissing his forehead, cheeks, his jaw, his neck, and even his lips. I lifted his hands and kissed them fervently. 'Wipe that. And that. And that,' I said, my voice trembling. We stared at each other and I realised I was shaking. And then once again we lunged at each other, until kissing was no longer a foreign activity to me. When the shock had worn off and the passion had waned, I put my head on his chest and he put his arms around me.

'I'm sorry,' he said, and I stiffened.

Without looking up at him, I asked, 'Why?'

'Because you're engaged.' His voice was flat. I shut my eyes at his words, refusing to let the meaning register.

'No, I didn't mean to ask why you were sorry,' I murmured softly.

'Then?' He had wound his hands around my braid and tugged it until I looked at him.

'Why this? Now?' I asked, looking into his face. How could I have hated him so much? Even till this moment? I traced his jaw with my finger and realised that it couldn't have been hate.

He shrugged. 'I wish I knew. It's not like I planned it.' His mouth trembled a little.

'Let's run away,' I surprised myself by suggesting something so dramatic but the moment I said it, it sounded perfect. He pushed me away angrily.

'Are you mad?' he asked.

'But… ' I bit my lower lip.

'I don't know, Mariam! I wish I had never come upstairs

looking for you!' he said, unfolding himself from the alcove and walking away.

'Wait!' I pleaded and he stopped.

'People will be looking for you,' he said evenly without turning around. 'It's better I leave and you come downstairs after a while.'

'But… '

'No, Mariam. Running away is not an option. I could never do that to Bhabhi. And neither can you, I'm sure,' he said, turning around to face me.

'You can't just… you can't just leave!' I exclaimed, desperately.

'At your fiancé's house, they've fixed your wedding date three months from now,' he informed me. I shut my eyes, anger filling every pore of my body.

'It's *best* if I leave,' he said, and I realised he wasn't just talking about going downstairs.

'What do you mean?' I asked, walking towards him. He walked backwards as though physically distancing himself from me.

'Someone from another terrace could see us,' he warned.

'Well, good then,' I said, not caring.

He sighed heavily. 'Things aren't so easy, Mariam. We can't get married, not now, not after your engagement to someone else. And there's no way your father will agree to our marriage anyway.'

'Why?' I demanded, 'Your brother was good enough for my sister!'

'Yes, but age matters. I'm way too young to get married,' he explained and I wanted to slap him as he calmly spoke about why he was all wrong for me. Why had he kissed me then?

'I just made a decision. I'm going to leave Vellore,' he announced. What? Now he was the one who sounded crazy.

'I… I can't stand around seeing you get married to someone else, so… '

'So you mean you're running away *without* me, you coward!' I spoke through gritted teeth, and he winced.

'I'm sorry,' he said, his voice bleak as he backed towards the door.

'I'll never forgive you.' Anger strengthened my voice, lending me a conviction that he was wrong and I was right.

I shook my head. 'Never,' I promised.

chapter 18

It was anger that sustained me through the next three months because true to his word, Aasim had disappeared from my life. Everyone was surprised that he had decided to go to Madras to study further, especially my sister, because until now he had always seemed laidback and complacent.

'I don't know what has happened to that boy,' she remarked one day when she came home. I looked up instantly, knowing that she was talking about Aasim.

'I'm a little worried about him actually, Ammi,' she said and both wondered what could have caused such a dramatic change in him. He never visited our house and I could see that it had upset Ammi and even Raheema bu.

I sat at the back, listening to them discuss him and I allowed the anger to fashion a hardened block out of my heart. I refused to remember the reasons he had outlined to me on the terrace because as far as I knew nothing else mattered – only the fact that being with him had felt so right. But apparently not to him.

As the day of his departure neared, I lingered on the terrace more than ever, refusing to even look at the alcove. It was one more thing he had completely ruined for me. I usually stayed there until dusk, looking at the stars, sometimes crying, sometimes just remembering what it had felt like to be in his arms. Despite the anger, I hungered to see his face, to talk to him, to hear his voice, but he never came home. I wondered if he would come to see Ammi before he left for Madras and casually asked her once while she was cooking lunch.

She looked at me and shrugged, and I marvelled at the blindness of adults, while being thankful for it at the same time. How could she not see it?

'I'm going to send word through someone that he has to come and meet me before he goes. How can he go just like that?' Ammi said as she blew out the wick of the kerosene stove.

I woke up one morning, sick to my stomach knowing that it was the day he was going away to Madras. Although I reasoned to myself that it was just Madras and not some place like Bombay or… or… Delhi and he could come back any time he wanted. But that was the important thing. *If he wanted.*

I waited that day, positioning myself near the door, hoping to catch a glimpse of him when he came to say goodbye to my mother. I knew that he wouldn't linger and there was no chance I wanted to miss him before he went. A part of me knew that he was probably a little wary. Or rather, afraid that I would tell everyone about what had happened on the terrace. Why would I? It wasn't important enough to him. *I* wasn't important enough to him. So, I decided around ten in the morning that he too wasn't important for me. I was going to play it cool.

He walked in as always, but I could sense the change in him instantly. He looked nothing like the boy I had known. It seemed that his personality had changed drastically and most of all, his eyes… there was something wrong with them.

He saw me sitting in the hall looking at him, but he ignored me and walked towards the kitchen where he knew my mother would be. I let the ball of hurt and anger roil around inside me, while at the same time, wishing for even a single moment to be with him, alone. He emerged from the kitchen and then went looking for the other aunts and sat down and spoke to Raheema bu. I didn't move from my place despite the strong urge to follow him wherever he went.

My mother came out from the kitchen with a cup of tea in her hands and she gave it to him when he came out. I observed everything from my place on the mat in the hall, emitting such strong vibes that I was sure he could feel them scorching his skin. He took the tea and she asked him to sit down. He was carefully sitting ten feet away from me. Not so much like last time, I thought nastily. I was angry, sad, lonely and hurt, and he was clearly not concerned.

'I hope you will be back in time for Mariam's wedding?' Ammi said, smiling at him. I flashed a look at him, daring him to look at me, at least now.

'I'm afraid I won't be able to, Ammi,' he replied, looking into his tea. I swallowed. He meant it.

'Why?' Ammi asked, surprised. 'You can take a couple of days leave from your college and come.'

He shrugged. 'I'll see. But don't expect me.'

'What happened to you, Aasim? How come this sudden urge to go to Madras and study?' she asked him, placing her hand on his shoulder.

Look at me, you fool. Me. I'm sitting right here. Look. Up. This way. I'm the reason you're turning around your entire life. I wanted to say the words aloud if only to elicit some sort of reaction from him, but I stayed quiet.

'It's been on my mind from quite some time, Ammi,' he said sipping the tea. She sighed and then walked back into the kitchen, leaving the two of us alone in the hall. There were a hundred things I wanted to do, and most of them involved throwing sharp, pointed objects at him, crying, pushing him down and hitting him until he hurt as much as I did. But the topmost thing that I could think of was to curl up on his lap, put my hands around his neck and kiss him.

He sipped the tea quietly, unaware of the nature of my thoughts. When he finished, he placed the cup carefully on the ground and got up. That was it. He was going.

'Aasim!' I called out, unable to stop myself. The despair inside me tipped the scales in favour of not acting so cool after all. He froze, as though he had realised only then that I, too, was in the hall. He turned to look at me and for the first time that day in nearly two weeks, our eyes met. I wanted to convey so much to him, tell him that until that day on the terrace, I had been walking around feeling sad and unhappy because a piece of me had been missing. And it was only when he had held me, the missing piece had slid into place and fit there snugly. How could he uproot everything after that? But my thoughts weren't coherent or lucid and neither was I able to express them the way I wanted to. Instead I found myself saying, 'Don't go,' and my voice shook, not with anger, but with fear that I would never see him again.

He pursed his lips and broke away his gaze, looking down at the mat as though entranced by its patterns. When he looked up again, I saw that his eyes were wet. Was he crying? Instantly, all my anger dissolved and in a flash, I was up. He shook his head furiously and got up, backing away, mouthing, 'Don't'.

Feeling foolish I stood there as he slid his feet into his shoes, looking at me all the while, his eyes blazing, but I knew instinctively that it wasn't anger. Just as he was headed towards the door, Raheema bu shuffled out.

'Aasim! You're still here? Wait, I forgot to give this to you,' she said, handing him the crocheted skull cap she had been making for him a day before my engagement.

'It's beautiful, Raheema bu,' he said. 'I'm glad you finished it in time.'

'Arrey, I finished it that day itself but you haven't come back home after Mariam's engagement!' she said, smiling at him.

He looked at me swiftly, nodded in my direction and then bent down to remove his shoes and came back inside the hall where he took the cap from Raheema bu and hugged her. 'I'll miss you all so much!' he said, all the while looking at me and I knew his words were meant for me. 'I'll miss you the most.' He stepped away from a surprised Raheema bu and then without looking at either of us, wore his shoes and walked out of my life. Forever.

chapter 19

I felt like I was in the centre of a raging storm. The whirlwind of chores, the buzz of activity, and the chaos surrounded me but did not involve me. On some days, men from the sari shop would come, bringing along bundles of saris packed in muslin, which they would open in front of Ammi and Apa. Both of them would sit a little further away, their faces half covered with their pallus as they nodded or shook their head as the men showed them the saris one by one. Abba usually sat down with them, helping them choose and when the men would go, Ammi and Apa would move forward and see the saris again.

The rest of the work was managed by Abba alone. He gave the order for the jewellery at our jeweller, and appointed the bawarchi who would cook the biryani for my wedding. He went to Madras with a friend and purchased various household items that would be sent along with me as my dowry. Finally, only the smaller items remained. Pretty but inconsequential things like laces, ribbons and petticoats. Raheema bu crocheted for me almost incessantly, peering over her hook myopically as she produced tiny squares of delicate lace that were stitched on the sleeves of some blouse or the other.

I spent most of my time in my room, refusing to go to

the terrace any longer. It hurt too much now. Ammi was glad because it meant I wouldn't be out in the sun any more. On some days, Raheema bu came and sat down with me and she would try and talk to me. I felt protective of her because Aasim was fond of her, and in her own way she reminded me of him.

I tried not to think of him, but that was impossible. I remembered every single one of his annoying words and gestures, but most of all, I remembered our staring matches. And of course, the kissing on the terrace. At times, I felt that I would have given anything to be able to revert to my old state of despondency, the time when I had no clue about what I was feeling or why. I would have loved to simply move on into my new life, not having known anything about Aasim, and I would have been able to continue my childish banter with him whenever we met. And he wouldn't have left Vellore.

But there were times, usually around three or four in the morning, when I would wake up to the sound of regulated breathing around me, punctuated with snores, and I would tiptoe outside to the courtyard where I would sit and stare at the strips of darkened sky. At these moments I was glad of what had happened, of what we both did, because imagine living a life not knowing that this had been just around the corner?

I took to crocheting some of the lace with Raheema bu because I felt sorry for her, hunched in one corner of a room over her hook, alone with her yarn. She was thrilled that I finally asked to learn and she showed me the basic stitches, which I picked up almost instantly. There is obviously a small but positive side to every heartbreak. Your mind is so addled with pain that something monotonous like crochet, with its constant and repetitive movements, can help you create such heartwarming beauty, the creation of which becomes second nature for you.

I started crocheting doilies with her help and Ammi was pleased that I was finally accomplished at something useful. 'Otherwise they would have said that we have not taught her anything,' she was telling Apa one day, unaware that I could hear her. 'She doesn't like to cook or sew; all she does is listen to Binaca Geetmala on the radio.'

'Actually, don't you think she's changed a little after her engagement?' Apa asked Ammi. The two of them were sewing the falls on my sari hems and hadn't heard me come.

'It's the fear of getting married and moving to another house,' Ammi explained as she snapped a thread with her tooth. 'But I'm glad that her mother-in-law will be pleased to see how well she can crochet.'

'Well, no one in her family will run out of namaz topis. That's for sure!' Apa laughed and was surprised when she saw me standing there, looking stricken. 'Mariam, sit down here,' she said patting the ground beside her.

I thought of Raheema bu crocheting the topi for Aasim and I shook my head, rage turning my tongue to ashes. It seemed like I couldn't say a word, and honestly I didn't know who was making me angrier.

'I am never going to crochet a namaz topi in my life,' I spat out the words and ran away to the backyard. I could no longer run to my refuge on the terrace and I really hoped that no one would follow me to the backyard to see what was wrong with me. I was afraid I wouldn't be able to withstand a round of questioning, no matter how well-meaning it was.

Apa came looking for me and I stared straight ahead at

the dead leaves on the ground, at the chattering birds and the myriad butterflies that flitted around.

'Mariam?' she said gently, placing her hand on my back. I flinched. 'What's the matter? Is everything alright?'

I didn't trust myself to speak. Briefly, very briefly, I considered coming clean to her, telling Apa that I was in love with her brother-in-law, but he hadn't even bothered giving us a chance. That he had preferred to turn his back on the whole mess. But I took in Apa's round, pleasant face and her trusting eyes and I knew I couldn't do it. Maybe, like Aasim, I too was afraid, but I might have had the courage if he'd been with me. I didn't dare step into it alone.

'I'm just sad about leaving you all and going, Apa,' I said finally and she looked sympathetic.

'That's okay. Even I felt that way. See, I'm back here with you? You will also come back and visit all of us,' she consoled me and pulled me into her embrace. I hugged her back, closing my eyes tightly, wishing for so many conflicting things that I didn't even know what I wanted any more.

'It will be alright,' Apa assured me as she patted my back, probably relieved that I was just suffering from a case of nerves like all brides. Apa and I had never been close as siblings because of the age difference between us. She was eight years older than me and although she was only twenty-six now, with her three children, she seemed more at par with my mother. I nodded bleakly, wondering if I would feel this way all my life.

chapter 20

Vellore, 2011

All four of them stopped and looked up at me expectantly. I tried to gauge what I saw in their eyes but my usual perceptiveness had disappeared. It probably had to do with dredging up old memories and telling them things that I had told no one.

'Then? Then what happened?' Arifa asked, her eyes shining for some reason. Or maybe it was a trick of the light.

'Did you get married, Amma?' Nimra asked without looking up. I saw that her corner of the bedspread was loose and instantly, I forgot what I was going to tell them.

'Nimra, hold your hook firmly. I cannot have this bedspread all tight in one corner and loose in the other!' Startled, Nimra fumbled over the row of double crochet stitches she was making. I pursed my lips and looked up, trying to stop my irritation from showing.

'Did you ever see him again, Amma?' it was Amreen who asked me the question softly.

'Yes, and of course I got married, Nimra. What a question!' I said a little scornfully. I was trying to dispel some of the nostalgia I had evoked by being brusque.

The usually silent and long-suffering Shaista looked at me squarely in the eye and asked instead, 'Were you happy?'

I rubbed the dry skin of my forehead with my callused palms, trying to buy time before I answered. But I needn't have bothered.

'I somehow find it hard to believe all this happened,' Arifa said, her usual scepticism at the forefront. 'I mean, how come no one saw the two of you on the terrace? Or no one realised that *both* of you were missing after your engagement?'

'You don't have to believe it if you don't want to,' I responded after a moment. After all, what else could I say?

'It's just so difficult to connect you to that Mariam,' Nimra said, still looking down at the bedspread and diligently working away. I smiled at her bent head.

'No, I believe it!' Amreen announced, shushing Arifa with her hand. 'Continue, Amma. You said you met him again. When was it? What happened?' They all looked at me expectantly. Even Nimra looked up, her eyes wide.

I looked at their faces, each with a story of their own, that they were willing to put behind for a few hours a day when they came here and listened to mine. My throat was parched, as though lined with prickly needles. I shook my head.

'Not today. I can't talk anymore,' I pointed at my throat and noted how disappointed they all looked. 'But come tomorrow and maybe I'll tell you more.'

Quiet murmurs preceded their departure as they all packed away their things and started shuffling out. I looked at the unfinished bedspread and sighed. Despite my age and my slowly ebbing eyesight, I didn't trust them to do as good a job of it as I wanted. So, one warm afternoon, I had started the quiet and unassuming centre, the core of the bedspread, myself. I crocheted out of habit, not even requiring to see what I was doing. Performing the simple, repetitive action brought a kind of peace to my heart that was hard to achieve in any other way.

The girls had naturally been surprised when they saw that I had started on it, but then I launched into my story and they listened quietly, each taking up a corner and working on it in their own haphazard fashion.

chapter 21

Vellore, 1958

I had been, married for nearly three years and there was no sign of a child on the way. Every day I would wake up and cover my face with my palms, murmur duas under my breath before stepping down from my side of the bed. Each day I avoided looking at *him*, as he slept, thankfully turned away from me, facing the wall.

It wasn't always like this. It wasn't. In the beginning, we were almost happy. I don't know if that was the term to describe it, but yes, there was a measure of contentment about me, knowledge that this was my life, and this was how I had to live it. The memories of Aasim seemed like a mere aberration in this journey, but I was wrong to have reduced it to that. If I had accepted that I would never feel for anyone what I felt for him, I might have fared better in my marriage. But I pretended that Aasim was the culprit, a man with no backbone, who had wronged me. To be honest, that was the only way I could deal with it.

So right before I got married, I looked around my familiar

home and at the faces of my loved ones, and decided that I was going to be happy. At that moment, it seemed as simple as making a decision. I went into my marriage, eyes wide open, and with no expectations except that I had a right to be happy, even without Aasim.

It was only after he left Vellore that I realised I didn't have any friends at all. I never spoke to the other girls in the family during functions, I didn't whisper with them about film stars, and I didn't giggle as much. I didn't have a single person with whom I could share these life-defining decisions that I was making. But I didn't know any better then.

Marriage was certainly an eye-opener though. It was only after marriage that I understood the value of my family and how easily they had let me off in everything. I had been the youngest in my family, considering that my mother had only two daughters, and I had been indulged and treated with affection. At my in-law's home, however, I was the only daughter-in-law, and it took me some time to understand the unspoken rules that I had to live by. For instance, anything that went wrong had to be my mistake and I had to bear the blame for it. On the other hand, if anything were done right, it was my mother-in-law who took the credit for it, because after all, it was she who had 'found' me.

Not having children immediately was of course lined up at my door. After the first three months of marriage my mother-in-law often stared at me speculatively. I worried about the moment when the unspoken words on her face would find a voice and come out into the open. At such times, I wished that communication with my husband wasn't such a problem.

He was a good man, but he was nearly ten years older to

me. We hardly spoke about anything outside the periphery of our daily lives, and that itself seemed a major accomplishment to me. It seemed inappropriate to discuss his mother with him over something that she *might* be thinking, so I left it at that.

The dull ache inside my chest that had morphed into a sharply splintered agony after the meeting with Aasim on the terrace, had throbbed in the initial days of my marriage but I ignored it, refusing to acknowledge its presence. As the days passed, I could bury it completely under the mediocrity of household life and I convinced myself that this was the happiness that everyone wanted and aimed to get. But it only transpired to me later that the happiness that I had been so bent on achieving was now centred on the possibility of a baby.

It wasn't for the lack of trying. So I didn't know why I hadn't conceived yet. The frustration of not getting pregnant was now wholly responsible for the uneasy feeling inside me, which told me that all was not well in my world.

With each passing month, my will to be happy at any cost crumbled till I was left with just the dust of my convictions. I almost never thought about Aasim now, except for the times when he slid into my mind without my knowledge. Immediately, I'd banish him to the darkest and deepest recesses where I hoped he languished and ached for my loss, just as I now hungered for a baby.

I didn't visit my home much, not because my mother-in-law was overly fond of me, but because she didn't want to let me out of her sight. So, not only did I miss my family, my sister and her children, I also didn't get to hear any news of Aasim.

I only went home on Eid or on rare occasions and during that time we would be so busy catching up with other things that there was no time to ask about him. And I had no plans of asking either. In the third year of my marriage, I had lost all hope of having a child and expected to hear any minute about how my mother-in-law was planning to get my husband re-married. It was one of those rare, non-festive occasions when I had been allowed to go home because my mother had fallen sick and sent word that she wanted to see me.

I draped my chadar and waited in the hallway for the rickshaw puller to come and call out. Obviously, I couldn't go alone, so I was being escorted by Razia bu, the old lady who had been living at my mother-in-law's home for what seemed like forever. I realised soon after marriage that she was nothing like the old women in my mother's home. There was something inherently sly about her; this combined with her rudeness, always made me feel uneasy in her presence. But there was no one else I could go with that day and hence, she helped me get into the rickshaw, and we weaved our way through the gallis to my childhood home.

Everything seemed the same, but it wasn't. Without Apa or me, the house seemed to have shrunk somehow, even though the rest of its occupants were still the same. It was something about the air—a lack of young energy probably—and I suppressed a sigh of sadness as I asked Razia bu to sit in the hall while I went in to see Ammi.

I slipped out of my chadar and sat down near Ammi who was sitting up on the bed, looking drawn.

'What happened?' I asked her, feeling a smidgen of fear for the first time. She brushed away my concerns, saying that she had the fever for quite some time now, and it was almost gone.

'But you look so thin and weak!' I protested, feeling bad

for not having come earlier to see her. 'Why didn't you tell me about your fever before?' I didn't like the way my marriage had crept up behind me unawares, eclipsing my life before it, until I ceased to even remember what had been important to me all these years.

'But you're a married woman now and you're busy with your life,' she said softly. I shut my eyes at that reminder. 'No... news?' she asked hopefully, her brow lined with worry.

I shook my head. The lines stayed on her forehead, not dissolving into her countenance. 'Don't worry. You came quite a while after your sister. It happens.'

'But you already had Apa, right?' I asked, allowing some of my bitterness to seep to the surface. She grimaced as she sat straighter.

'Yes, but she was a girl and your dadi was quite adamant that we have more children, preferably boys,' Ammi said, taking my hand.

I noticed how thin and veined her hands had become and I pressed them gently. 'Then you must have been disappointed that I was not a boy,' I said, although I knew that it was not the case. Ammi shook her head.

'Your father was a little disappointed at first and your dadi... 'Ammi left the sentence incomplete. 'But we couldn't have more children after you and I reconciled myself. But you made up for it all.'

I smiled at her, my first real smile in what was probably months.

'How come Apa isn't here?' I asked, looking around. The usual women in the house, the aunts and the relatives, those who just lived with us, were around but busy with their work.

'And where's Raheema bu?' I asked a little warily. In my mind, I associated Raheema bu with Aasim. On the day he had left, briefly, foolishly I had wondered if I could hug her and somehow absorb the touch of his body through her, but I hadn't. She would have been surprised to have received two hugs one after the other, especially since our family wasn't very forthcoming when it came to expressing affection.

'Nazreen came and saw me yesterday. She wanted to come and stay but she can't,' Ammi explained.

'Why?' I asked, looking out of the room, wondering where Raheema bu was.

'Aasim was in Vellore for his holidays and he had an accident. He fractured his leg. It's going to take quite a few months to heal and she needs to be there to take care of him,' Ammi said.

I turned back to her, my mouth dry and my stomach full of what seemed like hot lead.

'When?' I managed to ask.

'Last week, Thursday.' I thought back to last week, at what I had been doing on Thursday. He had been here in Vellore and… And what, I thought dully, trying to quench the different feelings that had snaked up from nowhere and caught me unawares, making me realise that I still yearned to see him.

'How's he now?' I asked, knowing that my face might have given away what I'd been thinking about and wondered what Ammi would make of it.

She smiled and patted my hand, consoling me. 'How the two of you used to fight! Poor fellow! He's in quite a lot of pain and it will take a while for him to get back on his feet.' I nodded, looking down, hoping that Ammi would not spot the single tear that surprised me by forcing itself out of my eye. I wanted to get away from here, put as much distance between myself and any mention of him, but that wasn't possible. Ammi, blind as usual to my feelings despite the fact that they were evident on my face, continued chatting about how responsible Aasim had become and how his brother was proud of him.

'There's one thing that your Apa's husband is a little worried about,' she said. I didn't care. I didn't care. I repeated the litany but I knew Ammi would tell me whether I wanted to hear or not.

'What?' I prompted her finally, in a bid to get out of the whole situation.

'Aasim apparently wants to become a writer! Can you imagine?' she exclaimed, and then in a bout of coughing that shook her, forgot all about him and I let it be, although I was burning to ask her more.

It probably made no sense to anyone. Except me of course.

chapter 22

As long as I'd known Aasim, he'd been entranced by the movies. He made sure he watched almost every movie that was released and would come back and trouble me by telling me the entire story, whether I wanted to listen or not. At that time, I thought it to be another one of his intensely annoying habits, but I would still wait for him to come. It never occurred to me that we were two bored children who had found each other's company through chance, and I never realised that what we had then was the very beginning of what I felt for him. What I would feel for him.

For Aasim, who starred in the movie was never as important as its story, although he was partial to Dilip Kumar, and didn't quite like Raj Kapoor. He would come back and narrate the entire story to me with actions and energy, his eyes bright with excitement. One day, an elderly member in our family sat down to hear him narrate a story with passion, I think it was Dilip Kumar's *Deedar*. When he became conscious of the fact that he had an audience, it made him very uncomfortable; he liked to limit his audience to me.

Initially, his storytelling sessions would annoy me, but later I had started looking forward to him recounting the tales. It almost didn't matter that I didn't get to see any of the films myself. I did watch *Deedar* though, months after he had narrated the story to me, and it felt like I was watching it for the second time, so vivid had his description been.

'I wish I could join the movies,' had been his refrain since the time he was around twelve or thirteen. I would snigger and tell him off soundly for having such foolish dreams.

'Don't you know that Bombay is such a bad place and no decent Muslim boy thinks of joining the movies?' I would scoff.

'What about Yusuf saab?' he would ask immediately. 'He's a Muslim too.' I would brush off his repeated reference to Dilip Kumar and pretend that he was just being stupid. Within, however, I always felt the quicksilver dart of envy—the fact that he could contemplate something of the sort!

'Well, your brother will never allow you,' I would tell him and stomp away.

Maybe he had realised he didn't want to act in the movies but wanted to write the stories, I thought as the rickshaw puller cycled his way back to my galli, my kingdom. After all, it had been the stories that had intrigued him the most. Razia bu, who had been chatting with some of the other women in the family, looked at me pointedly for some reason. I didn't know why. But what would have irked me at any other time was of no consequence to me right then. Thoughts of Aasim filled my head, and I wondered if he ever thought of me too.

In this same town, not very far away from my own house, Aasim lay cooped up in bed with his broken leg. A part of me throbbed when I thought of how much pain he must be in, but a smaller, insidious part was viciously pleased that at least he was experiencing some sort of physical pain. Overriding all other thoughts was the wish to see him again, a wish that was impossible to fulfil considering my own marital status and my mother-in-law's diktats.

Each day I wondered how he was, whether his leg had healed, and how he planned to become a writer. At times I wished I'd never known about him because now it seemed as though he was never too far away from my thoughts. I would be in the kitchen, blowing air into the pipe that we used to light the fire, the hollow sound echoing in my ears, and his name would simply pop in my head, and I would look around uneasily wondering if someone else had heard it too.

I was half afraid I would mention his name in my sleep and my husband would get wind of something that, had been, that wasn't there, that could never be, even though it had the power to still twist a knife in my chest.

Ammi's health had improved considerably and there was no further reason to visit my mother's house after that, even though they lived so close. I often wondered at the unfairness of my situation, where my mother-in-law welcomed her daughters with open arms but held mine so I couldn't go to my mother's house. However, I knew what was better for me and for my state of mind, so I didn't even clamour to go because I didn't want to come back with more news of Aasim. It was best if he stayed nebulous in my head.

Then, the unthinkable happened. I became pregnant. I really don't know why it happened *now* instead of the past so many years, but nevertheless, I was glad it did. It took me two months to realise that I wasn't going to get my period for some time, and that the slight weight gain I had noticed was due to my pregnancy. I began noticing small things about myself, my reactions to the world in relation to my body, and I was sure that this too seemed some sort of aberration to my mother-in-law.

I don't know what she expected from me, but I wasn't given any special status in the house just because I'd finally become pregnant. I carried on as usual and when my mother found out, she came to visit me, beaming, bearing homemade mithais, a cloth bag packed to the brim with almonds and a small tin of saffron.

She requested my mother-in-law to let me stay with them for a few days and to my surprise, she relented. I was a little ambivalent about staying in my mother's house where inevitably news of Aasim was bound to filter through, but the thought of reverting to my life before marriage, even for a few days, was a temptation I couldn't resist.

I went to Ammi's house the following month and stayed there for a few days where I did nothing except lie down and read magazines or books. I didn't go to the terrace or to the backyard now, but chose to remain in my room as a sort of rebellion against my own feelings, and was successful most of the time.

My sister came to visit, me when she heard I was here and I almost dreaded her visit, because she was sure to talk of Aasim. Her children increased the noise levels in the house as they ran from one end to the other, ate aamchur from my mother's special tin, and generally brought the house down. Apa was very happy to learn that I was pregnant and we shared some stories about morning sickness and nausea and she reminisced about her own pregnancies. Then she sighed loudly and I braced myself.

'I don't know what is wrong with that boy,' she said.

I didn't pretend that I didn't know who she was referring to.

'Why? What has he done now?' I asked, picking up a sliced apple from a plate and nibbling on it, wishing she would come out with it. She scratched her chin and then sighed again. 'Your brother-in-law is very worried about him. Now that he's done his BA, he wants to become a writer! Can you imagine? What kind of money will he make?'

I remained silent. After all, what could I say? But Apa continued, 'He says that he wants to write books and not get into business. Have you ever heard of anything as silly as that? Your brother had finally convinced him to come back to Vellore after his studies, but even then I don't know what will happen.'

I frowned. 'Isn't he already in Vellore? I heard his leg was fractured,' I mentioned casually. No one would know the effort it had taken me to sound less than concerned about him.

'Yes, but he went back last week. His leg has still not healed completely but he insisted that he couldn't miss any more classes, and so he went. He's got a slight limp now,' Apa shook her head and I closed my eyes, my mind instantly conjuring up images of Aasim limping around in the wide open spaces of his college.

The thought that he was no longer in Vellore sent another shaft of pain and I hated my feelings, especially the way they see-sawed where he was concerned. Apa lingered for some more time and then left with her children, taking away what seemed like a vital source of noise and energy from the house.

Gloom and despair loomed inside me as I tried to understand myself better. Had I been hoping to see him in some way, while I was here? No! But then, why would I feel this way on hearing that he was no longer here? I felt cheated. I closed my eyes and willed myself to sleep, fervently wishing he had never been a part of my life.

chapter 23

I did not expect the changes in my body to be so dramatic. I had seen pregnant women before but very objectively, and I had rarely paused to notice why they seemed short of breath, or why they had puffed up so easily. Even the minute changes in my body caused me to wonder how women could go through it multiple times, sometimes every year. But the larger changes made me wish for normalcy again, for the times when I could walk or run like I used to, before marriage made a woman out of me.

My feet swelled up easily and in the afternoons when I didn't have any work, I took a nap in my room with the curtains drawn. When I woke up around four, with raging hunger and nausea, I would cry, missing my home and my mother, but I would often quell it by thinking of the baby and how everything would finally be alright when it arrived.

Aasim was no longer a pressing concern because with all the things that I was going through, alone, he rarely figured in my head. I didn't care if he became a writer, if he joined his brother's business or if he decided to live in Madras all his life. As the months progressed and my belly expanded, all I wanted was the baby to be born, more so because the thought of giving it to someone else to take care of once in a while, seemed very tempting.

Each day dragged, stretching and pulling at my nerves until it was finally the ninth month and my mother-in-law had no choice but to send me to my mother's home for the delivery. I arrived, bloated and moody, angry with the world and myself for thinking that my life would be a sheet of smooth, uninterrupted glass once I was pregnant.

Ammi took good care of me, fed me my favourite dishes, and I didn't do any work although Raheema bu and the other aunts tut-tutted, telling me that they did the housework right through their pregnancies, sometimes right till their delivery. I would listen to them, roll my eyes and then promptly turn around and fall sleep. I heard them complain to my mother that I needed to be a little more active if I wanted an easy delivery.

'Make her sweep the house. It's the only way her muscles are going to loosen up,' an old aunt proclaimed. 'If she sleeps all day, Allah knows how she will be able to deliver!' Ammi would protest then, telling that I deserved to rest a bit because I had been working hard in my in-laws' home.

The diwan in the hall was my friend in those days, where I would sleep all day, my ample body covered with the pallu of my sari, rising gently, slowly, jerking awake to a hard kick from the baby sometimes. I had my meals on the diwan and read magazines and books that Abba got for me. I even received visitors there, like my sister, or my husband who would drop by to see me after his day's work at his shop.

One day while I sat flipping through a magazine, I stopped and felt myself grow still. I had just seen Aasim's name under one of the stories. I stared at it, the Urdu calligraphy burning my eyes until I sat up with some difficulty and read the story, gulping, my hands shaking, wondering if he had indeed become a writer.

I had to read the story twice before I could understand it and I tried to smile through the sudden ache that his name had evoked. It was a well-written story, an action-filled spy thriller that I could completely envision him telling me. Even though I read the story in my head, I could hear him telling it to me with his excited voice and his gestures as he tried to make me see what was in his head.

I wondered if someone would think it odd if I removed the pages from the magazine. After pondering for some time, I decided that the best way would be to do it openly. I called out to Ammi and showed her the story. She looked at it, her eyes shining.

'Our Aasim!' she exclaimed with pride. 'He's writing stories for magazines now? Maybe he *will* write a book one day!'

I smiled grimly and then nodded. 'Do you think he's written more stories?' I felt a measure of hope grow inside me. Ammi shrugged.

'Do you think Apa knows?' I asked, struggling to remind myself that just the mere mention of his name had been enough to make me feel morose and upset all these days and here I was, actively asking about him. But it was completely legitimate. And I did want to know if there were more stories.

I ambled off to my room where I blew the dust off some of the magazines under the bed and brought them back to the diwan where I spent the rest of the evening, flipping coarse pages in the hope of seeing his name elsewhere. I found two more, and each story sprang out of the pages into my hands as though it was him I was touching.

I stopped analysing my thoughts and actions and decided to just go ahead with what I wanted to do. I got a pair of scissors, cut out the pages neatly and touched his name when no one else was looking. Then, I pasted them in a notebook that had been lying around, using some mashed rice because I didn't want to wait till Abba came back home and bought me glue.

Ammi helped me in the project. Of course, she never saw it as anything more than a way of preserving his achievement because we knew him and because... well... I used to play with him when we were small. For me, the three stories collapsed the distance between us and blurred the boundaries, and I refused to think anything further than that.

I kept the notebook with me in my room and I don't think Ammi noticed it. Although I continued spending my time on the diwan every day, I now took my afternoon naps in the room where I would read the stories again, slowly, savouring each word he had conjured.

One such afternoon, around ten days before my daughter was born, I was feeling extremely uneasy and short of breath. I snapped at everyone and the hairs on the back of my neck were constantly raised as though I were anticipating something unpleasant. Raheema bu was the only one who dared to talk to me despite my temper tantrums, but it could well be because she was almost deaf now.

Despite my insistence that I wasn't interested in crochet any longer, she remembered my short stint with it before my wedding and brought in a hook and yarn for me, asking me to help her with something. I immediately thrust it back into her hands but she kept pushing the hook into my hands over and over again until, sighing, I took it and started making the chain and then a design for a doily from memory.

The two of us sat on the diwan, crocheting in silence, thoughts making abrupt entries and exits in my head and then, flexing my fingers I told her I wanted to take a nap inside. She nodded and I waddled in, grimacing as I climbed the bed and lay down on my heaving side. I put my hand behind me on the window ledge and felt around for the notebook with Aasim's stories. I pulled it out and read them again.

By now, I knew each word, each nuance and I couldn't wait for the next story which I was sure would come the next month. I wondered if I would be back at my mother-in-law's house then and if so, how I would get hold of the magazine, because reading anything other than the Quran was not encouraged there.

I rubbed the side of my belly in circular motions, as the baby jostled inside me and I felt the panic that had become familiar to me over the past few months. The realisation that I was housing another human being in my body suddenly seemed absurd and unnatural to me. I took deep breaths, trying to calm myself and in one of those rare moments I allowed myself, I let my thoughts take me back to that starry evening on the terrace.

Then suddenly I opened my eyes in shock. I could hear Aasim's voice and it wasn't just inside my head.

chapter 24

What happens to all those profound proclamations that we make about other people? That we will never see them again, never talk to them again, never forgive them… for something that they didn't actually do? I didn't know. I heard Aasim's voice in the hall outside, Ammi's loud reaction at seeing him and I knew that it wasn't a dream. He was here in Vellore, in my mother's house.

'Aasim! When did you come to Vellore?'

'Just this morning, Ammi,' Aasim replied and I knew then that he had sat down next to Raheema bu on my diwan. I knew because he was talking very loudly to make himself heard to her.

'I asked, how are you!' he nearly shouted, and I shut my eyes as I let his voice seep through my senses.

Raheema bu murmured something and then Aasim spoke aloud again, 'For whom are you making this?'

I think it was then that Raheema bu said something about how I had been making it but had abandoned it and went inside to sleep. Aasim didn't speak loudly but I think I heard him ask, 'Mariam?'

Just then Ammi, too, joined them and I could clearly hear her tell him about how I was here for my delivery and that she was going to get me to come outside. I think he protested saying he didn't want to disturb me and I quickly turned around to face the window and closed my eyes, the notebook under my pillow.

Ammi opened the door and called out my name. When I didn't respond, she didn't leave. She came in and tried to shake me awake. 'Aasim's here!' she said like an excited little girl. I refused to budge and continued to pretend sleeping all the time she stood there, but her focus had changed from me to something else.

'Where's that book?' she asked herself as she searched for the notebook where we had pasted Aasim's stories. I was glad that she couldn't find it and I felt sad yet relieved when she left the room, telling Aasim that I was fast asleep.

He murmured something about not wanting to disturb me and I opened my eyes, not surprised to find them full of tears. I wanted to see him, absorb his face and note how he had changed over the years. I wanted to see if I still felt something for him, but there was no way I was going outside when I looked like this.

I looked down at my swollen feet and hands and shut my eyes again. I could hear Ammi talking to Aasim about his stories and he was telling her how he had just sent off one for a lark, and was pleasantly surprised when it had been accepted.

'Our Mariam is very proud of you,' she continued innocently and I closed my eyes, feeling mortified. Now he would know about the notebook. 'She's cut out your stories and pasted them in a notebook and everything. I was just searching for it to show it to you. We're so proud of you, Aasim,' said Ammi.

I couldn't hear what Aasim said but would have happily given an arm and a leg to see the expression on his face at that moment. But it was my sense of vanity and a tiny speck of self-preservation that stopped me. Meeting him at this juncture would be disastrous for me.

'Will you be here for long?' Ammi asked. I strained to hear his answer. I couldn't hear it and then after sometime all conversation ceased. It was dark, and I knew he had left. There were times when my heart felt like a rapidly sinking block of stone, and this was one of those. I yawned and stretched, feeling my body shift and re-adapt itself to my mood and breathing deeply, the way I seemed to be breathing all the time these days, I stepped outside.

I was surprised that Ammi hadn't switched on the lights and I walked towards the switchboard slowly and pressed the black nub down, bringing a yellow bulb to life in the hall. I had been mistaken when I thought the hall was empty. I pursed my lips and stood still, watching Aasim as he slept on *my* diwan.

I took a few tentative steps closer to see his face, my heart beating madly all the while. Why was he still here? Why was he sleeping? I looked down at him and shifted my focus to his face, while all the time feeling as though I was on the edge of a precipice, barely managing to hang on to the rock with my slippery hands... such was the state of my heart at that moment.

His face had filled out a little but apart from that tiny fact, he was still the same. I had to angle my head to see him better and I quickly tried to note everything about him. It was a bit like a starved person being presented a large meal and not quite understanding what to eat. Everything looked so good.

'I can't believe you're still doing it,' he said, the moment he opened his eyes and I stepped back, horrified. What did he mean? He must have seen the questioning look and he smiled, his old familiar half smile and got up shaking his head. It was such a wrong moment for me to note how graceful his movements were compared to my own lumbering body.

'Stop staring at me like that, Mariam,' he said easily with a grin and I looked down, almost ashamed and then I lifted my face to meet his eyes defiantly. Somehow, seeing him in the flesh had made me a little less wistful about him and more angry. I forgot about my pudgy face and my dimpled shins and spoke with what I hoped was hauteur.

'Why are you sleeping here? This happens to be my diwan,' I knew I sounded recalcitrant and not regal, but it was too late. The words had already been said.

'No wonder I hardly got any sleep. You must have made the mattress all lumpy,' he countered, looking up at me. I wondered what kind of a tableau we made – a heavily pregnant woman standing, looking down at a young man on a diwan. So I looked around for a chair, waddling up to it and sat down.

Gone was my bashfulness and unease and it seemed like the evening on the terrace had never happened. I quickly glanced around me to see if there was anyone around, in case he was playing an elaborate game to cover up his feelings for me. But there was no one. Ammi and the others were probably in the kitchen making dinner and... here I was... face to face with Aasim once again.

I trained my eyes on my swollen wrists and thought that maybe it was for the best. The pretence that none of it had happened or held any meaning for him. But how could I just let it go so easily? How could I pretend that my heart did not beat a little faster every time his name was mentioned? Maybe he could, because he had never had any feelings for me, I decided. Instantly I felt hurt, angry and miffed, but decided to bury my emotions under the surface. If he was going to pretend, well, so could I.

'Let me see, let me see… what is it that's different about you?' he asked in a teasing manner, looking me up and down and my face flushed in mortification. Surely he wasn't going to talk about my pregnancy!

I looked up at him squarely and for the barest of seconds, something in his eyes shifted, and then he was back to his usual ribbing.

'I swear I had no idea that you would love the food in your mother-in-law's house so much,' he teased. I narrowed my eyes.

'I asked you to get up from my diwan,' I shot back, feeling that the whole situation was quite unreal. For nearly four years I hadn't seen him and now when we did meet, he was behaving exactly like before. What about the… the kisses and that meaningful hug he had given Raheema bu, which had been meant for me? Surely he couldn't have forgotten, I thought in horror. Maybe he had, and I was the only one who had pined for him and cried and made more out of what had been.

'Why? It's my house as well. And I can sit wherever I want,' he defied me. Suddenly it was too much for me. I couldn't quite accept that he could sit there so easily and talk to me like when we had been kids. I wanted to make a statement by walking away, but I found it most difficult to even get up from the chair.

'You know, we're going to need a lever to lift you out from that soon,' he remarked and I swallowed the sudden rush of tears that threatened to make a fool of me. I turned my face away from him pointedly, hoping that it would make it apparent to him that I didn't want to talk to him. There was silence for a while and I really wished I could turn my face back to see what he was up to but I continued staring at the pillar which was in my line of vision.

'I heard someone's become a big fan of my writing,' he remarked casually and it took all my willpower not to turn towards him and scoff.

'Apparently she's even kept a scrapbook of my stories hidden safely somewhere.'

I blushed, feeling appalled. There was silence and then a sound of sudden movement and before I knew it, he was in my line of vision, hunkered down on his knees.

'Hey!' he said softly and waved in front of my eyes. I tried to look the other way but he held my chin.

'I'm sorry, Mariam. I… I tried being mean and nasty like how I used to before, but it's no fun now,' he said. I moved my face away from his hand, dismayed that he still had that melting effect on me, and I tried to back away while being seated in the chair. That was a mistake because the chair tipped back a little and I scrambled about in the air before he caught the chair swiftly.

'Wow. You *are* heavy!' he said and laughed. I pursed my lips mutinously and then right in front of my face, it seemed as though his entire face transformed. The boy on the terrace who had kissed me *hadn't* been a figment of my imagination. But it seemed that we had no words for each other.

'How have you been?' he asked instead, still on his knees. A second later, he winced as he got up and turned away.

'Good,' I replied tightly. The playful banter from his side had buffered the pain and hurt of losing him. I almost wished he would go back to it.

'Happy?' he asked, with his back to me.

'Very,' I replied, wishing he would turn back and look at me. He finally turned around to face me and shook his head.

'How's your leg?' I asked him, because the silence was confusing. I didn't know what to make of it.

'Still hurts at times,' he said, flexing his knee. 'And I limp a little.'

I nodded, unwilling to let my sympathy show on my face.

'So it all turned out for the best then,' he murmured, sitting down on the diwan.

'What do you mean?' I asked him, feeling the first spurt of anger and although I knew what he was referring to, I needed him to spell it out.

'This whole... ' he gestured in my direction and let his hands fall in his lap.

'Oh yes, it turned out very well indeed,' I said, a nasty edge to my voice. 'But what if it hadn't, dear Aasim? Would you have come and rescued me? You?'

I had called him a coward on the terrace and I wanted to fling the word at him once again but the way he looked up, his eyes blazing, I decided not to say anything.

'Why can't you just forget it ever happened?' he asked suddenly and I flinched, realising what it looked like to him.

'Forget what happened?' I asked after taking a moment to collect my wits. 'I have no idea what you're talking about.'

He stared at me, disbelief writ on his face, and then he laughed. 'Not bad for you, Mariam. I thought you were above all this, playing games and everything.'

'Do I look like I can play any game?' I asked him, finally exerting myself to get up from the chair.

'I meant mind games,' he muttered, looking a little concerned when I wobbled on my feet.

'I stopped playing games with you when I was twelve. Mind or otherwise,' I exhaled and before he could retort, Ammi came back from the kitchen.

'Oh! You two are fighting again,' she said happily, as though that fact alone had set the world back on its feet.

'Ammi, I had better go home now. Bhabhi will be waiting for me,' he said, getting up with a sigh.

'Did you show him your notebook?' Ammi asked. I winced but pretended it was because of the baby. Immediately Ammi grabbed hold of my arm and made me sit down on the diwan. Aasim, who had been sitting there, literally jumped up to give me place.

'Drop by again, Aasim,' Ammi said, dismissing him as she helped me lie down on the diwan. Oddly enough, he seemed reluctant to leave now.

'Can I just talk to her for a bit,' he asked and I felt surprise cause a small flutter in my stomach. I was positive that it wasn't the baby.

'Sure, go ahead,' Ammi said, as she covered my feet with a shawl and waited for him to speak.

'Umm… take care,' he said half-heartedly because he'd been expecting Ammi to leave.

'Ammi, can you get me some milk?' I asked and she nodded and left. Swiftly, Aasim sat down on the chair and pulled it up to me.

'Listen. I'm sorry. For everything,' he bit out and I turned my face away from him. I didn't want his apology. I didn't know what I wanted any more.

'Mariam,' there was a slight pleading tone to his voice and I turned around.

'What?'

'I really am sorry. For being mean now and… for… ' he looked down, unable to complete the sentence. I wished I could articulate to him that the two of us had been like two parts of a puzzle, meant to be together, but we had discovered it too late.

'Do you want Ovaltine in it?' Ammi called out and Aasim looked in the direction of the kitchen, tense and wary.

'I… I will never forget that evening on the terrace,' he confessed finally, picking up my hand and giving it a small squeeze

'I really hope you'll read my story next month. I… I… wrote it for you,' he said, and with that, he left.

'Yes, Ammi. I'll have Ovaltine in it,' I answered Ammi, hoping it would delay her arrival. But I would need more than five minutes to understand everything. His departure left a hole of despair in my heart, until I recalled his last words to me about his story.

It was also then that I realised that no matter how much I denied it, how much I tried to dress it up in my domestic happiness, I would never feel as alive as I felt when I was with him.

chapter 25

Vellore, 2011

'Were you obsessed with him?' Arifa asked, distaste evident on her face. Oh, you poor judgemental creature, I thought, and smiled slowly, shaking my head.

'No. It wasn't like that,' I said.

'Then it was love, wasn't it?' Nimra asked softly, looking down, blushing as she said the words.

'But how can you love someone other than your husband?' Arifa asked, and I had to laugh a little. For all her obstinacy and attitude, she was as naïve as Shaista at times. I looked at Shaista who had been quiet and was observing me as she crocheted around her corner.

'You don't have any questions, Shaista?' I asked her. She pursed her lips, shaking her head. She didn't look five months pregnant yet, but the changes were slowly becoming evident.

Amreen looked the most anxious of all for some reason, although I could sense that all of them, except Arifa, were invested in my story for their own personal reason. Of course, Arifa was another matter altogether. She lifted her corner of the bedspread and flung it down, almost in disgust.

'I'm tired of making this. My back aches. I want to go home,' she declared, getting up abruptly. The others looked at her and I was surprised to see that they were annoyed. Maybe they felt I wouldn't continue the story if any one of them wasn't there.

'Stay for a little longer, no?' Amreen pleaded, but Arifa shook her head. She seemed glad to be able to deprive someone of something, and packed her bag. I watched Arifa as she got ready to leave and although my mind was presently blank, she seemed to sense something as she wrapped her scarf around her head.

'I don't like this bedspread that you're making us do,' she said, tying a knot at the base of her neck angrily. 'If I didn't know any better, I'd say you're making it for that man!' she added, her eyes narrowed.

Her words were so absurd that I started laughing, unable to stop myself and I found that my eyes were watering. It had been so long since I had such a good laugh but the tears hadn't been entirely triggered by laughter. They had been lurking under the surface for quite some time now.

'Is it true, Amma?' Amreen asked wide-eyed. I controlled my laughter and wiped the tears from my eyes.

Everyone now seemed to be waiting for an answer and I shook my head.

'It's not for him,' I said, shaking my head again at the sheer idiocy of the notion. It would seem that the girls had been caught up in the immediacy of my story and were transferring it to the present day.

'Then?' Arifa asked defiantly. I sighed.

'The story I was telling you girls is not just a story. It's what happened to me. But then you have to remember that

I'm talking about events that took place fifty years ago. Why would that have any bearing on what you're doing now?'

Arifa still didn't look convinced. 'Then tell us who it's for and we'll believe you.'

I looked around at the expectant faces, at the crochet hooks paused in the air, and at Arifa standing at the door looking wary.

'It's for my granddaughter,' I told them, lifting the unfinished bedspread and caressing it slowly. The white thread that held the stitches bunched together in my hand, and I spread them out again, wishing that this bitter-sweet ache that seemed to weigh down my heart so much these days would go away. 'My granddaughter,' I repeated.

chapter 26

Vellore, 1959

Some events shape our lives, mould them, and change their functions forever. One such event was the birth of my daughter in the January of 1959. Barely a few days before she was born, I had been hungering to read the next story that Aasim had promised would appear in the magazine. But when my daughter was born, there was no way I could think of anyone, not even Aasim. It was like being trapped inside your own body and there was another prisoner that you had to free before you could free yourself.

It's not that I didn't have feelings of tenderness towards my daughter, but they didn't appear immediately. I was just glad that the pain was over and my body was finally my own again. But I was too fast in thinking that, unfortunately. The aunts at home reprimanded me for every little thing, right from the way I sat to the food I ate. They made me tie a cotton sari tightly around my waist, so that my huge, flabby stomach would recede. I had my doubts about whether the remedy would work, but I went ahead with everything they said, just to get them off my back.

Since I had to feed the baby, even my food was under their control. I ate bland food for most of the forty days that I stayed at my mother's house. Among the several other rules that I was made to follow as a new mother was one that said that I couldn't do anything to strain my eyes. Things like reading, or crocheting. Not that I had time for those anyway. When the baby was awake, I had to take care of her and when she was asleep, I just fell back on the bed, dead to the world.

Aasim hadn't crossed my mind at all, although a quiet voice in my head kept telling me to read his story. However, absent-mindedness was one of the side effects of becoming a mother apparently. When January came, I completely forgot that the new magazine would be in stores and Abbu, of course, didn't get me any books or magazines to read because Ammi had told him not to.

When the first forty days were over, Ammi organised an elaborate ceremony for me and the baby and sent me back home to my in-laws. Everyone had been invited, even Aasim. I wasn't sure if he would come, so I tried to keep myself neutral about it because there really was little else I could do. Besides, he wouldn't come all the way from Madras for something like this, right? Especially since he hadn't come for my wedding.

On the day of the ceremony, Ammi had invited my in-laws home for a big feast. My husband, his mother, and his sisters came. I was in one of the rooms where we were dressing up Asma in the gaudy pink frock that my mother-in-law had brought for her and there was a lot of noise in the house. When I finally emerged, holding her, I saw that there were many people seated outside—relatives, uncles, cousins and it was nice meeting everyone again. I was a little disappointed that Aasim hadn't come but since I hadn't been expecting him, I was able to gloss over it with my daughter's constant cries for attention.

My sister had told me that Aasim was in Madras, and I knew he wouldn't come; so I was able to behave normally although it felt as though a certain part of me had been switched off, doused in a tiny, throbbing pool of darkness.

Ignoring the feeling, I went through the motions of the day. When everyone had finished eating, the ceremony was performed during which my husband and I had to be seated in the centre of the hall with Asma in our laps. We were garlanded, and Ammi gave us various gifts of gold. I was feeling a little awkward about sitting this way in front of everyone, a little conscious of my husband sitting next to me, and of course Asma, who was now thankfully asleep.

When everything was done and I got up with Asma in the crook of my arm, I faltered when I looked up and saw Aasim. He had come! For a moment I forgot about the reason for the ceremony. I smiled at him and then looked away quickly. There were so many people milling around, I couldn't allow anyone to catch the passing look between us.

I changed Asma's clothes (once again) and handed her to my mother who took her out. Meanwhile, I packed my clothes and Asma's nappies, towels and various other paraphernalia and was ready to leave in twenty minutes. Although my mother's house was just two streets away, I wouldn't be visiting again very soon.

I suppressed all thoughts of Aasim, wondering why he had decided to come and then with a final click of the clasp on my bag, I stood up. I glanced at the mirror in the room and appraised my face. My face had thinned down considerably, although it wasn't like before and I felt a little more comfortable in my own body now.

Outside, the guests were leaving and my husband lingered, waiting so he could take me and Asma home. His mother and sisters had already left. Soon it was only us—the immediate family, my sister, her husband, children and Aasim, along with my parents who remained in the hall. Ammi was tired after having organised such a big feast. She sat down while someone brought her tea.

'Shall we leave?' I voiced the question to my husband, my eyes on the ground. It felt odd to interact with him in Aasim's presence. Various thoughts were clamouring for attention inside my head but I refused to give any one of them credence. I would examine them later when no one else was around.

'No, no! You have to have tea!' Ammi protested, and she picked up the cups and started handing them around.

It was surreal. Aasim, my husband, and I drinking tea calmly as though we did this every day. In fact, my husband even asked Aasim about his college and his studies and my eyes bored into the ground, wishing for me to be anywhere but here. I wanted them to hurry up so we could leave and I could strive for some normalcy. I didn't want to examine my feelings for Aasim now, at this moment.

'Our Aasim is a writer,' Abba thumped Aasim on the back.

Apa's husband gave a short laugh in response. 'I've told him that he can write stories for magazines but he has to do business with me!' At almost the same moment Aasim and I looked at each other and our eyes met. Mine lit with understanding. His new story! He had said that it was for me! He looked at me speculatively and then hung his head and shook it slightly.

He looked resigned and despite the presence of my husband and Asma, I felt sorry for him. Had he expected me to read the story? Had he been hoping that I would gain some special understanding after I did? I would never know.

I felt frustrated all of a sudden and I got up, picking up the tea cups from the ground to take them to the kitchen. Asma was in Ammi's lap.

'I'll help you!' Aasim offered and before I knew it, the two of us were carrying the tea cups to the kitchen which was empty as all the aunts were resting in the rooms. In silence, we deposited them on the ground where they would be washed later.

I pursed my lips not knowing what Aasim could possibly expect from me.

'So, you didn't read it?' he asked, his face drawn.

'Why did you want me to read it?' I asked him, thinking of the absurdity of the situation.

'I... I wrote it because I couldn't tell you what I wanted to... ' he stammered and I shook my head, backing away. Surely he couldn't mean...

'What?' I asked and he sighed.

'Nothing. It was just a silly story. Don't bother,' he said, moving away.

'Wait! Why did you say it was for me?' I asked him, looking at the door. My sister or mother could come in any moment.

'Because you will be the only... ' He swallowed, his Adam's apple bobbing and then without completing his sentence, he stepped out of the kitchen.

I dipped a glass into a mud pot of water and splashed my face with it, hoping that the red flames his words had caused would ebb away. How could he tell me anything now? *Now!*

I thought of my husband sitting outside and in a sudden surge of affection for Asma, I shook my head and hardened my heart. 'Too little, too late,' I muttered to myself as I fanned my neck with the pallu of my sari. I decided I wouldn't read the particular story although I knew that curiosity would propel me towards it eventually.

When I went back, he wasn't in the hall. Almost relieved, I draped my chadar around my body, holding Asma in my arms and looked at my husband, indicating that we ought to leave.

As I edged towards the door, I felt a plummeting sensation inside me once again as I saw Aasim emerge from one of the rooms with Raheema bu slowly trailing behind him.

'I can't see so well these days, Aasim!' she called out. I wondered what she meant.

A second later, Aasim responded, 'It's okay, Raheema bu. I'll send them anyway.' Saying this, opened the door which led to the exit even before my husband could reach it and strode out.

'Send what?' I turned to ask Raheema bu although my mother was tugging at one end of my chadar to pull me outside where my husband was now waiting. The rickshaw puller had also come apparently.

She made a face and then spoke. 'He's found a shop in Madras where they sell old crochet magazines. Imported ones!' she said, looking and sounding important. 'He said he will send them for me,' and in a gesture typical of old age, she raised her eyes and her hands above saying, 'What will I do with them… but he doesn't listen!'

She smiled at me and I smiled back, trying to see if there was any hidden meaning behind his actions. But then, I wouldn't know because I would be back in my husband's house. Nodding to her, I turned around and stepped out.

Chapter 27

Marriage between two people is not the hazy, hope-filled ending that is hinted at in books and stories. It is a relationship fraught with discussions about the future and the present, but never the past. I was okay with that. I didn't want the past intruding on my life, an unwelcome reminder of what might have been. But I knew that somewhere in my heart, I'd been expecting more.

It seemed that my initial problems with conception had somehow been erased after my daughter was born. Barely a few months later, I became pregnant once again and I wondered if I, too, would end up being like those women who had children almost every year. I shuddered at the thought of never being able to call my body my own. But since I knew what to expect from the process, the pregnancy was smoother than before although there was hardly any time to rest, as I had to take care of Asma as well.

My husband's shop wasn't doing well. He sold hardware and paint and we had always been comfortable until the year my son was due to be born. Losses piled up one after the other and there were constant lines of worry on his forehead. I felt bad for him, wished I could help by simply being a source of strength, but he preferred his mother over me, especially when it came to confiding his troubles.

After a point I gave up caring because even when I brought up the topic with him in the privacy of our room, he would lie down on the bed and stare at the ceiling in silence. The only time I saw him animated was when he played with Asma and there were times he looked at me speculatively, more so at my bulging stomach, probably hoping that it would be a son this time.

Somehow events towards the end of my pregnancy led me back to my mother's house, because his mother decided that she wanted to complete her Haj that year. Despite all his losses and worries, my husband had agreed, hoping that a visit to this most cherished place would eradicate his problems. The process had already been initiated before I had even become pregnant and so when the news came that my mother-in-law and husband had to leave, I was around five months p regnant.

Haj travel was complicated and it usually took around three to four months to complete the journey because it had to be done by sea. I moved to my mother's house when they left, feeling that my life was off kilter for some reason. I was barely twenty-one and soon to be the mother of two children, and it seemed as though half my life was already over.

There was something comforting about being in Ammi's house, and although everything had changed in my life, it was wonderful to see that some things just stayed the same.

In the evenings, I took Asma with me to the terrace and we watched kites soaring in the sky, or sometimes we would just stand as still as the mountains in the distance. I never looked at my alcove again because of the memories it inspired and with a definite purpose, thought of my life ahead.

Yet, I didn't know why it seemed as though my life hadn't begun. That I was still waiting for it to embrace me. At times, especially at night, I would miss my husband. Even though we barely spoke, there was a measure of security in his solid presence. His absence made me aware of the vacuum more prominently and I was a little surprised to find that I cared more about him than I had assumed.

Those months I spent at my mother's house were special—time seemed to become meaningless and responsibility was only limited to my daughter. I didn't sleep as much as the last time, but I let the delicious miasma of nothingness sweep over me.

It was around the same time that I discovered my genuine love for crochet.

As promised, Aasim had been sending Raheema bu crocheting magazines almost every month. These were imported magazines, but nearly two or three years old. How they found their way into second hand book stores in India, I never knew. I loved looking at the pictures in the magazines, rubbing my fingers against the glossy sheen of the pages and imagining the lives of the people who posed for the pictures, wearing gorgeous crocheted scarves and other items of clothing. With my discovery of crochet, I discovered that creating a beautiful object was within my own hands.

My eyes goggled when I saw the number of things that could be crocheted, and my respect for the craft grew. It didn't have to be a way of making namaz topis alone. Raheema bu was strangely possessive of the magazines. She never let me look at them for long, clucking and murmuring incoherent phrases before pulling them away from me.

A part of me wondered if she had any inkling about Aasim and me. I kept thinking of how Aasim had gone to the trouble of looking for the magazines, how he had handled them, and posted them, obviously with a lot of care. Was Raheema bu aware of the attraction that had been there between us? Then I would look at her peering at the crochet hook myopically as she continued with her namaz topis, and I would decide that she couldn't possibly know. With the brief time she allowed me with the magazines, I gleaned as much as I could, rapidly imprinting the images in my mind so I could try and replicate them later. Sometimes, I wondered about Aasim and the story he had purportedly written for me. I had left my notebook here when I left with Asma the previous year because I felt I couldn't take it to my house. It was enough that I carried him in a part of my heart, a physical reminder was out of question.

I didn't know what he was doing now; the last I had heard was that he had stayed back in Madras and opted to start a branch of his brother's shop there. In fact, he had been doing so well that apparently my sister and her husband were thinking of moving to Madras to live with him. That was all I knew and to be fair, I wasn't digging up information about him.

I convinced myself that I had changed and that I didn't need the added tinge of hurt when I thought of him, so it was for the best. I heard that he rarely visited Vellore except for Eid and for his mother's barsi, and I thought it was a good thing. By then, I reconciled myself with the thought that our lives were like parallel train tracks that could never cross or meet; and it was probably the way it was meant to be.

Abba was his usual indulgent self and brought me all the yarn I needed, and I managed to recreate quite a few of the designs that I had seen in the magazines. Over time, I became quite proficient with the hook and Ammi was really impressed.

'You must thank Aasim for sending these books the next time you see him,' she beamed as she picked up a doll that I had crocheted for Asma. I didn't say anything.

'Really sweet of him, isn't it?' Ammi asked. I stayed silent, wondering how much of our exchange Raheema bu could hear. Since she continued crocheting impassively, I assumed it wasn't much.

Those days that seemed to stretch almost endlessly had their ups and downs. We finally got to know that my sister and her family were moving to Madras. Ammi was a little upset about it because she had got used to Apa being around and accessible, but she got over her initial disappointment soon enough.

'The children will have a good life,' she intoned and I nodded, a little catch somewhere in my throat, thinking of my children. Life in Madras suddenly seemed more glamorous and even meaningful compared to this existence in Vellore.

My husband and his mother returned just a few days before my son was born but Ammi insisted I stay with her for the delivery. I noticed numerous changes in my husband when he came to visit us and I wasn't sure what to make of them. He looked different, older and more sorted, somehow. He seemed more spiritual and religious and he had a beard. I was still the same. I felt a little cheated that he had moved ahead in some plane of life and left me behind, but I didn't blame him for not taking me along. With Asma and my pregnancy, performing Hajj was unthinkable. Nevertheless, when my son was born and I returned home after the requisite number of days, I felt the subtle changes everywhere. The only thing that kept me rooted was my love for crochet that hadn't diminished, even though there was now a squalling infant in my arms.

chapter 28

My husband's business did not improve even after he returned from Hajj. In fact, things quickly progressed from bad to worse, and one day he announced solemnly that we would have to sell the house and move to Sathuvacheri. In those days, Sathuvacheri wasn't the posh locality that it has become now. It seemed like we were being sent on exile.

My parents were very upset when they heard about our move, but my husband refused any manner of help from them. Nevertheless, it seemed like one more momentous occasion in my life had flipped us over on its back, until there was nothing left to do but scramble frantically in the air.

It seemed that the sheer drudgery of ordinary life had sapped my capacity to quantify life in terms of years. And although it seemed that the years just dragged on, it was 1965 and I realised I had been married for ten years. A lot had happened in the interim, such as the death of Raheema bu sometime in 1962.

My mother's house was no longer the happy place it was in my mind or memories. There was a sadness there, a tenacious longing for the old days, such that I often wanted to head back to my own house within minutes. My parents had grown old, and most of the aunts who lived with them had either moved out or passed away like Raheema bu. Each visit made the neglect of the house apparent to me, until one day I picked up the courage to tell Abba and Ammi that they should sell the house and move to a smaller place. Abba shook his head sadly.

'We can't leave our house, Mariam,' he said, sighing and looking around at the cobwebbed ceilings and cracked rafters. 'Too much of us is here. We would never be happy anywhere else.'

'But are you happy now?' I cried out, looking at the empty house that rang with the echoes of forgotten laughter and the heady scent of jasmine flowers that my mother had worn every single day; there was so much here that had been reduced to dusty memory. 'Look at this place! It's crumbling!'

When Apa visited them in the summer, I told her what I thought should be done. She was upset initially, but she, too, agreed that it would be easier for them if they lived in a smaller place. I noted the changes in Apa's face, at the lines that seemed to have sprung up although she was just in her mid-thirties.

'How's everyone?' I asked her cautiously. She sighed unhappily and then turned to tell me the reason why she looked so worried.

'It's Aasim.'

I nodded, happy to realise that the mention of his name didn't do anything to me now. Time had eroded the pain and the feelings.

'What did he do now?' I asked. I thought his success story was something all the youngsters in Vellore might want to emulate. Not only had he got himself an education, but he had turned around his brother's shop into a hugely profitable venture in Madras.

'We want him to settle down, get married, but he just

refuses,' she raised and dropped her hands in a helpless gesture. I looked down at the mat and its patterns, observing that the churning in my stomach had slowly started again.

'Why?' I asked, my voice even lower.

Apa shook her head. 'He says he doesn't want to get married! Can you imagine that? Such a successful young man, and he's finished writing a novel too. I've had the most difficult time all these days fending off proposals for him.'

I nodded, not quite knowing what to say to that. Why didn't he want to marry? Was it because… no, impossible. Our meeting on the terrace that evening seemed to have happened eons ago, a time when life was different, when each day shone with promise. Over the years, I had edged out its memory into a part of my mind where I didn't have to relive it at all. I rarely dwelt over it now, but today when I took it out and dusted it, it seemed that the years and the distance had dissolved, leaving me with a bittersweet sensation.

'He'll come around,' I said gruffly, and I was right. The next time I heard from Apa, it was to invite me for Aasim's wedding. I took the card in my hands and willed myself to smile, shaking my head when she asked if I could come.

'But he's your childhood friend! You should!' she insisted. I made up an excuse about being unable to attend because my mother-in-law was sick and needed care, and that was that. Aasim got married to a girl in Madras and I never got to see her because within a year of his marriage, he moved to San Francisco. Yes. America. I don't know how he pulled it off but he went there with his wife, leaving his brother to handle the shop, and he started writing in English.

Towards the end of 1965, my life came to a sudden stop when

both my parents died within months of each other. I couldn't understand how it happened. They were fine, or seemed fine but they had been sick and hadn't really taken care of themselves. Guilt played a heavy hand and I broke down when I visited the house that was now truly alone. Apa and I decided to sell it because we couldn't take care of it, and since she lived in Madras, it fell upon me to take care of my parents' belongings.

With the help of Razia bu, the old lady who continued living with us even when we went to Sathuvacheri, I sorted their clothes and other belongings, sobbing all the while for the lives gone and the pain that didn't seem to go away. And that was when I chanced upon the magazines that Aasim had sent Raheema bu.

They were a dusty bunch, tied together with a frayed string, untouched since Raheema bu passed away. I fingered the string unhappily, thinking of her life and how she had spent it entirely at my house, crocheting away namaz topis for others. Crochet hadn't really taken a back seat in my life despite all the problems that had arisen. I continued doing it despite the tedium of everyday life promising to smother me with its demands, because crochet kept me sane. And although I didn't know it then, it was the vaguest of my connections to Aasim.

I remembered how lovely those magazines had seemed then with their pretty designs, and a small hope seemed to rise inside me. I would take these magazines home with me. I remembered how protective Raheema bu had been of them, never letting me linger over them for too long. It was sad how they had been relegated to a forgotten corner of the house and I was determined not to let them be destroyed. They would serve me as a reminder of Raheema bu's legacy.

Days later, when the children had gone to school and my mother-in-law was napping, I pulled out the magazines from under my bed and sat down cross-legged on the bed. I wasn't planning to make anything new. I just wanted to browse through them and revive the old memories. I flipped through the dulled glossy pages.

That was when I saw it. Writing in Urdu, neatly inscribed over the page number. How did I miss seeing this before? I narrowed my eyes and peered at it closely, trying to decipher the words. When I did, I clapped my hand over my mouth. Trembling, I dropped the magazine into my lap.

chapter 29

It took me a good part of an hour to reconstruct all the messages that Aasim had sent me, month by month, page by page, chronologically, so I could make sense of them. At first, there was the shock of the message out in the open, but once it wore off, I began to smile. Whatever messages Aasim had left for me were years old, but still, they were something from him.

I realised that the feeling of being alive had somehow wormed itself back into my being, and it was because of him. It took me a good ten years to accept that what I felt for Aasim would always be special, a part of my life where I had been teetering between adolescence and adulthood, where I had stepped out of childlike innocence and right into his arms. But then who was I fooling? I had been aware of him much before that evening on the terrace happened, and maybe it was all just meant to be.

As I rearranged the magazines, I wondered if I should cut out the messages and stick them on the pages of a book so I could read them as a letter. But that would be foolhardy. Surely, if someone else chanced upon it, there would be no mistaking it for anything but a love letter. So, painstakingly I pieced together the messages that he had inscribed on random pages, all the while feeling the fullness in my heart.

In the very first magazine he wrote that he missed me after I got married and went away. He took the whole of that magazine to just say those words. I touched the faded ink, running my finger along it gently, right to left in the opposite direction of the printed matter on the page. I looked at the ceiling as if it would offer me some answers. Could my parents see me now, I briefly wondered. What would they make of it? Was I doing something illicit? But then, I was just piecing together messages, letters from someone they, too, had loved as a son, I told myself.

In the second magazine, he described how disappointed he'd been to find out I hadn't read his story. It all seemed so long ago to me that it took me some time to retrace those moments in my life before Asma was born, when he had visited me, squeezing my hand, telling me that he would never forget the evening on the terrace. I could almost hear him berating me, calling me foolish names, and I hugged the magazine to my chest impulsively.

Why did you go so far away, Aasim, I murmured and then sat up, a sudden thought blowing up like a cloud in my head. Had he expected me to do something with these messages? Had he waited for me in some way? And when I hadn't responded, had he finally decided that he had waited enough and decided to get married and then go away to America?

This new thought seemed to make my hands tremble. Surely, he wouldn't have expected me to do something rash? After all, I had been the one to suggest we run away and he had been the one who walked out on us. Even so, I rushed through the magazines, wondering if he had indeed left some crucial message for me, and I had received it too late.

I flipped the pages, finding words, stringing them together but there was nothing unusual in them except that he had proclaimed his love for me sometime in 1960. I paused, the frenzy of finding a hidden message suddenly evaporating in this declaration that had come five years too late. My feelings of happiness were quickly replaced by despair when I realised how hopeless our situation had been. But why now? Why had he told me that he loved me? I turned the pages of the same magazine until I came across another message.

'It's probably wrong to love someone else's wife,' he had written. I shut my eyes, almost laughing at how ludicrous he sounded. Or desperate. Had he asked me to run away with him in the following magazines?

Had he made some elaborate plan for us, which I had thwarted by merely being unaware of it? I remembered how I had spent time with Raheema bu, making those crochet dolls during my second pregnancy. Had Raheema bu seen these messages too? Was this why she never left me alone with the magazines, never let me enjoy them as much as I wanted to? I'd never know. She was certainly the reason I hadn't been able to see the messages until now. Feeling uneasy, I flipped through more of the magazines.

'But there are some things that cannot be helped,' he continued, on another page and I shook my head, feeling indulgent at his naiveté. In another magazine, he wrote of how he would never dream of hurting my marriage or my children by taking me away or doing anything of that sort. I scratched my head in confusion. Why was he telling me all this now?

It was then that his tone changed and I sat up straighter. In the subsequent magazines, he outlined a plan, something so outrageous and almost audacious that I curled my hand into a fist and bit it because I didn't know if I wanted to laugh or cry. When I was done reading them all, I felt a deep sense of loss, a feeling of finding something precious, only to lose it. It was so acute that I could barely understand where I was or what I was doing. With a sigh, I neatly stacked the magazines, aligned them perfectly and then placed them inside my cupboard. These were too precious now to be stashed under the bed, where dust would inevitably find them.

I had never been a manipulator of events at any point of time in my life. Even when Aasim had accused me of playing mind games with him (he had reminded me of that in one of the magazines), I was too naïve and self-absorbed. So, to orchestrate my life the way Aasim had suggested seemed far-fetched and quite impossible for me. Well, let's see.

chapter 30

Vellore, 2011

'We are not going to finish this in time,' I grumbled as I looked at the girls who were at different stages of completing their respective corners. I could see the bedspread taking shape, but there was so much more to be done and so little time! I had picked up a random corner to work on my own but it caused a stinging pain behind my eyes and I had to reluctantly relinquish it to their inexpert hands.

'What's the hurry?' Arifa muttered, dropping her hook and then bending to retrieve it. Shaista moved aside to give her space and then winced as the movement caused her pain.

Are you okay?' Amreen asked her, looking wary.

I had been observing the dynamics between Amreen and Shaista since the time the bulge of the pregnancy became visible. Amreen almost never looked at Shaista directly, but I had caught her observing the way Shaista sat, or how she sometimes rubbed her belly without realising it and I could feel Amreen's crushing disappointment at not having experienced any of it. But there was a new bond now, that tied them together, and held them enthralled as they listened to my story.

'Yes, I'm alright,' Shaista replied and Amreen nodded before continuing with her stitches.

'What had he said in the magazines, Amma?' Nimra asked, twining the white yarn around her finger to give tension while weaving her hook in and out dexterously.

'Yes, what was his plan?' Amreen asked. I smiled remembering how shocked they had been when they heard that Aasim had been sending me messages in the crochet magazines for so many years. Nimra had clapped her hands to her mouth, her eyes had become big and round.

Arifa looked incredulous as always. I kept getting the feeling that she listened to my story but was unable to think of it as something that had happened in reality. I could sense that she immediately discounted it in her head as a piece of improbable fiction.

'I already told you that he said he loved me,' I said the words slowly, relishing them as they formed in my mouth. It was so liberating, being able to speak about it finally.

Shaista shook her head. 'No, Amma, there was a plan. What was it? You didn't tell us what it was.'

I sat back and smiled. Even demure and quiet Shaista had been taken in by the story, and I could sense that for the little time she came here, she forgot all her troubles.

'As plans go, it was a most contrived and stupid plan,' I pronounced. A collective gasp followed. I could see that they had already taken sides in the story.

'Well, it was! I had no idea if it would ever come about and even then, there was nothing really to be gained from it,' I added.

'But what was it?' Amreen persisted. Arifa also looked at me keenly.

I took a deep breath and then spoke. 'Well, Aasim believed that even though we couldn't get married, there was another way in which we could… we could share something that belonged to both of us.'

Arifa narrowed her eyes. 'Huh? What does that mean?' I looked around at the puzzled faces and then felt a jolt as I saw Nimra cover her mouth in surprise. She had been the only one to figure it out.

'What? What?' Amreen asked, looking around in confusion and when she saw that everyone else looked equally perplexed, she looked back at me. 'What did he mean?'

'Ask Nimra,' I said, flexing my fingers. Nimra looked at me and shook her head, although there was a smile on her face.

'Is it true then?' she asked, her customary diffidence evolving into assertiveness. Her eyes were shining as she looked around at the others and then spoke, 'This bedspread we're making, Amma said it's for her granddaughter, right?' she asked. Everyone nodded.

'Well, it's not just her granddaughter. It's Aasim's granddaughter as well,' Nimra declared triumphantly. I shut my eyes, time sliding back to those golden days when Faiza had just been born.

'What? How?' Arifa asked and I had to admit that for someone with a deeply suspicious nature, she wasn't very intuitive.

'Arrey! Amma's son married Aasim's daughter. Right?' Amreen asked excitedly, clapping her hands in delight. I nodded, unable to stop smiling because her excitement was so contagious.

Shaista and Arifa, who had been the last to understand, looked shocked and then there was laughter, and as a sort of celebration Deepa made tea for everyone. I forgot that she, too, had been avidly tuned into the story.

'But... but where is she? Your granddaughter? Why do you live alone? Where's Aasim?' the questions flew thick and fast and I had to put my hand out to make them stop.

'When I next saw Aasim, he was my son's prospective father-in-law and we never spoke, never even looked at each other or acknowledged the plan in the magazines,' I lied, watching them absorb it completely.

'Oh!' Everyone looked disappointed.

'You have to understand. There was a good twenty-five year gap after the magazines. We had grown older and I had almost forgotten about his plan when I heard that our relatives had come from America, looking for a son-in-law.

Everyone was surprised when Aasim agreed to get his daughter married to my son, because for a girl who had been living in San Francisco all her life, he could have chosen anyone he wanted. But he chose my son, and only I knew why.'

The girls were shaking their head in wonder and I smiled at the memories that were unwinding.

'Was his daughter a good bahu?' Amreen asked. I shifted a little uneasily.

'Well, I wasn't a perfect bahu myself, so... I was mostly okay with her,' I said, looking down at my lap.

'She was a horrible girl, wasn't she?' Nimra asked and I looked up, shaking my head.

'No, no! She was a nice girl but can you imagine someone who has lived in *America* all her life, trying to live *here*?'

'She took your son and went away, didn't she?' Shaista asked, and I sighed.

'Something like that. They went away and never came back,' I whispered, my eyes feeling prickly with unshed tears.

'What do you mean?' Shaista asked, her eyes wide.

'My son and daughter-in-law died in an accident a few months after Faiza was born.' The words seemed unnaturally big, leaching all the moisture from my mouth.

There was another collective gasp.

'Oh no! What about Faiza?' Arifa asked. I looked down, shaking my head, waiting for the tears that came inevitably.

'I almost wished I had never listened to Aasim!' I said, surprised at the anger in me, residual even after twenty years. 'My son would have married some girl from around here who would have lived with me and I would have had grandchildren to love.'

There was a round of solemn nodding. 'But what happened to Faiza?' Arifa persisted.

'Aasim took care of her, sent me letters, pictures, telling me all about her. But… but it was never enough!' I slowed down.

'Amma, what about your husband? Why didn't he intervene?' Amreen enquired, looking at me avidly.

'He had been against the match from the beginning,' I reminisced. 'He had correctly guessed that a girl from there would never be able to adjust here. But I was so caught up with the thought of the success of our plan, that I didn't stop to think, and neither did Aasim. I learnt an important lesson then.'

'What?' Nimra asked.

'No matter how many plans we might make for our lives… they're all useless because everything rests in His hands,' I explained, looking up.

'So, Faiza never came to India? You never saw her?' Arifa queried pointedly.

'She did. Aasim brought her once a year and let her stay

with us for a month,' I replied, my eyes glazed with memories that sometimes brought tears.'

And you met Aasim then, right?' Shaista anticipated. I had to smile.

'We met as grandparents, Shaista, who had each lost a child.

'Nimra's face, which had been so animated sometime back when she had figured out the details, now had a moue of unhappiness. 'But... but... '

I shook my head at her unvoiced questions and looked at the others who wore a varying range of expressions. There was sympathy, pity and disappointment.

'Is she fond of you?' Amreen asked. I looked down at my lap again.

'I... I haven't seen her since she was five years old,' I admitted, my eyes still trained on the faded pattern on my sari.

'Why?' Nimra wanted to know. I looked up to see her anguished face. I didn't know if I had the heart to tell her the truth, but it was so odd. It was my life that they were listening to, experiences that had shaped me into who I was and yet, they were reacting to it with such heartfelt emotion.

'Why, Amma?' Shaista asked. I looked at each of their eager faces and realised the story had to continue.

Part Three

chapter 31

If distance were to be measured in mere numbers, one could say that San Francisco was approximately 14,000 kilometres away from India. But for millions of people, distances have collapsed into a mere difference in time. All it took was one look at the clock and a quick calculation in the head to know what time it would be there and then a flipping open of the laptop and switching on of the internet. But for Mariam, it was every bit of those 14,0000 kilometres and more. She found the distance and difference harsh and unacceptable. In fact, she couldn't understand the time difference at all and in the early days when Aasim would call to update her about Faiza, she would click her tongue in annoyance.

'You always call at the oddest of times, Aasim!' she would complain and he would sigh. In the late 80s, the internet hadn't made its appearance yet, so all communication was limited to weekly phone calls and regular letters.

'But at least I call, Mariam!' he would retort with a fair amount of exasperation and she would have to agree. She had been amazed at the way the walls between them had fallen when their granddaughter was born. Now, Aasim could call her and talk to her and no one would find it odd. They rarely talked about anything other than Faiza, but Mariam knew that the calls were as important to him as they were to her.

'She reminds me of you sometimes,' he said and Mariam would shake her head, even though she knew he couldn't see it.

'Don't lie!'

'Arrey, you have to see the way she makes faces at me when I try to make her eat something, Mariam! Exactly like you! Here, ask Faisal. He will tell you,' and he would give the phone to her son whose sheepish-sounding voice would come over the receiver across all those thousands of kilometres.

'Don't tell me he's making Faiza *eat* things!' she had asked him incredulously. 'She's just a five-month-old baby!'

'No, no, Ammi! Abba was joking,' Faisal said, laughing at how easily his mother and father-in-law could fight like they were teenagers. Mariam closed her eyes and smiled at the way Faisal referred to Aasim as Abba.

In those short days between the time when her son had moved to America and before he had died, Mariam hadn't really felt any anger towards Aasim or her son. Faisal was still the treacherous man who had abandoned his parents for the lure of America, but for Mariam it was alright because she knew that he would come back eventually with more grandchildren. Little did she know that that was not to be.

If anyone had found it odd that the two grandparents had taken to discussing their granddaughter with such enthusiasm, it was often overlooked on account of their childhood connection. Then, her son and daughter-in-law died in that horrible accident. Aasim had called her, his voice broken with his sobs and she had yelled at him, screamed at his selfishness, and stopped just short of blaming him for their deaths.

Her husband had taken their son's defection hard, but after the accident, he withdrew himself into a tight shell within which he slowly wasted away. Mariam didn't know how she managed to console him and herself, but between the two of them, she had been the one who had emerged stronger, willing to continue living for Faiza.

'I want her back here in India,' she had told Aasim firmly when he called a week later. 'I want my granddaughter back.'

They argued back and forth and Aasim told her he could take better care of her because Faiza was already used to living with them and he had a large family that would absorb a single, lonely child with ease.

She had shut her eyes in pain because she knew he was right. Aasim's other children, his two sons, loved Faiza and would take care of her as their own. While what would she have to offer her here? An empty house with a grandfather who slept most of the day and refused to talk to anyone? In every aspect, Faiza would have a better life there, and so she agreed.

'I'll bring her to you every summer,' he promised. Mariam hung on to the promise and waited for him to bring Faiza to live with her in Sathuvacheri.

The very first time he came to her house, Mariam had broken down when she carried Faiza in her arms. It was the first time she was seeing their granddaughter, this baby of extended love and she didn't know how to react. There was so much of her son in her, the eyebrows, the forehead, the nose, and she felt a tight bud at the centre of her chest opening, inch by inch.

'Thank God she doesn't have your forehead,' she murmured and only then turned to look at Aasim. In her mind, he was still the cocky teenager she had fallen in love with but she knew that he looked much younger than his fifty years.

'You haven't changed,' he remarked easily as he sat down. Mariam looked lovingly at the seven-month-old Faiza in her arms, refusing to meet his eyes. He was joking. Although they were the same age, there was a difference in the way their lives had shaped them. Then she realised he wasn't referring to her appearance.

'Was it… instantaneous?' she asked him, pausing, her breath coming in short gasps. She couldn't believe she was asking him about her son. And his daughter. But she had to know and she had to learn how to move on from the pain.

Aasim nodded, his face grimacing in pain and then together they cried for the children they had brought together. It took time for Mariam to forgive Aasim. Slowly, she got used to his presence in her house during that one month in 1988. He was staying in his old house in Vellore, the one where he had lived as a child and although his brother and Mariam's sister still lived in Madras, he stayed the whole month in Vellore, visiting Mariam and Faiza every single day.

'What about… your wife?' Mariam asked hesitantly. She had never met this woman who shared Aasim's life.

Aasim sighed. 'She's broken down, unable to accept that Raina is gone.' His eyes teared. 'I can't believe it myself sometimes. It's just… so… '

The two of them had fallen silent, watching Faiza sleep in her makeshift jhoola. The question that remained unasked but still evident on their faces hung heavy in the air—was this baby worth it?

Mariam bent and picked up Faiza and hugged her so tightly that she woke up and started crying. Aasim had to take her and console her. It was a question that couldn't be answered. Ever. The two of them were still cooing at Faiza as Aasim rocked her in his arms when Mariam's husband came out of his room. He rarely left his room now and his condition had deteriorated since Faisal's death. He took in the picture of his wife standing with a man who was cradling a baby and he blinked.

chapter 32

Nimra turned on the tap, cupped the warm water in her hands, and splashed it on her face. She ran some of it over her head, the heat in the air dissipating any coolness she might have felt momentarily. Stepping out of the bathroom, she wiped her face with the edge of her dupatta and then leaving the wet edge dangling from her shoulder, she sat down on the bed and crossed her legs.

Listening to Amma tell her story had been interesting at first, then shocking, then amazing and finally a tiny part of her began to be in awe of Amma's enduring love for Aasim. Despite that, a part of her had felt uncomfortable. After all, Amma and Aasim had been married to different people and yet they continued to love each other. How sad was that?

She allowed herself the luxury of rocking on the bed because no one else was there. She closed her eyes, thinking back to that one crystal-clear moment when Rocky had given her the butterfly brooch. It was almost as if wings had sprung out from her back, which she had extended, flapped and then soared into the sky.

Rocky had smiled at her and then she had watched as he went his way to the restaurant where he worked. She went back to the café and waited for her cousins, the brooch still clutched in her palm, its sharp edges poking her soft skin, making its presence felt.

Her cousins came and in the flurry of shopping bags and gifts that they had got for her, she allowed the memory of the walk and the gift to be swept away as they hurried into the Masjid Jamek station. In the LRT, the train swayed and stopped at regular intervals. It had also started raining. The Petronas Towers were still visible from the foggy glass inside. Nimra thought of Rocky, waiting tables and living his life here in Malaysia, so far removed from hers, back in Vellore.

She wondered if she would be able to make it back to the café again before she left and even if she did, what could she possibly do? She was always accompanied by her cousins everywhere and there was no way they would leave her alone again.

That night after dinner, Nimra and the cousins played Scrabble. Nimra was distracted, unable to form the right letters. With a sigh, Shireen packed away the board. They were in the room where they slept, Shireen had been observing Nimra carefully.

'Is everything alright?' she asked her.

'Huh? Yes, yes it is!' Nimra assured her brightly. But her mind had been occupied with the brooch, which now rested inside her handbag, almost seeming to pulse with a life of its own.

'You don't seem yourself today,' Arshiya remarked as she sat on the bed and adjusted the AC controls so that the cool air fanned them better.

Nimra deliberated if she could confide in her cousins but she hardly knew them and really, what was there to confide?

'No, I'm fine,' Nimra insisted, smiling at them. She then stretched out on the bed, curling away from them, inviting the world of dreams to take over. But sleep didn't come easily to her. She sat up an hour later to the gentle, breathy snores of her cousins and gingerly got down from the bed for a drink of water. She pushed aside the heavy curtains and looked at the empty road below. It was quite indescribable, this odd mixture of sadness and elation that had sprung up inside her.

The following morning when Shahzad mamu left for work, he smiled at them and suggested they spend the day in the city, as Nimra was leaving the following day.

'But we just went there yesterday, Abba!' Shireen complained. They had already taken Nimra to Genting on the first weekend of her visit, and Nimra had been amazed by the cable car ride up the mountain to the amusement park.

'But who knows when she will be back?' Mamu had insisted. 'If I didn't have to go to work today I'd have taken you all somewhere.'

'It's okay, Mamu. I'll stay at home today and pack,' Nimra had said quietly. Shireen and Arshiya had already been so nice to her, getting her gifts and taking her shopping. They happened to have holidays at their university, so it had been fun for everyone concerned.

Shahzad mamu looked guiltily at Nimra and then smiled. 'Okay. I'll come home early and we can go for dinner at that restaurant where we went when Nimra came here first. Be ready!' and saying so he left. Nimra had felt the slightest thud inside her body when Mamu had said those words but she was afraid that the girls would protest and insist he take them elsewhere. However, they didn't say anything, and Nimra sighed in relief. She could see Rocky again, even though it would be in the company of her uncle and his family. That evening when they made their way into the city, Nimra was surprised when they walked past Rocky's restaurant.

'Isn't that the restaurant we went to last time?' she asked hesitantly. Mamu looked at her and blinked.

'Oh yes! But a colleague told me that this restaurant here has some good offers, so I thought we could check it out,' he said as he led them into another restaurant. Nimra's appetite vanished instantly and her mood plummeted. Her cousins chattered on excitedly but she merely toyed with the food on her plate, feeling a little sick. She had made an effort to dress up that evening and her cousins had helped her wear make up and now she just felt like a fool.

The food kept getting stuck in her throat and the effort of pushing it down was too much. Finally, she got up and went to the restroom where she took deep breaths, trying to calm down, wondering if she would leave Malaysia without seeing Rocky again. She was supposed to fly back to India the following evening.

When she got back to the table, her uncle looked at her, concerned.

'Are you alright?' he asked and she nodded, unsure if she could get the words out.

'This restaurant doesn't have many dessert options. Shall we head down to that old place and see if they have something good?' he asked. It was like being on one of those terrifying roller-coasters, Nimra thought as they headed towards Rocky's restaurant. What if he wasn't there? And then another thought struck her with full force. What if he came up to her and spoke to her! What would she do? How would she explain his familiarity to the rest of them? How would she explain his gift—the one she was wearing on her hijab even now? They were sitting outside as before and Nimra looked around anxiously, not sure if she wanted to see him again. But he was there, dressed in black like the last time, and there was a smile on his face when he saw her. But he didn't approach them and she was glad. Only then did she realise that both Shireen and Arshiya had noticed him too.

They whispered to one another and since Nimra was sitting between them, she was privy to all their conversation.

'How did we miss seeing him last time?' Arshiya asked her sister.

'I wonder if he's new here! We eat here quite often and I haven't seen him before.' Shireen replied.

'Just look at that jawline! He's so hot!' Arshiya exclaimed and then straightened up when she noticed Nimra turning red in the face.

'Don't mind her!' Shireen giggled and Nimra smiled automatically before looking down at her lap again as her icecream sundae was brought to the table. Nimra ventured a look at Rocky who wasn't busy but casually lounging against one of the walls, watching them with amused interest.

She blushed as she dipped her spoon into the dessert and ate it, feeling extremely self-conscious. It seemed that the rest of her family had melted away and only she was sitting there, eating a chocolate icecream topped lavishly with nuts and cherries, while Rocky watched her from his corner.

She kept her head lowered as she ate and a fat spoonful of icecream fell on her salwar.

'Oops! Better go and clean it up!' Shireen suggested. Nimra nodded and got up in a hurry, refusing any offer of help as she rushed into the restaurant's restroom. It wasn't really a restroom, just a washbasin and a set of toilets, but it was located inside the restaurant.

She wiped away the traces of the icecream from her clothes and washed the stained area. As she looked up she was startled to see Rocky in the mirror, grinning at her.

'Hey!' he said.

She smiled at him uncertainly. She didn't know what to say to him but she washed her hands and turned away from the basin.

'You're wearing the brooch,' he observed with a smile.

She blushed, nodded and then pursed her lips.

'I'm leaving tomorrow,' she forced herself to say the words. He nodded his head knowingly.

'I kind of hoped you would come to the café today,' he smiled. Nimra started giving a long-winded explanation but stopped because he had closed the distance between them.

Up close, her eyes darted to his, fear and excitement writ large on her face as she took in his presence. His clothes gave off an odd mixture of smells that spoke of his association with the kitchen and without being aware of it, her nose wrinkled slightly. He smirked as he touched her nose gently with the tip of his finger and then tweaked it slightly.

Then he stepped back and Nimra realised he was going away. She should be relieved and not disappointed, she told herself firmly as she watched him step outside the restaurant. She turned back to the mirror and saw her face; she splashed cold water to cool down her heated cheeks waiting for her breathing to return to normalcy, but when she looked up, there he was again. She was startled when he bent down and kissed her gently, A moment later, he looked up and rubbed his rough thumb over her lips.

'Goodbye,' he whispered, and walked away once again, leaving Nimra shattered.

Nimra closed her eyes as she remembered that moment when it seemed her world had started spinning and there was no way it was going to stop. She didn't remember much about the rest of the evening, which she spent in a daze after she went back outside. As they left the restaurant, she turned around and saw him standing there, lifting his hand in a half wave and she nodded.

She wore the brooch on the flight back home, touching it lightly and dreaming about the only kiss she had received in her life, while her uncle who was escorting her back, kept telling her how nice it had been to have her there for the holidays.

'I wish you could have stayed longer,' he said as they snapped open the seatbelt when the plane landed in Chennai.

'Thank you for everything, Mamu,' Nimra replied, wishing that she, too, could have stayed longer. 'I will never forget this trip!'

'Next time, I'll get you a visa for a longer period and convince your father to let you stay for a few months at least,' Mamu offered thoughtfully. We both know that there's not going to be a next time, Nimra thought ruefully, but she was glad she had gone to Malaysia anyhow. It wasn't that she was coming back with a broken heart, but it was the hopelessness of the situation that had saddened her so much.

Nevertheless, she accepted it with equanimity because she had known all along that this trip was a brief interlude in her life. When she got back home, she was subjected to intense stares from Saira who wanted to see everything that Nimra had got. Saira didn't understand the concept of ownership. For her, anything she liked belonged to her. So, with a great deal of sadness, Nimra watched Saira usurp a pair of shoes her cousins had got for her, along with a couple of pretty scarves and some costume jewellery.

'I have gifts for you too,' Nimra protested weakly but Saira was adamant. 'I like these and I'm taking them.'

When Saira had finished rummaging through the last of Nimra's bags, her eyes fell on the butterfly brooch still pinned to the hijab that Nimra had removed.

'And I want this too!' Saira demanded, her hands moving towards the hijab to unpin the brooch. Nimra's eyes widened and she grabbed the hijab before Saira could reach it.

'No!' Nimra almost shouted as she held the hijab close to her chest. 'I'm not giving this to you. It's mine.'

Saira pulled the hijab from Nimra's hand but Nimra didn't relent. Finally, she played her ace card. She called her mother.

'Why aren't you giving a small thing to your sister?' Saira's mother asked, unmindful that her daughter had already taken away most of Nimra's things.

'It's mine,' Nimra said forcefully, clutching the hijab in her hand tightly.

'Come, Saira. I'll get you something better than this cheap trinket,' Saira's mother snapped, as she led away a mutinous Saira.

Nimra released the hold on the hijab and breathed with ease. She unpinned it and kept it in the box in her cupboard where she stored all her precious things. That very evening when she opened the cupboard to check it, her heart sank—the brooch wasn't there.

chapter 33

Arifa pressed the red button on her phone, ending the call. She dropped the phone carelessly beside her. She leaned back against the headrest of the bed and opened her eyes, training them on the ceiling. Armaan was watching TV outside and she expected him to come bounding into the room any moment now, demanding attention, but she prayed he wouldn't.

Since the time the old woman had started her story, Arifa had been enthralled. Surely the old bat was making it all up. Surely it couldn't have been true. She'd looked around at the other girls listening to Mariam, equally entranced, and she had felt a little uneasy. And then there were times when she observed how Mariam spoke about that man Aasim. There was a faraway look in her eyes that spoke of stolen moments and a carefree youth that none of them had ever experienced. Well, not she at least.

Finally, grudgingly, Arifa began to accept that Mariam's words were indeed true. She was recounting her life to them and while it sounded too fantastic to be anything but fiction, Arifa was quite sure it wasn't. The realisation had made her feel angry and cheated. She didn't know why. She should be glad she was young and she had a life ahead of her and she loved her husband. Not like that Amma who had secretly nurtured a love for another man all her life. But listening to the end today, the fact that Amma hadn't done anything scandalous, that she hadn't had an affair with this Aasim and had instead managed to share a grandchild with him had released a slew of feelings inside her, none of which she could understand. Except the phrase 'What now?' that kept reverberating in her head.

She came back home and without even consulting the clock, dialled her husband's number from her mobile phone. It was engaged. Feeling impatient, she tried again and again and finally gave up. His call wasn't due until tomorrow. He called every alternate day and since he had spoken to her yesterday, there was no chance he would call today.

But she wanted to speak to him, to hear his voice and... to ask him to come back. There was only so much a woman could manage and she was truly fed up of doing it alone. She wanted to convince him that they could have a good life here, one that involved him entirely. She was about to disconnect when he answered the phone.

Feeling foolish, words dried up in her mouth and she didn't offer any explanation as to why she had called him out of turn.

'Is everything alright? Has something... has something happened to Amma?' he asked, referring to his mother. Arifa rolled her eyes before exhaling a 'No'.

'Then?'

Something has happened to me, Shuaib. I need you, she thought, extremely angry at herself for being unable to articulate the words to him. Just say it, she kept thinking.

'You called for no reason?' he asked, and it was the tiredness in his voice that made Arifa sit up straight.

'Come home,' she said quietly. He thought he hadn't heard her properly and asked her to repeat the words. He seemed taken aback when she did.

'Is everything alright at home?' he asked again, his concern for everyone but her seeming to tip her off some edge.

'No, it's not! I'm not alright. I need you!' Saying this, she disconnected the call. She wondered if he would call again to ask her what the matter was, but she knew him. This man. This man living so far away from them. She could picture him, looking at the phone in disbelief.

She covered her eyes with her hands and feeling overwhelmed, began to cry. She didn't know why but the tears that had collected somewhere deep inside her refused to abate. She had instantly identified herself with Aasim's wife, that unknown woman who hadn't known how much her husband loved another woman. What of her? Didn't she deserve a man whose heart was whole, who was not torn between affection for his wife and love for his childhood sweetheart?

What if Shuaib too had some childhood sweetheart he still had feelings for? What if *she*, Arifa, was the other woman in their equation? The tears sprang up with full force and although a small part of her tried to remind her that her husband wasn't Aasim, it seemed that she needed the nudge of self-pity before she could indulge in a bout of crying.

Wiping the tears with the back of her hand, she dialled his number again.

'What?' he snapped. 'What is the matter with you?'

Arifa stayed silent, listening to his voice and the spaces in the conversation that she was expected to fill. She hated this uncertainty of not even knowing what she was going through.

How could she tell him what it was when she didn't know it herself? Her mouth curved downwards and she pulled her upper lip inside, biting down on it with her teeth.

'Arifa?' he asked. 'Tell me. What happened?'

She took a deep breath. 'I don't know. I... I don't think I can manage like this any longer. I can't live life like this. I want you back home.'

There was silence at the other end as he measured her words. 'What has made you decide this?' he asked finally.

'I... ' she couldn't possibly tell him that an old woman had set off this chain of events by her nostalgic reminiscence of her life.

'It's just that... I can't do this anymore. I want you with me,' she managed to tell him. She chewed the inside of her cheek while waiting for his answer.

'It's a bit sudden, isn't it?' he asked.

Arifa looked down at her folded knees and nodded. 'Yes. But I don't care for money. You can do something here. Please come?' she closed her eyes as she realised she was begging him.

'Arifa, try and understand. I can't just leave my job here and come there. I... have some responsibilities too,' he reasoned.

'And what of your responsibilities towards me?' she asked.

There was silence. And in that chink of nothingness, a new sound crept upon them. A baby crying.

Arifa felt her stomach plummet. 'What was that? I heard a baby cry!' she said, getting up from the bed.

'Huh? Oh yeah! That's the baby next door,' he said easily.

Arifa couldn't accept the explanation. 'It sounded too close,' she said, her voice seeming to dry up as she gathered the courage to accuse him.

'So? What are you trying to say?' he asked her, sounding exasperated.

That you got married there and you have another family. That's why you don't want to come back here. The words reverberated in Arifa's head, but she couldn't voice them. What if he accepted her accusation? What if it were true? Instead of a childhood sweetheart, what if Shuaib had found a new wife in Dubai? It wasn't so uncommon after all. Oh, why had she agreed to let him go to Dubai, she thought as she hastily disconnected the call, tears running down her face.

Was it true? Had he got married there, was that the sound of his baby? But she had never heard any other such sound before. It could be because *he* was the one who called all the time and obviously chose to call at a time that was convenient for him. When the baby wasn't around. Another thought made a forceful entry. Maybe the baby was newly born. It was followed by a flurry of thoughts that jostled around inside her head, drowning the sound of the phone that kept ringing by her side.

chapter 34

'So, are you famous?' Mariam asked Aasim that first year when they were new grandparents. Both of them avoided looking at each other whenever Aasim came home Instead, they focussed completely on Faiza. But that day, for some reason, Mariam remembered the old Aasim, the boy who had wanted to tell stories and had her captivated by his mere retelling of the movies he had seen.

Aasim shrugged. He was sitting on the sofa and Mariam was on another chair while Faiza slept in the improvised jhoola Mariam had fashioned for her with an old sari looped through a hook in the ceiling. A gentle breeze fanned them, and with the aid of a small length of the same sari, Mariam rocked the jhoola gently, ensuring the baby slept soundly.

'I'm afraid she'll get into this habit of being rocked to sleep, and what will I do back there?' Aasim mused.

'How difficult is it to set one up?' Mariam asked in return.

'Very difficult. Especially since you're not there,' Aasim retorted and then took a deep breath and let it out as a big sigh. They had avoided talking about personal things, unless it was something related to Faiza and it was understood that they wouldn't ever bring up anything from the past. But there were rare times like this when they seemed to forget that decades had lapsed since those stolen moments on the terrace.

Mariam pretended she hadn't heard the last sentence and loosened the grip on the sari, letting the jhoola slow down its momentum.

'So, you didn't answer,' Mariam said, hoping that talking of his professional life would ease the tension that had sprung up between them. Ever since Aasim had returned to Vellore with Faiza, Mariam had felt a tiny well of happiness open inside her, a place where she believed fervently that something had died along with her son. It wasn't just happiness. It was something to look forward to, an hour of stored memories to keep her going when she felt bleak. Even though her husband was in their house, it seemed as if it was just them with Faiza.

'I don't know what you mean by famous,' Aasim replied finally, inspecting his hands as though they fascinated him. She knew he didn't want to look up at her.

'How come you started writing in English? Urdu isn't good enough for you?' Mariam asked, hoping to prod him into giving an answer.

'No! No, it wasn't like that,' Aasim protested, shaking his head. 'Urdu will always be my first love, but I had to start writing in English to become a mainstream writer.'

'And did that help?' she asked, curious about his life there.

'Well, sort of,' Aasim replied, not willing to divulge any more. Mariam sighed and he looked up in surprise. 'What?' he asked.

'I've known you for so long, Aasim. I know when you're trying to avoid giving answers.'

'Too bad you know me so well,' Aasim muttered, cracking the knuckles of one hand with the palm of the other.

Mariam let go of the jhoola completely and faced Aasim with a grim smile. He looked at her squarely and for the tiniest of moments, the two of them felt that thing again. That which had been a raging, thundering thing when they were teenagers and had become as elusive as a butterfly, spotted one moment, gone the next. But for this moment, they held the fluttering winged creature in their outstretched palms.

Aasim cleared his throat and the butterfly vanished, leaving them with an odd mixture of relief and disappointment.

'You could say I am famous,' he admitted gruffly.

Mariam raised her eyebrows in mock appreciation.

'I've been interviewed hundreds of times and they've even adapted one of my novels into a television series,' he said slowly. 'I-I'm not boasting. You asked,' he reminded her when Mariam narrowed her eyes.

'But I don't think of it much. Just telling a story gives me happiness and that's what's important to me,' he added. Mariam looked down at the frayed border of her grey sari.

'I'm happy for you,' she said. 'So happy you followed your dreams.'

'What about you? I remember you were very keen on crochet,' he prodded, folding his arms across his chest. Mariam looked up swiftly. He hadn't brought up the crochet or the magazines in all these months. Mariam found that she was unable to form the right words. She could say it so easily now. She could tell him that she had found the magazines and his messages. But then, that was a bit redundant. It was *because* of those damned messages that she had got her son married to his daughter.

'Yes, I do crochet now and then,' she said, biting her lower lip but unable to meet his gaze.

'Namaz topis?' he persisted.

'No, Aasim. Not just namaz topis,' she replied, looking at him finally.

'Then?'

'Do you want to see my work?' she asked him. It was more of a challenge and before he could answer, she got up.

She walked away from there, resolutely avoiding his gaze, wondering what any of this could accomplish. But she put away the thoughts from her mind as she rummaged in her cupboard for the crocheted doilies, table cloths, runners and dolls that she had made in all these years. For some reason, she had never put them out on display. She had just hoarded each little thing she had created with the help of the magazines, going through them once every few months as one would check on an old acquaintance to see if they were alright.

Then her eyes fell on the baby clothes she had made when she heard that Faiza was going to be born. She had kept meaning to send them to her son, but hadn't been able to and now they were too small for her.

She put those also on the pile of crocheted items, turned to look at her sleeping husband and felt something catch in her chest. Before she lost courage, she went back outside and deposited everything on the sofa where Aasim was sitting. He looked impressed as he looked through everything and kept shaking his head, but soon Mariam realised that he seemed to be looking for something in particular.

'What are you searching for?' she asked him curiously.

'I... I don't know if I should be relieved that you didn't make the bedspread,' he said finally.

Mariam didn't know what he was talking about but she

had a feeling that if she told him that, he wouldn't tell her a thing. In a moment of sharp perception, she decided not to let him know that she wasn't clued in to what he was saying.

'Why?' she asked. He covered his eyes with his hands and rubbed them none too gently.

'I… I felt bad about it, Mariam. I… I shouldn't have said what I said and I think… you realised it too,' he said, his eyes still covered.

Mariam scratched the side of her neck briefly and decided to just let him continue talking. Maybe he would fill in the blanks himself.

'I don't know what got into me that day,' he continued, dropping his hands from his face. 'I posted the magazine as usual and then… I wanted to take it back and tear away the page.'

There had been so many magazines he had sent but which one was he talking about? The one in which he had professed his love for her? There had been no bedspread in that one. She should know. She had memorised each of the pages, not just his messages but the contents, the layout, the figures, the clothes, the colours.

'It was just that… I suddenly realised I would have to live my whole life without you. I would have to continue living that half-life and you would never be a part of it. It overwhelmed me. And I… I just wrote impulsively that day,' he explained, his palms facing upward in a gesture of despair. 'I felt really bad about even suggesting such a thing to you, especially as I had told you I would never take you away from your family but for that one moment, I was selfish. I...' he stopped when he saw Mariam's shocked expression.

'You have no idea what I'm talking about!' he exclaimed,

almost accusing her, and Mariam didn't know how to react.

'I didn't see any such message,' Mariam finally admitted. Aasim stared at her, mouth open.

'What?' he asked, shaking his head as if the action would clear the confusion.

'What had you written in that magazine?' Mariam asked him after a moment. She wished she had kept her face impassive but it had been impossible as she listened to him speak, especially the emotions that played across his face.

'You're not pulling my leg, are you?' he asked her suspiciously, and Mariam shook her head impatiently.

'I really don't know what you're talking about. The thing is, Raheema bu never let me look at those magazines when you were sending them. I brought all the magazines from my mother's house only after Raheema bu and my parents had passed away, and these were the only ones there. Maybe if you tell me what you had said in it… '

He shook his head slowly. 'Raheema bu didn't let you see them?'

Mariam nodded. 'She never let me linger over them. I think she must have read your messages and didn't think it was right for us to stay connected this way.'

Aasim looked down. 'Then she must have seen that message. Maybe she tore out that page.'

'Which message? And why would she do that?' Mariam asked. Faiza awoke and squirmed in the jhoola but the two of them couldn't move their gazes towards her yet.

'Maybe she understood my desperation and realised what I asked from you was wrong. Maybe she was trying to save the two of us from doing something… '

'Doing what?' Mariam asked, her voice rising over the sounds of Faiza crying.

'Running away. I asked you to run away with me. I told you that you had been right, that day on the terrace. We should have run away together when we had the chance,' Aasim confessed, bending to pick up Faiza and cooing to her, without looking at Mariam.

chapter 35

At this time of the evening, Amreen was always expected to be in the kitchen preparing dinner. She would be wrist-deep in the atta she kneaded, or wiping sweat that trickled down her face as she cooked aloo-kheema, a staple in the house. But that day, instead of heading towards the kitchen, she found herself walking up the stairs to their terrace.

Her mother-in-law had looked at her, startled, and even called out to her when she went. 'Why are you going to the terrace now? Did you leave something there?'

Amreen shook her head but continued climbing the stairs. She, too, lived in Vellore like Amma had, and as Amma's tale unfolded, it was probably easiest for Amreen to visualise the terrace and Amma's strong connection to it.

A warm wind met her face like an old companion before moving away to ruffle some of the persistent kites in the sky. The sun's warmth still lingered in the air. Amreen walked towards the parapet and placed her palms on it. Dust rose in a cloud and she felt the grittiness of sand on her hands, as she looked out towards the mountains.

Even if everything else in Vellore had changed since Amma's time, the mountains hadn't. They were mute spectators to the kite fights that boys indulged in, to the shy glances that were exchanged across terraces and to the occasional but passionate discovery of love, as in Amma's case.

She looked up at the darkened sky, at the stars that blinked unwaveringly each day, and thought of her own life and situation. She leaned closer towards the parapet wall, its warmth touching her stomach, and shut her eyes. This obsession over a baby had to end. She was letting it override everything else in her life. But it wasn't only her obsession, she reminded herself. It was her mother-in-law who looked at her expectantly, sometimes asking questions straight away, eliciting surly answers from her.

Amreen never went down that road where she wondered what would happen if she'd never be able to have children. She couldn't. She panicked every time and back-tracked. Her husband was more laid back. He hadn't let the scrutiny of others affect their personal equation and that was what she loved most about him. Even now, she knew that he would come upstairs looking for her. It was as though he was tuned into her in some primal way and while it was something neither of them understood, she was glad of it. Unlike that poor Arifa who constantly seemed on edge with her husband away, or Shaista who was plainly unhappy with her pregnancy. She had to stop mentally shouting the word 'unfair' every time she looked at Shaista. Why did it happen to her and not me? Why, why, why?

It wasn't as though she had found any answers to her questions, she realised, as the darkness intensified. She had stopped asking the questions. She smiled then, a true, happy smile that lit her from inside as she felt her husband's arms slide around her waist.

'When did you come?' she asked, leaning back into him. She hadn't even heard him come upstairs.

'Sometime back,' he replied, bending down to nuzzle her collarbone before straightening up.

'Come downstairs. Someone might see us,' he said, moving away, but she held his hand and turned around to face him.

'So? I'm your wife,' she challenged him, tugging him closer.

'Amreen,' he said, a warning tone in his voice as she squeezed his hand.

She shrugged and without even thinking of why she was doing it, asked him straight away. 'Are you unhappy that we haven't had a child yet?' It was odd how the two of them were so close to each other in every sense of the word, but had never really voiced this question. Amreen had preferred to believe that as long as she didn't ask it, the question would remain a question and not a glaring reality.

His eyes narrowed and he remained quiet for a while. Amreen's heart sank. 'Did anyone say anything to you?' he asked and Amreen couldn't help but guffaw at that. Oh, her dim-witted, thick husband. People had been plaguing her with questions, asked and unasked since the *day after* they got married!

'You can't answer a question with another question,' she prodded, touching the tip of his nose with her finger. He held it firmly. He was not joking.

'I'm happy with you, Amreen,' he said, looking into her eyes. 'If we had a child, I would be happier, and I really believe that if Allah wills it, we will have one.'

'But what if we don't?' Amreen asked quickly, asking the question before it could evaporate from her tongue. 'What if we never have a child?' she winced as she said the dreaded words.

He cupped her face in his hands and kissed her on the forehead gently, turned around, and walked downstairs. That was not reassuring, Amreen thought shakily as she followed him. Later, after dinner, when he was watching TV outside, Amreen went back to her room and rummaged in the cupboards looking for her old books.

He came inside and looked surprised. 'What are you doing?' he asked, sitting down on the bed and picking up the remote to switch on the TV.

For some reason, Amreen found that annoying. 'You just watched TV outside,' she grumbled, her head still inside the cupboard.

'So?' He did, not bother to elaborate.

One day, Amreen decided fervently, one day she was going to unplug the TV and smash it to pieces. Until then, her books would have to do.

'What are you looking for?' he asked her over the sounds of Vadivelu being beaten to pulp.

Amreen popped her head out and looked at him. 'The next time you go to the market, can you look for any books by Aasim?'

'Aasim what?' he asked, his eyes still trained on the TV.

Amreen scratched her head thoughtfully. She had never asked Amma what his full name was. She would ask her in the next class tomorrow. All the rummaging had yielded a book that she hadn't read before. Grasping it to her chest, she went back and sat on the bed, feeling the same happiness she had felt on the terrace seconds before her husband had come.

She flipped to the last page, read the ending and then went back to the beginning. Her husband shook his head in amusement. He had apparently moved his eyes from the TV for the barest of seconds to watch her do this.

'Why do you always read the end first?' he asked, nudging her shoulder.

'Because I want to make sure there's a happy ending,' Amreen mumbled, her head buried in her book. She didn't see the look of confusion dart across her husband's face.

chapter 36

The last thing Shaista wanted was this baby.

At first, she had thought that she would develop maternal feelings when the baby would start moving inside her body but that momentous occasion didn't bring any changes in her mindset. She continued feeling trapped and angry and she wished it were Amreen who had been pregnant, not her. She knew how much Amreen coveted for a child of her own. She could sense it in the hungry glances that Amreen sent her way every day at Amma's place.

As her pregnancy advanced, Shaista found small movements, such as lying down and sitting up, become a challenge. When Amma started talking about how she had felt when her daughter was born, Shaista could connect to her immediately. She knew what it felt like to be trapped in your own body. She understood how difficult it was to even take three or four steps without feeling the pain knife through the centre of her spine. But she didn't know if this was how every pregnant woman felt.

Overcoming her shyness and initial fear of her mother-in-law, one day she asked her if all pregnant women felt this way.

'What way, ma?' her mother-in-law asked her, as she peeled off the skin of an onion with the blade of a sharp knife.

Eyes watering, Shaista briefly explained to her about the aches and pains that plagued her body, but not her mind. Her mother-in-law put down the onion in surprise.

'Why didn't you tell me before? We should ask the doctor when we go visit her for your next check-up.'

Shaista shrugged. The doctor might give her some medicines to alleviate the pain. But what of this gaping hole in her heart that she carried around with her every single day? At least Amma had her feelings for this man, this Aasim, which eclipsed everything else in her life. What did she have? She, Shaista, had no one who loved her that way. She closed her eyes, feeling sadness settle over her like second skin.

Her pregnancy put a visible barrier between her and her husband and that was the only thing for which she was glad. He seemed to find the sight of her body distasteful, and as usual plunged the room in darkness the moment he entered. However, these days he was a little wary of reaching out for her; she would curl up in her corner, a grim smile on her face.

Each morning, the routine was the same and Shaista knew that a child would do little to change it for him. It would change everything for her though, but everyone expected that.

She took a nap and found herself transported into Amma's world—the one they had all inhabited with her these last few days. She wondered if it was just her or were Amma's words reverberating in the mind of each of them long after they had been spoken. Why did she feel that Amma was telling this story *for* her? It almost seemed as though Amma was sending some sort of subliminal messages for her, not unlike those that Aasim had left for Amma in the magazines.

She didn't have much time to dwell over it as her mother-in-law came and woke her up, telling her that her parents were in Vellore and coming over to see her.

Shaista had visited her town only twice after marriage and not even once since the beginning of her pregnancy. She talked to her mother every other day, but it was more a collection of 'umms' and 'aahs' than any real conversation.

'How come they have come?' she asked without thinking. The older woman smiled at her, shaking her head.

'You are so naïve, ma. They have come to see you because of your condition.' Her mother-in-law glanced at her round belly as if to confirm she was still pregnant. Saying so, she left the room and Shaista twisted her mouth into a scowl so deep, her unborn child would have flinched, had it seen her face.

Later, when her mother was sitting with her in her room, Shaista summoned the courage to tell her of the constant claustrophobia that this baby had cast over her, like a slithering net over a school of unsuspecting fish.

At first her mother couldn't understand. She insisted that Shaista was looking too pale and that she should soak almonds in water in the night and eat them in the morning. At this Shaista shut her eyes and let out a growl of sorts to communicate her impatience to her mother.

'What?' her mother looked at her, surprised. When Shaista finally explained everything to her, she looked confused and a little scared.

'Shh! How can you say such a thing? Why don't you want this baby?' her mother whispered, looking around fearfully. True. Walls could sprout ears at the most inopportune moments.

Shaista shrugged and sighed. If her own mother couldn't understand her, who would? Her mother hunched forward in the chair, looked up at Shaista and finally spoke in a rush.

'It's all because we didn't let you finish school, isn't it?'

Shaista looked up at her mother, surprised. She had almost forgotten she was just fifteen.

chapter 37

Guilt is a tricky creature. It creeps up behind us and grabs us by the chest when we are not prepared at all; no matter how hard we try to reach back and fling it away, it sticks around, its acid fingers slowly corroding any feelings of happiness that may have existed in the heart.

Mariam's relationship with guilt was a long-standing one. They greeted one another as enemies who knew and recognized each other only too well. It had bobbed around when Mariam was pregnant and Aasim returned to her life, confusing her with his feelings for her. It reared its ugly head each time Mariam confronted her own feelings for Aasim. After the discovery of the magazines, guilt and she had plateued, coasting along together. Mariam accepted that it would always remain an omnipresent emotion, no matter what she did.

Nevertheless, she wasn't prepared for this deluge of emotions that hit her after Aasim left with Faiza that first year. She looked at her emaciated husband and guilt whistled in her head, a tuneless song that threatened to spill out into the emptiness that was her home, now that her granddaughter was gone along with the only man she had ever truly loved.

She firmly put both Aasim and Faiza to the back of her

mind, as she tried to undo the damage that her son's death had done to her husband. She refused to consider that the carefree moments she had spent with Aasim and Faiza had been anything but a healing process. Guilt made her think otherwise. She didn't deserve to heal, not when her husband was suspended in grief.

Her daughter, Asma, lived in Madras with her family, and although Mariam had never involved her in anything, she felt compelled to do so now. Asma was only thirty and yet, there were times when Mariam felt a little wary of her, as though she could see through her in ways no one else could. When she did come to Vellore with her husband, Mariam's foremost feeling was relief—that there was finally someone else she could share the burden of her husband's condition with.

Together they took him to hospitals and doctors and hakeems but were turned back from everywhere. He was not suffering from any pathological disease. His son's death had been a slowly expanding pain in his heart, leaching away his will to live.

Frustrated one day after returning home from yet another unfruitful visit to yet another doctor, Asma turned to her mother and slapped her forehead in anguish. 'This is all your fault. You should never have got Faisal married to that girl in America,' she blurted.

'Asma!' her husband warned her. Feeling uncomfortable, he stepped out of the house. Mariam looked at her son-in-law leave and wondered if he, too, felt the same way. How could she explain to Asma that she blamed herself too? And yet, there was Faiza, that gorgeous baby who belonged to both her and Aasim. How could she negate her existence?

'It's fate,' she said finally, internally wincing at using that word. Fate? Hadn't she and Aasim meddled with it and been punished enough for it?

'Fate!' Asma spat out. 'Abba was against that match from the beginning. But would you listen?'

'It's not as if Faisal died alone. His wife died with him, Asma!' Mariam's voice rose in anguish.

Asma shrugged with the nonchalance that only the very narrow-minded can pull off. 'So? That man has two sons. You had only one and you lost him too!'

Mariam made a decision there and then. She would not involve her daughter in anything to do with Faiza or even her husband ever again. Judgemental people were a dime a dozen and she had enough of them right here in Vellore, she didn't need to import any from Madras.

'If you've said what you had to say, you can leave,' she told Asma quietly. Many years later, Mariam regretted saying these the words to Asma that afternoon. Asma had kept away from her ever since, refusing to visit Vellore unless it was absolutely necessary, like when her father passed away in the summer of 1990. Mariam's husband finally lost the inner battle he had been waging with himself and departed to another world, leaving her truly alone. There was no one with her now. Her mother-in-law had died years ago, Razia bu had left after that, then Faisal went, and now her husband was gone too. The only person who stayed back was Sarita, their old retainer and maid with her three-year-old daughter, Deepa.

There were many times during that four-month period of iddat when Mariam thought of the day her husband died. It had been one like any other, warm and still. She had spent it coaxing her husband to get up, to eat a little, to live a little more.

He had refused to sit up, and finally when she had made a move to leave the room with the bowl of ganji in her hand, he had called out to her.

She retraced her steps to the bed, the warm ganji bowl still in her hands as she stood near him. It was so unfair, the way his life had turned out. Why did Allah favour one man with success and another with the deepest, darkest failure?

His eyes were closed but Mariam knew he had called out to her. 'I'm sorry,' he said slowly, his eyes flickering open. Despite the heat in the room, the warmth in her hands, Mariam felt a chill coursing down her back. It made her shiver as she placed the bowl on the table nearby and sat down beside him.

'What are you sorry for?' she asked, pushing his sparse hair away from his forehead.

'Everything,' he replied. Mariam closed her eyes, wishing life had turned out different for them.

'You didn't do anything wrong,' Mariam said, and he shook his head slightly.

'I know you... weren't... ' he couldn't finish the words and Mariam felt the chill more intensely now. She wanted to prod him until he explained what he meant.

'Faisal dying,' the words broke out, sweat popping up on his forehead, 'was not your fault. I kept blaming you, but it's fate.'

Mariam shut her eyes, pain swamping down upon her. If only he knew.

'I know,' he said suddenly and Mariam opened her eyes quickly. What did he mean?

'What?' she managed to ask him, her throat thick and clogged.

'About you and Aasim.'

Mariam turned pale. She got up immediately and brushed

her hands as though his words had implied something that could be dusted off physically.

'I don't know what you're saying,' she managed to mumble, picking up the bowl to take it to the kitchen.

'I've known since the time Asma was born, and I also know that he wrote that story for you.'

Mariam froze. She turned around slowly, unwilling to believe what her husband was saying.

'I don't know what you're saying.' she repeated. 'I didn't read any such story.'

'You must, you must,' he whispered, his eyes closing as he drifted off into sleep, as though exhausted by the longest conversation they'd had in years.

In the kitchen, Mariam sank to the floor, where guilt wrestled her down and reduced her to a weeping wreck. She allowed her old enemy to punch her, push her, and shake her hard. He knew for all these years! The words wouldn't stop ringing in her ears as she thought back to her life since Asma was born. The past thirty years he had known everything and kept quiet. Why bring it up now, she thought wearily as she made her way back to her room to tell him that all that was in the past. Now, only he mattered.

But guilt had won the last round. She could almost envision it raising its hands in the air like a victor as it straddled the unmoving body of her husband.

chapter 38

During the entire period of Mariam's iddat, she refused to take Aasim's calls. Her daughter would often hand her the receiver with a disdainful look, saying, 'It's that man and he wants to talk to you.' Mariam would shake her head without saying why she wouldn't talk to him.

It wasn't that she was punishing Aasim for anything; it was just that she didn't want this process of grief for her husband to be muddied by her feelings for Aasim, whatever they were. Her daughter stayed with her for the first forty days although she went to Madras frequently and came back. There was often an undistinguishable look on her face—something between awkwardness and embarrassment. Mariam couldn't figure out what it was until one day after the chehlum, the fortieth day fatiha for her husband, Asma sat down beside her, fidgeting with the pallu of her sari.

'Ammi, I was thinking that maybe you should come to Madras and stay with us in our house. How will you live here alone?' she asked, all the while looking down. Mariam knew that Asma was only being dutiful and had asked because she must make the offer.

'I'm not leaving this house to go anywhere, Asma,' she replied softly.

'Why?' Asma almost looked relieved, but also indignant.

'Because this is my home and I intend to stay here till I die,' Mariam replied, her eyes going back to the page of the Quran she was reading.

'But, Ammi, how will you manage everything? It's so difficult for a woman to live alone!' Asma protested with more enthusiasm, now that she knew Mariam's chances of moving to Madras were minimal.

Mariam shook her head and refused to listen to any more of Asma's arguments.

'What about money?' Asma asked hotly and then clammed up all of a sudden. She probably hadn't meant to ask that question because it could mean that she would have to offer her mother money in case she didn't have any.

'I have,' Mariam replied confidently.

'What? How?' Asma's curiosity was aroused as well.

'I saved some when your father sold his shop. I'm a single woman. How much can my expenses be? I'll manage. You go back to Madras, to your life there,' Mariam reassured her daughter. Instead of assuaging her guilt, Mariam's words seemed to have inflamed some sort of resentment inside Asma.

'What will people say? That I've left you alone to fend for yourself? They will say all sorts of things about me.' Asma's voice had started rising and quivering.

Mariam shrugged. 'Look, I cannot impose myself upon you and your family. I'll manage here,' she said with finality.

After the death of Mariam's husband, Sarita had stayed on as full-time help, and she became indispensable to her in numerous ways. After the iddat was over, Mariam remained shut inside the house, unwilling to embrace the normalcy of life because there was nothing really left for her to do. She often thought back to her husband's last words and grimaced, because they had been about Aasim.

She finally took Aasim's call nearly six months after her husband's death and his voice exploded into her ear, across all those thousands of miles.

'Why haven't you been talking to me? Are you alright? How have you been? Don't you even care about Faiza? Why wouldn't you come on the phone?' he railed on and Mariam shut her eyes, a tear escaping silently as she thanked Allah for the miracle of the telephone that seemed to deposit Aasim's voice right inside her ear. She hung on to the quality of his voice, the rough timbre that she adored so much, and bit her lower lip, knowing that she wouldn't be able to talk to him without crying.

'Are you alright?' he asked her again, but this time his tone was softer and more gentle. Mariam sighed. 'Say something, Mariam! If you hadn't answered today, I would have come to India to see you!'

'I'm fine, Aasim,' she replied finally. He was silent.

'I'm really sorry about your husband. He was a good man.' It felt as though he were almost parroting the words. 'Are you alone? Is there anyone with you?' he asked.

'No, Aasim. They all left. Now it's just my memories and me,' Mariam replied, wishing she didn't sound so maudlin. She didn't want pity.

'You know what? You should come here to San Francisco!' Aasim suggested, and it was the first time in ages that Mariam laughed.

'No, I'm serious! You should,' he continued.

Mariam thought of his life there with his children and his wife and what she would possibly do there and the very thought made her quail.

'No, Aasim. I'm not going anywhere,' she said firmly. The very thought of sharing a roof with his wife... 'Please don't bring this up again.'

'Do you know that Faiza has started saying words? She's saying "dada" and "dadi"!' Aasim said, trying to tempt her. Mariam closed her eyes and pictured her chubby Faiza, then shook her head.

'I'll see her when you bring her here the next time.'

'That won't be until next year,' Aasim warned.

Time could stretch or collapse as it saw fit, Mariam thought. 'Fine,' she replied, knowing that there was little else she could do.

'Mariam,' Aasim's voice had softened further.

'What is it, Aasim?' Mariam had started feeling tired by the mere effort of talking to him politely.

'Please come back with us to San Francisco? If you say you'll come, I'll arrange everything for you!' he sounded a bit like a recalcitrant child.

'I'll see you next year, Aasim,' Saying this, Mariam replaced the receiver on the phone with a sense of finality. It did not ring again.

From then onwards Aasim calmly disrupted the routine that they had developed all these months. Instead of calling her weekly, he would call her whenever he felt like it and although Mariam was glad to hear his voice, she felt fettered by his demands at times.

Sometimes she would let the phone ring because she knew

it would be him wanting to ask her what she was doing and whether she had changed her mind about moving to his city. When she had missed around four or five of his calls, she would answer the next, knowing that he would be mad with worry.

'Why do you do this to me, Mariam?' he would ask her, refusing to listen to her explanations or excuses.

Finally, at one point when he was accusing her of deliberately ignoring him, something inside Mariam snapped.

'Stop this, Aasim! You and I, we are samdhis. We share a granddaughter. Nothing more. Don't call me so often! Just because my husband died, you think you have all the freedom you want?' she was unable to stop the words from tumbling out of her mouth.

'What do you mean?' His voice low and angry. Mariam's thoughts went back to that last day when her husband had calmly told her he knew everything about Aasim and her before he died. So, she told him.

'My husband knew about us, Aasim,' she finally managed to say, finding it supremely difficult to get the words out. Although she wondered what 'us' could there really be after being haphazardly bound together for more than three decades? Of loving each other but never experiencing fulfilment? Us. The word itself referred to some sort of arrangement between the two of them, something that had never existed.

'What do you mean?' he asked her. Mariam was glad he hadn't asked her, 'What *us*?'

'I… he… the day he died, he told me he had read that story you'd written for me the month Asma was born,' Mariam stuttered.

'The story you didn't read? The one you still haven't read?' Aasim asked, his voice flat.

'Yes. That one,' she replied finally.

'So?' he asked and for a minute, Mariam forgot why they were arguing.

'So, it's not right that you and I... should become so close again, so soon after his death.' Mariam hoped he would understand what she couldn't convey to him in words. 'I'm a widow now, Aasim,' she reminded him.

'We have not done anything wrong,' he spat out, and before she could tell him that doing wasn't necessary, thinking about it was enough, he disconnected the call.

He didn't call her for two months after that and Mariam went through each day, staring at the black telephone, her connection with Aasim, that now lay silent. At first, she enjoyed the freedom from his attention and his overbearing nature, which she knew was merely a cover for his feelings for her. Often, she would think about his wife, wondering where she was whenever Aasim chose to call her and spend at least ten minutes talking to her.

But after that last argument, he stopped calling and Mariam schooled herself to believe that things had changed. He was hurt and angry and although she missed him terribly, she felt this was better for them.

After two months had passed, relief gave way to indignation. What about Faiza? Why wasn't he calling to inform her about her progress? Surely, this was a mean way of punishing her. In the days before their fight, he had even let Faiza talk to her on many occasions—Mariam had stored Faiza's spit-infused babble in her memories for a long time. Now, each day became painful for her, getting up, going through the motions of life, wondering what he was doing, and why he wasn't calling her.

How odd, she would think on days when the despair wasn't calling out to her, that they hadn't spoken to each other for thirty years. That it was Faiza who connected the two of them again. Finally, he called again. Their conversation was stilted and revolved mostly around Faiza, but Mariam was relieved to hear his voice again. When it was time to end the call, Mariam was surprised to note that he didn't.

'Aasim?' she asked, and the single word collapsed all the boundaries she had set between them.

'Mariam,' he responded, his voice gruff and it seemed, short of breath.

'Hmm?' she asked.

'Marry me.'

chapter 39

Aasim had reverted to calling her weekly and Mariam felt a mixture of relief and anxiety for he had now stopped asking her to move to San Francisco with him. Or that he wanted to marry her.

His words had rung in her ears for days after that call. She would often lie down on her bed staring at the ceiling, wondering what her life would be like if she says yes. She knew she would be his second wife and yet, she would be the one he loved more. Then she'd turn in the bed she had shared with her husband for three decades, look at the pillow where his head had rested and shut her eyes in anguish. How could she even contemplate marriage?

Mariam stewed with her feelings all alone, unable to tell anyone because once again, there was no one she could tell them to. She thought of her sister, the only person who had loved Aasim and her equally, but she just couldn't imagine telling her anything now. Not after all these years. Also, Apa wasn't keeping too well these days and was mostly confined to her bed. Her husband, Aasim's brother, too, had become old, and Mariam often felt a flash of irritation at Aasim. Why couldn't he be as bothered about them as he was about her? Why couldn't he take his brother and the sister-in-law, who was like a mother to him, to San Francisco?

Tentatively, she asked him once when he called her for his weekly report on Faiza. He was silent for a short while and then he spoke. 'You think I haven't asked them? I've asked them repeatedly to come back with me now that their children are married and have their own lives.'

'But why, Aasim? Why do you want everyone to come there? Wouldn't it just be easier if you came back?' Mariam asked softly, voicing a thought that had been jostling in her head for a few days.

'Come back and do what? My life is here. My work is here. I couldn't survive back there!'

'You've lived there for so many years now. Isn't it enough?' she asked him again, unable to stop herself.

'Mariam. I just can't.' Something in his tone made Mariam a little angry.

'Then don't expect others to just leave their lives and come with you because you have such a nice life there!' she exclaimed, her voice rising.

'What do you mean?' he asked and Mariam sensed that he, too, was angry.

'You're nothing but a child who hasn't grown up. If you can't get your way, you sulk and d-don't call for days. Why on earth should I l-leave my city and country to come live there with you?' Mariam stuttered, forgetting that the conversation hadn't been about her, but her sister and his brother.

'Because I love you, Mariam. And I want to marry you,' he said the words simply, unaware of how much turmoil they caused in her heart.

'How?' she whispered, her voice anguished. 'Think about your wife! The woman has lived with you for so many years! And yet... '

There was silence on the other end and Mariam thought that maybe he had ended the call.

'I told her about you a few months after we got married, Mariam. She knows.'

Mariam couldn't speak after that. It was suddenly too much for her to take. Her husband knowing about them surreptitiously and Aasim's wife learning about her all those years ago... if anything, she felt empathy for these two people who had soldiered on, married to two individuals who had no place for anyone else in their hearts.

'You can't do this to her, Aasim. She deserves more,' Mariam found herself taking the place of his wife. 'I'm surprised she stuck around with you for so long!'

'This isn't about her. It's about you and me and what we should have done years ago,' Aasim said, his voice fierce.

'We can't be so selfish, Aasim. Think about your children! They're all married, right? We'll be the laughing stock of the community!'

'I don't care. I just want us to be together at least now, Mariam.' Aasim's voice had taken on a strange tone.

'We're fifty years old, Aasim! It's time we cut off this... this connection we have with each other instead of... making it stronger. We can't get married, and I won't come to America. Just don't ask me again,' she blurted, and ended the call.

'Too late, too late,' the words mocked her as she clutched her head in despair. There was no way they could cut off their ties when they had Faiza.

The following year when Aasim brought Faiza, Mariam was worried about what he would say to her, in person. He hadn't brought up the topic again on the phone but she knew that the reprieve was temporary because he probably wanted to convince her when he met her.

Mariam stacked her defences high and decided she would meet him only as Faiza's grandmother. She would ignore him, yes, plainly ignore him if he brought up the topic of marriage or San Francisco again.

She opened the door to see him standing there with Faiza who was now a year and a half. Faiza looked around nervously and clung to his trousers and Mariam's heart melted for her son's little girl, all alone in the world now, just like her.

'Come in!' she said, realising she would have to befriend Faiza now, instead of just taking her into her arms like last time.

With all her focus on Faiza, she finally looked up at Aasim's face. Deep in her heart, she was glad he had come. Perhaps it was because she was deprived of companionship. Perhaps it was just the love she still felt for him, despite her own objections. She smiled at him but he didn't smile back.

Aasim had brought with him a suitcase filled with Faiza's toys and clothes and he deposited it in the hall before sitting down on the sofa warily. The silence between them wavered and stretched and Faiza tottered back towards Aasim, and lifted her arms, indicating he should pick her up. He picked her up with an indulgent smile, and she turned away from Mariam.

The awkwardness of the situation became even more evident when Mariam heard Faiza's muffled voice as she spoke in English to her nana, 'I want Nani!'

Aasim's face reddened slightly and he looked at Mariam, a

little apologetically. Mariam suddenly became conscious of the fact that this was how it was going to be all the time. Faiza would always be a stranger for her and would prefer her nani to her dadi. She lived with them after all. The excitement that Mariam had felt the past week slowly dissolved as she realised that Faiza might not want to stay with her at all.

Faiza buried her face in his neck and Mariam got up, feeling wretched. This was bound to happen, she told herself as she went to the kitchen. Her mind was blank as she arranged the mithai on a plate and then found that she couldn't go outside. Faiza wouldn't eat it. She just knew it.

In a flash of recognition, Mariam understood that she would always be on the periphery of her granddaughter's life. The thought had immobilised her but unleashed all the tears that had hardened her heart in the months since her husband's death.

Silently, she stood near the sink, crying, waiting for the sadness to subside but if anything, it seemed to continue burgeoning in her chest. Mariam had no sense of time but she knew she had been in the kitchen for too long. She had to go outside. What if Aasim had left with Faiza? Was that why it was so quiet?

She stepped out cautiously and saw that Faiza was asleep, curled in Aasim's arms. Aasim, too, was sleeping. She moved towards them slowly, absorbing the planes and angles of Aasim's face and Faiza's chubbiness, reminding her of a time many years ago when she had watched Aasim sleep in her house.

Maybe Faiza was just tired from the journey. Maybe she would be a little friendly when she woke up. Mariam sat down on the sofa nearby and watched the two people she loved the most in the world, sleep peacefully.

chapter 40

It had been a combination of many things, namely jetlag and tiredness, that had made Faiza cranky on that first day. Aasim coaxed her gently and whispered something in her ear. Mariam felt a shaft of jealousy—she would never be so close to this special child. Repressing it, she smiled when Faiza looked up at her and opened her arms, hoping the little girl would take the hint.

Faiza didn't move from Aasim's lap where she had woken up some time back and Mariam pretended that it didn't matter so much as she dropped her arms. Only then did she note that Aasim was staring at her with a blazing look in his eyes. She had let down her guard a minute ago and hadn't been able to put it back soon enough; he had probably seen her expression.

They stared at each other, Mariam uncomfortable and Aasim intense, before Faiza stepped down from his lap and ventured to explore the crochet dolls that Mariam had brought for her.

They didn't need to bandy words to know what the other was thinking, Mariam thought as she relished the powerful silence that echoed between them. But she had been living in silence for too long with no one to talk to or understand her. Now, there was a surfeit of words in her head that tumbled over each other to get out, and yet she suppressed them.

Faiza was trying to pull the head of the crochet doll, but it wasn't detachable and she flung it away in disgust, the scowl on her face a replica of her son Faisal's. In that instant, she forgot everything about taking it slow with Faiza. She dropped down and picked up Faiza who looked startled and hugged her tightly, as though her small, warm body could heal the broken spaces inside her.

'Nana! Down! Down!' Faiza screamed and Mariam put her down immediately, startled at the faint accent that rolled around in the air long after she had spoken.

'She'll get used to you, Mariam,' Aasim spoke finally, and smiled at her tentatively. Mariam nodded as Aasim opened the suitcase and took out Faiza's familiar toys and gave them to her. When it was time for Aasim to go, Faiza refused to let him leave. Heart aching, Mariam told Aasim that maybe he should take Faiza with him to his house in Vellore till she became accustomed to Mariam.

'I can't!' he shook his head. 'There's nothing there. I can't take a small baby and go live there. No gas, no milk and… '

'How do you manage?' Mariam asked, surprised. He shrugged.

'Then… maybe you should stay here tonight,' she suggested, the words finally released into the air.

Aasim stared at her for what seemed like ages although it was merely a few seconds. He shook his head.

'I'm not staying here, Mariam,' he murmured, and without another word, left the crying Faiza and a stunned Mariam together.

Faiza stood at the window and cried for her grandfather for nearly an hour, and Mariam was tempted to join her. She, too, wished she could bawl like Faiza and simply demand that Aasim come back—the very thought made her start laughing.

Faiza turned around and stared at her balefully before she resumed her crying.

It had to be one of the most unforgettable nights of her life, Mariam thought. Even when Asma and Faisal had been small, they had never kept her awake all night like Faiza did. She had simply refused to come inside the room to sleep with her and together both of them had sat outside, watching TV. Mariam's eyes blurred with sleep and yet she fought to keep awake as Faiza picked up all her toys and threw them away before crying out for her nana again. All maternal thoughts flitted away as Faiza refused to eat or drink and then Mariam realised with dismay that she needed to change Faiza's diaper. Only, she didn't know how.

These new-fangled things, she thought as she tried to remove Faiza's diaper while trying to ensure Faiza lay still on the sofa. How did Aasim manage her on the flight? How had he become so good with children? Or maybe he had always been this way, she thought, remembering her own husband who hadn't even seen either of their children's bottoms.

In the early hours of the day, bone tired and feeling dead with the exhaustion of staying awake, Mariam closed her eyes for a moment and promptly fell asleep. When she woke up minutes later, she saw that Faiza had crawled to a corner of the sofa and had tried climbing up but had fallen asleep near the foot.

Shaking her head, not knowing whether she ought to laugh or cry, Mariam picked up the stubborn child and together the two of them slept in the room. Mariam would have slept the day away if it hadn't been for the doorbell ringing. Thinking it must be Sarita who had taken the previous day off, Mariam stumbled to open the door and saw Aasim standing outside, looking fresh and squeaky clean. Feeling foolish, she admitted him inside but without offering any explanations, she went to lie down next to Faiza and promptly fell asleep again. When she woke up, she sat up in horror. She had asked Aasim to come inside and then… she turned to look at Faiza who was not there.

Aasim emerged from the bathroom then, holding Faiza wrapped in a towel. He had given her a bath. Oh. Mariam felt like she needed one too if only to clear the cobwebs from her mind.

She waited until he had dressed her and taken her outside, unwilling to look at the picture of domesticity he made, as he blew into Faiza's ears till she squealed. Thinking he had gone, she got up sighing only to find him still standing on the threshold.

'I'm sorry,' he said. Mariam shook her head but he continued. 'I shouldn't have left Faiza that way with you but I thought it was the only way she will get to know you. I've been telling her that you're her dadi and she… she'll be fine now,' he promised.

Mariam nodded as she went inside and shut the door, her hand over her thudding heart. How was she going to manage seeing him for a month without capitulating to his proposal? If it was still on the table, that is. She shut her eyes and instantly the picture of him as he emerged from the bathroom holding Faiza formed in her head. His blue shirt splotched all over and his trouser legs rolled up to his knees. Obviously, Faiza must have splashed a lot of water on him as he gave her a bath.

She dressed carefully, not willing to acknowledge why her heart was singing just because he was in her house with their granddaughter. She had stopped wearing colourful saris a decade ago, and now that she was a widow, she chose only pale, lifeless hues. But today, she wasn't in the mood for a grey or beige.

She remembered her favourite pink sari, the one she had been wearing that night on the terrace and although she didn't have that sari anymore, there was another pink one that she had bought some years back. For some reason, she was unable to wear it without thinking of Aasim. She decided to wear it today, refusing to pay heed to the very loud and obvious protests in her head. Today, she would be the Mariam from all those years ago, the one who used to act on impulses just because she felt like it.

She stepped outside, feeling a little self-conscious of the towel wrapped around her head and saw that Aasim had busied himself in her kitchen and was now feeding Faiza a roti. He didn't look up at her as she watched him coax Faiza into opening her mouth to eat some more, but Faiza was busy with her toys.

'I take it you two didn't get much sleep last night,' he said, smiling and looking up at her. His expression faltered when he saw her in the pink sari, looking fresh from her bath, water droplets still on her neck. Mariam thought she saw him swallow. It was amazing that he *still* had those feelings for her. They watched each other in silence and before Mariam could lose her nerve, she spoke.

'Yes, Aasim. I'll marry you.'

chapter 41

Arifa dropped her end of the bedspread and covered her mouth with her hand, letting out an audible gasp. The others, too, looked at Mariam with surprise, shock even.

'You disgusting old woman! You married him? You didn't even think of his *wife* there in San Francisco with their children and grandchildren?' the words rushed and tripped over each other and Arifa stood up, her eyes shining with anger.

Mariam stared back at Arifa, unable to decide what stance to take. But even as she chose her words, Arifa went on.

'Do you know what it's like to be the wife who waits for her husband to come back to her? Do you even know what it feels like inside, knowing that he loves someone else?' Arifa asked, her words echoing loudly in the room.

Mariam abandoned the words that were on her lips, and instead asked Arifa softly, 'No, Arifa, I don't. But do you?'

Arifa was caught unawares. She looked around helplessly at the others who were staring at her, and suddenly understood she had given away too much. That which she had guarded and kept safe inside was open for everyone to view now. She clutched her stomach tightly, shook her head and sank down in her corner, tears streaming down her face.

No one approached her because they were scared of her

reaction to Amma's story. For some reason, each of them knew there had to be more to the story than what Amma was telling them. It was Nimra's beseeching look that made Mariam relent and tell them the rest.

Nimra's eyes had grown round with each little nugget of information that Mariam threw their way, but it was Arifa who had troubled her the most, right from the beginning, as she told them of how Aasim had turned up at her house with Faiza in his arms. She hadn't interrupted even once, but unlike before there was something about her stillness that was at odds with her frantic crocheting, and it rankled Mariam.

Arifa was crying in a corner, her hands covering her eyes. Mariam felt her heart go out to her. She stepped down gingerly from the bed and walked up to Arifa and everyone moved out of her way. Wincing, she clutched her knees as she sat down next to Arifa who stiffened at her proximity.

'Don't!' she blubbered, wiping her eyes with the back of her hands. 'Don't come near me!'

Mariam put her hand on Arifa's arm and she flinched. 'Arifa, it's okay. Look at me,' she said, her voice strong and deep. Arifa sniffled and then with a deep sigh, she looked at Mariam.

'What?' she asked belligerently.

'My life and your life are not the same. Your husband is in Dubai earning money for the two of you. He's working hard. If you have a doubt, clear it with him. In fact, you should just go and spend some time with him there, in Dubai. Take your child and go. You deserve a holiday.'

Arifa had started shaking her head the moment Mariam brought up the word 'doubt' and her shaking increased when Mariam ended her little speech.

'I can't just go there! You need visas and you need money for plane tickets and… '

'You just need to decide, Arifa. If you decide it, it *can* happen!'

'No! It doesn't happen that way in real life!' Arifa protested but she sounded unsure.

'Look at me. Just look at me for a moment,' Mariam persisted, her eyes boring into hers. 'Do you think I don't have any regrets in life? I have. Many. But I've lived my life and I embraced happiness where I could. Do you want to wait as long as I did to do that? Do you?' she shook Arifa's shoulder.

Arifa was silent as she shook her head. 'But… how… I… ' It seemed as though everyone else had disappeared from the room, it was that silent. Except for Arifa's sobs, no one else made a sound, unsure of how to approach her, offer her comfort or solidarity.

'Don't wait until it's too late. Go now. Call him. Tell him you want to come and stay with him for some time,' Mariam urged her.

'But… but what of my mother-in-law? Who will be with her? Who will take care of her?' Arifa asked, looking confused. Mariam suppressed a flash of irritation at her.

'If you *have* to go, something can be arranged. It all depends on you,' Mariam replied.

'And what if… when I tell him that I want to come… what if he doesn't want me to?' Arifa asked, looking every bit like a lost child.

'You won't know unless you ask,' Mariam replied.

'What if… what if he's married someone there? What if that was the sound of his baby?' Arifa couldn't finish the sentence and broke down again, burying her face in her hands and sobbing. Everyone else looked uncomfortable and shocked. From the outside, Arifa had seemed so hard and strong. Turned out, she was so brittle and shattered easily.

'Again, you won't know unless you ask. Maybe you should just go home now. All of you!' Mariam addressed the rest of them. Nimra shook her head, and then looked at the clock and sighed. One by one, they all left.

chapter 42

For reasons best known to her, Mariam had insisted that they keep their marriage a secret. Aasim tried reasoning with her, telling her that he wasn't planning on keeping her a 'hidden second wife' like some other men, when something in Mariam snapped. They were in her hall, and Faiza was taking a nap in the room.

'You want to flaunt me to your wife who has been married to you for more than two decades?' she put her head in her hands and refused to look up. It had been worth saying yes to him for just the look in his eyes. It had been worth it just to feel his arms around her again as he murmured promises to her that everything would be alright. But she hadn't realised the price she would have to pay for it and her old enemy, guilt, made sure it was a heavy one at that.

'Mariam, if you come back with me to San Francisco, it will be better if we go as a married couple. I know you're concerned about my wife, and I feel terrible about doing this to her, but… it's you. It's finally you. Don't you get it?' he had gently lifted her chin with his fingers.

Mariam shook her head. 'Don't say anything that will make me regret saying yes. Or will make me want to change my mind. And I am not coming back to San Francisco with you.'

Aasim sat back, looking stumped. 'What do you mean?' he asked, his eyes registering anger and defeat.

'I… You know how I feel about you, Aasim. You will always be that special person in my heart and… ' Mariam stopped when she saw the anger in his eyes had indeed become more visible.

'Stop it,' he whispered fiercely. 'Stop it. You and I. We were supposed to be together years ago and if I hadn't been a coward then… yes a coward as you rightly pointed out then, we would have been married, been together all these years.'

Mariam swallowed, wishing he would stop. Ever since she had accepted his proposal, her nerves were constantly on edge, as though she had given permission for them to be raked over hot coals.

'You were not a coward, Aasim. I was wrong. We were just seventeen. How could we have possibly got married? You were right.' Mariam admitted, but Aasim shook his head.

'I walked away from you then because it was the right thing to do. Because I didn't want to hurt your family or mine. And now, where are they? They're nowhere in the picture. They're all gone,' he said, looking down at the floor.

'But your wife… she is still there and… don't you think she deserves something better?' Mariam asked, and unable to look at him she joined him in scrutinising the floor.

'Did I contact you even once after I got married to her? Did I ask you to run away with me? I gave her everything she deserved, Mariam. I gave her whatever was possible,' he explained softly, his hand edging toward hers.

Mariam shook her head, somehow unable to obliterate the image of the woman Aasim was married to. She had seen her only during that fateful wedding of their children and had kept out of her way, feeling uncomfortable in her presence.

'When Raina and Faisal got married, did you… did you tell her that I was the person you had told her about after your marriage?' Mariam asked, unable to decide whether it would be better or worse if his wife had known.

'She guessed,' Aasim spoke with a sigh. Mariam closed her eyes and leaned back into the sofa. Why had the two of them messed with the lives of other people? Why?

'Mariam, when I told her about you, I… thought I was doing the right thing. Telling her that I had a past. I had no idea if you had read those messages I left for you in the magazines and I really didn't think we would be able to get our children married. I… I have been true to her all my life and even now, I don't want to be unfair to her by marrying you behind her back.'

Mariam shook her head. 'How can it be *fair* to her if she knows that her fifty-year-old husband is hell-bent on marrying his childhood sweetheart?' At that the two of them looked at each other and Aasim picked up her hand and squeezed it tightly.

'Don't ask me, Mariam! I don't know what's right or wrong anymore! Just… just the thought of you all alone here… knowing that you could finally… be mine… ' he whispered and pulled her towards him. They sat that way in a quiet embrace, her head on his shoulder and for the first time in years, Mariam felt that spot in her chest throb and come to life. She lifted her head and touched his cheek, unable to decide if they were being given the gift of a second chance or if they were being cruel to those who loved them. At that moment, it didn't matter.

'Did you mean it when you said you didn't want to come to

San Francisco with me?' he asked, lifting her hand and unfurling her fingers one by one.

'Yes,' Mariam replied, her eyes closed. She knew she should get up before Sarita came back from the market. Before Faiza woke up and saw her grandparents this way. But for the shortest of moments, everything felt like a dream. Maybe when she woke up, her whole life would be a dream and it would just be the two of them on the terrace, *before* Aasim had made the momentous decision to walk away.

Aasim sighed and then Mariam sat straight, not feeling shy but knowing that it wasn't right to sit with him this way.

'You are still the most stubborn woman I have ever known,' he declared, understanding her need for space and not pushing her.

'You are still the only man who can make me feel so alive inside,' she said softly and got up before he had a chance to reply, because Faiza woke up just then.

Despite all her misgivings, Mariam agreed to accompany Aasim to Madras, where they got married in a quiet ceremony. Aasim asked two of his oldest friends to serve as witnesses and Mariam was tempted to visit her sister and confide everything in her. But she knew that she couldn't unburden herself at the cost of a maelstrom in the lives of her sister and Aasim's brother.

Aasim's thoughts were also moving in a similar direction and the two of them sat in the taxi pondering for nearly half an hour if they should involve the two people in their lives who had brought them together all those years ago. Finally, Mariam shook her head. Faiza was sleepy and tired and if they left now, they would be able to reach Sathuvacheri before evening.

They were quiet on the way back, each lost in their own thoughts, wondering if they had done the right thing.

'How did I become the other woman?' Mariam wondered, as she saw the trees whip past her as their car sped on the highway. The two of them turned towards each other simultaneously, and their gaze fell on Faiza who was sleeping between them.

'Regrets?' she asked him, her voice catching in her throat. He gave a firm shake of his head.

'Actually, yes,' he said and her eyes filled with tears. What had they done?

'We should have done this thirty-three years ago. That's my only regret,' he said, his hands reaching out for hers and squeezing it, reassuring her, adding the tiniest bit of hope in her heart.

Their second marriage was like a joke in many ways, Mariam thought as they reached her house. No one would guess that she was the bride and he was the groom. There was no external display of happiness anywhere, but then she realised that all those decorations and dressing up, jewellery and flowers, were merely that. Displays of what people *expected* the bride and groom to feel inside. But why would they need anything to *tell* them what to feel, she thought as she saw Aasim pay the taxi driver even as he held a sleeping Faiza over his shoulder.

What they had with each other was enough.

chapter 43

Three women sat in their respective houses, each holding a phone in their hands, wondering if they had it in them to make the life-changing phone call. Unless they pushed themselves to grab whatever chance they had, they would never know.

By now they had all accepted that listening to Mariam tell them about her life had changed them in some infinitesimal way. Her words had fractured their reality, little by little, until they had nothing but the glaring cracks to stare at, and it wasn't a pretty picture. However, the decision had been made. If Mariam could choose to marry Aasim and become his second wife, find happiness for whatever short period of time that had been allotted to them, why couldn't they—these three women—stop being so short-sighted about their own lives?

The first of the three, Arifa, dialled her husband's number and took a deep breath, mentally preparing the speech she would deliver to him, but the moment she heard his voice all her thoughts scattered. Biting her lower lip uncertainly, she stuttered, telling him that she wanted to visit Dubai with Armaan.

'I want to spend some time with you there,' she said, shutting her eyes tightly, wondering how he would react. This was the cue for him to tell her he already had a wife there, and he didn't need her. Shuaib sighed and Arifa opened her eyes, her breathing getting heavy. Here it comes, she braced herself, biting her lower lip again.

'How come?' he asked her gruffly and she eased the pressure on her lip. A reprieve.

'I… I miss you and since you said that you have work there, I… I thought we could come there and be with you.'

'You know my living quarters aren't suitable for a family,' he started. Arifa felt a shaft of disappointment rush through her.

'Armaan and I will manage,' she said faintly, aware that she was making a fool of herself. His reluctance in no way meant that he had another family there. Or did it? She would never know unless she asked, she thought, and taking a deep breath, she took the plunge. 'Actually, Shuaib, I have been getting some crazy ideas in my head for the last few days,' she admitted, surprised at how calm she sounded. Thin rivulets of sweat were making their way down her back and she pressed her pallu to her lower back, sponging them off.

'Yes, I wanted to ask you about the last time you called. You got upset for no reason and you haven't spoken to me properly ever since! You always give the phone to Ammi and disappear. What's the matter?' he asked.

'I… I was… ' Arifa shut her eyes in embarrassment. What if she was wrong? Wouldn't it be worse if she were right?

'I… thought you had married there and it was the sound of your baby I heard that night,' she said the words quickly and noticed the silence on the other end. She held her breath as she waited for him to speak.

'Um?' she prompted him when he still didn't respond.

'What will you do if I tell you that you're right?' he asked finally and Arifa's eyes grew wide as she bit her knuckle hard.

'You mean... '

'No, answer me first,' he insisted. Arifa looked away from his side of the bed, at the wall, at the ceiling, unable to understand why everything looked so blurred and cloudy. Only then did she realise she was crying.

'How could you do this to me?' she whispered, her voice broken and she cursed all the second wives she could think of, including Mariam.

'I asked you, what will you do?' he repeated slowly. Arifa took a deep breath and then wiping her tears, she steadied herself and unleashed all her anger on him.

'I will sell whatever jewellery I have and buy two tickets to Dubai, come to your *unsuitable* living quarters and that woman will wish she had never married you. No, she will wish she had never met you. I will make her wish she hadn't been born. And when I'm done with her, you have no idea what I will do to you,' Arifa stopped, pausing for breath but also because she didn't quite know what she would actually do. Her free hand flailed wildly in the air and then she clutched her forehead with it, wishing she had the courage to do whatever she had said.

'Well, it's a good thing then that I don't have a second wife or a second family,' Shuaib spoke slowly into the silence. Arifa refused to believe him.

'Okay, I think the only thing that will assure you is if you come over here and see for yourself,' he admitted and Arifa stopped in her tracks, surprised. 'So, I'll arrange for your visas and get the two of you tickets to come here. Then you can see for yourself whether it's true or not,' he added.

'You would probably get rid of them for the time I'm

there. You might send her off to her parents' place for some days. What proof is that?' Arifa asked, unable to stop the words forming mental pictures in her head.

Shuaib snorted. 'Yeah well, that's some imagination you have. I won't say that people don't do it, getting a second wife and all, but since I haven't done it, I don't deserve this treatment from you.'

Arifa faltered. 'You mean it? There's no second wife?' she asked softly, willing herself to believe his words.

'The one I have already complains too much of how little time I give her. So, a second wife is really out of the question,' he said simply.

'Also, I do love the one and only wife I have. I just haven't been able to show it enough.'

Arifa pictured him, sitting at the edge of his bed, running his hand through his beard, smiling at her idiocy.

'Oh, Shuaib, I… I don't know what happened to me,' Arifa said, breaking down for another reason altogether. She couldn't tell him about Mariam and how listening to her had sparked off these feelings inside her. It had been some sort of unspoken code—that no one would talk about Mariam's life outside the class.

'I would never do something so sneaky and mean to you, Arifa.' Arifa nodded, wiping the tears from her eyes.

'You know, I have some leave coming up. I had been planning to come to India but I think I'll spend it here with you and Armaan,' he offered, and Arifa smiled.

'About Ammi… ' she started and Shuaib surprised her when he interrupted her.

'Don't worry, I'll get someone to take care of her when you're here with me.'

They spoke a little longer and Arifa realised how little they had communicated all these days, these months. Whenever he would call, she had always launched into telling him about some problem that she was facing and they hadn't ever really spoken. He teased her a bit about her obsession with his fictitious second wife, and Arifa thanked Mariam in her mind for pushing her to take this step.

For Nimra, it wasn't so easy. She kept checking the balance on her phone, wondering if it would be enough to make the call to Malaysia. Perhaps she could call and quickly tell Shahzad mamu to call her back. She hated imposing upon him in this manner but this was nothing compared to what she wanted to say to him. She thought back to the moment she had made her decision, when she realised she had to do something about her own life. It had probably been when she had come back from Mariam's house in the afternoon and her stepmother asked her to sit in the room because the neighbour's daughter was coming to apply mehendi on her palms, again—yet another family was coming to see her the following day.

'And there's no need to go for those classes anymore,' her stepmother had coolly said without looking away from the TV.

Nimra had opened her mouth to tell her she couldn't discontinue now, as they had to complete the bedspread but then she shut it. This wasn't about the crocheted bedspread at all. She had gone to her room and waited for the neighbour's girl to come. Nimra stared at her open palms where the faint outline of last month's mehendi still lingered, and she took a deep breath. She was not doing this again. Before the girl came and froze her hands for two hours with the musky scent of mehendi, she was going to call Shahzad mamu.

She paused for a moment, thinking of why she was doing it. It wasn't for Rocky, she knew. Rocky was only one of the reasons. But what if her uncle refused? They had spoken only once since she came back from Malaysia, and that had been on Eid. The conversation had been easy-going and friendly and her cousins had spoken to her for quite some time. She paused when she thought of them and then shaking her head, she realised there was only one way to put her doubts to rest.

She dialled the number, her stomach clenching in uncomfortable agony as she waited for Shahzad mamu to answer. She knew that Saira could walk in any minute or worse, her mother could come; there was also the impending visit of the neighbour's daughter. This was a bad time she thought frantically just as her uncle answered the phone.

'Mamu?' she spoke softly, hoping against hope that the network wouldn't give out.

'Nimra?' he asked, sounding surprised. 'Is everything alright? Shall I call you back?'

'Okay,' she said and ended the call, feeling grateful. When the phone rang again, she answered it quickly, knowing that Saira and her mother knew that she hardly received any calls from anyone, and they would be immediately suspicious.

'So tell me, what's happened?' he asked, his voice on edge. Nimra didn't know how to say the words without sounding like she was begging or asking for help.

'Mamu, I want to come and live with you in Malaysia,' she said the words quickly, shutting her eyes, her heart thudding madly in her chest.

'What?' he asked surprised. Nimra didn't know how to elaborate, to tell him that her life here was miserable and she was constantly picked upon by her younger stepsister. It would sound like something from a fairy tale that had been hung upside down.

'I understand if you can't,' she added hastily, wanting to give him an easy way out. She didn't want to trouble him or embarrass him more than she had already.

'No, no! That's not the point,' he insisted, sounding thoughtful. 'Any particular reason?' he asked then.

Nimra's mind presented her with a quick but blurred image of Rocky, leaning against the counter, smiling at her, kissing her lightly. She shook away the image and taking another deep breath, she said, 'I was really happy with you and your family. Mamu, I've never been that happy in my life.'

There was an intake of breath and her uncle asked her, 'Do they treat you badly? Does your father know?'

'It doesn't matter, Mamu. I feel... I feel suffocated here. I thought if I could come there, then maybe I could... I could get a job somewhere and I won't trouble you much. I... I don't want to make any drastic changes in your house by becoming an unwelcome guest there. I'll be like a paying guest if you want, once I get the job... I'll...'

'Will you just shut up for a moment?' her uncle said fiercely. 'Have you discussed this with your father?'

Nimra pursed her lips. Her father was aware of what happened in the house and yet he chose to ignore everything.

'No.'

'He won't like it,' Mamu warned. 'And that woman... '

'She's been making people come and see me from the time

I got back from Malaysia. Even now, tomorrow, someone is coming. Mamu! They come and see me and then… they go away… and she blames me… and I feel so worthless,' Nimra whispered, getting startled when the doorbell rang. It was probably the mehendi girl.

'I… I can't just take you away to Malaysia. I have to speak to your father and really, you didn't have to say all those things about becoming a paying guest in my house. It's ridiculous. You're my only niece and I wish I had done something for you earlier.' Shahzad mamu's words gave birth to a tiny bubble of hope in Nimra's heart, her mind opening to the possibility of going away to Malaysia. There was something that still nagged her though.

'I know, mamu, but I don't want to make Arshiya and Shireen feel like I've… I've imposed on you and… '

'Look,' he cut her short. 'All this is a very long shot and we don't know how it will work out. I will have to speak to your father, arrange for your visa, and then come and get you. Just worry about that woman and how she's going to react once she knows that you're going to be out of her clutches.'

A picture of Saira's mother formed in her head, an image where her face was merged with the body of an eagle and unexpectedly, Nimra began to laugh. She was still laughing when the puzzled mehendi girl walked into her room.

♣

Shaista rubbed her stomach in slow circles, feeling the baby's kicks and steeling herself to not be moved by them. She decided against calling her mother. What was the point, she thought. Anyhow, her mother-in-law was planning to organise a big ceremony in a couple of weeks to send her off to her mother's house for her delivery. Shaista was just planning on not coming back.

chapter 44

'What do you think she did with that magazine?' Mariam asked Aasim one night when they had put Faiza to sleep in the big room and left quietly, leaving the door open.

'I told you, right? She must have torn it up or thrown it away,' Aasim said, not even asking her which magazine she was referring to as he reached out for her hand. He continued holding it as they walked to the other room in the house. Aasim had made it clear that he didn't want to spend any time in Mariam's house, especially now that they were married, but the other alternative was his house in Vellore. There were two reasons why they couldn't move there. First, it was in a state of disrepair and second, gossip was more rife there, and neighbours and relatives were sure to begin speculating about them.

'I often wonder what she must have thought when she read all those messages you had written for me.' Mariam sat down on the bed and Aasim massaged her neck, easing out the tension in the muscles.

'Hmm,' Aasim said. It was obvious to Mariam that he didn't want to think about Raheema bu now. As it was, they had very little time left together. Aasim was due to leave in another week. She closed her eyes when he stopped his ministrations, and began kissing the spot below her neck. She eased back into his warm chest, letting him continue.

'Why do you always close your eyes?' Aasim whispered a little later, and she turned towards him, unable to answer because of the fullness in her chest. 'You don't like to see me when we—'

'No, it's not that!' Mariam covered his mouth with her hands.

'Then? Because I'm old now?' he asked, and Mariam was touched by how serious he sounded, even though there was a teasing glint in his eyes. 'I have grey hair?'

She shook her head, trailing her hands through his hair, unable to believe she was doing this even now, that it was possible and perfectly alright for her to do so.

'It's because *I* am old,' she whispered, pulling his face close towards her own to kiss him gently.

'We're both old, but you know what?' he said, balancing himself on his elbows as he looked at her. 'When I see you like this, it's like the years between us have dissolved like this.' He snapped his fingers to emphasise the point.

Mariam had her doubts but she kept her mouth shut and her eyes open.

Much later, as Aasim was drifting off to sleep, his arm looped around her waist, Mariam spoke again. 'What was that bedspread like? The one in that magazine?'

She felt his sigh on her back, his heavy breath tickling the tiny hairs on her neck and she smiled. She turned around and for a moment was struck by how much he looked like the old Aasim. Maybe he was right. The years didn't matter.

He picked up her hand and kissed it gently and then went on to describe the bedspread in detail.

'You remember it so well?' she asked, surprised.

He shrugged. 'Maybe I'm making it up. I don't know. I stared at that page for so long, the one on which I had asked you to run away with me that… I think I must have memorised the image of that bedspread.'

Mariam poked his chest with her finger. Within a second, he grabbed it, pretending to bite it and they both started giggling, continually amazed with each other.

'Why are you asking now?' he asked, as he tugged her closer so she could rest her head in the crook of his neck.

'I wanted to try making it,' she replied softly, closing her eyes to the world outside.

When Aasim left with Faiza the following week, Mariam stood at the doorstep and waved to them with a smile on her face even though she felt sick inside. Aasim knew that her bravado was an act because she had broken down a little while earlier, wetting his shirt with her sobs and cursing him for coming back into her life.

'I'll be back soon,' he promised. She believed him. He had told her the previous night that he would visit India twice instead of once a year and she battled with emotions that wondered what his wife would make of it. Especially since she didn't know that her husband had another wife. She finally gave up her struggle and told him that he should stick to the plan and come only once a year.

'Would you look at yourself? I'm spending just two months in a year with you!' Aasim had exploded. 'Why can't you stop feeling bad for her and just take what's given to you?'

She didn't want to part with an argument and so she nodded, giving in to his caresses and kisses and declarations of love.

Aasim called her when he reached and they spoke softly but the familiar guilt had wedged itself between them and she hung up quickly, wondering where his wife was and whether she was privy to their conversation.

A week later, Mariam figured that the sum of all the parts of Aasim—his voice, his face, his tender lovemaking—was still less than the whole. His companionship. For the brief time he was here, she had gleaned what it would be like to have a partner. Someone she could trust, someone she could talk with, someone who would massage her neck without her asking for it, someone with whom she could just lie down on the bed.

'What have I done?' she thought as her eyes moved back to the telephone, wishing it would ring so she could hear his voice again. She knew that she had to only give him a tiny indication of her feelings and he would come flying back to take her away to San Francisco. But despite the fact that she missed him fervently, that was one thing she would never do, she vowed.

She busied herself with crochet, using her imagination and Aasim's memories to recreate the bedspread he had seen in that magazine. She would often think of Raheema bu, that silent catalyst who had brought them together, albeit unwillingly, and would smile silently. What would she say if she saw her now?

Aasim had made it a point to call her every day at a certain time and she waited for his calls, to listen to his voice like a lovelorn woman, even though she quailed inside when she thought of what his wife might think of it. She knew that they had cordless phones and that he would talk to her only in a private place, but what if his wife picked up an extension and heard them talking? She didn't know why it was so important to her that his wife did not know that they were married.

Aasim returned the following year with a very talkative Faiza who wouldn't keep quiet for even a minute. Mariam opened the door to see him standing there while Faiza looked around and prattled on in an enchanting manner. Her accent was already more pronounced. They both knew that they couldn't reach for each other in the presence of this precocious little girl; she was sure to go back and tell her nani that Nana had been hugging another woman.

Mariam watched Faiza as she walked through the hall, picking up some of her old toys, all the while keeping up her commentary.

'My god! Doesn't she ever keep quiet?' Mariam whispered to him when Faiza walked into the larger room to inspect it. Aasim took the opportunity to scoot up closer to Mariam so he could cup her face and kiss her.

'No,' he said, shaking his head with a smile.

'Why haven't you let her speak to me on the phone?' Mariam demanded even as she kissed the side of his jaw. The two of them sprang apart guiltily when Faiza came out from the room and went to the kitchen.

'I wanted it to be a surprise,' Aasim said, laughing as he took Mariam's hand and kissed her palm.

Together the two of them followed Faiza who finally stopped talking as she looked around at the kitchen in silence.

'Waterrr!' she said as though finally remembering what she wanted. Mariam dipped a glass in the mud pot and handed it to her, and Faiza drank it eagerly.

'All that talking you do! No wonder you're thirsty!' Mariam laughed as she bent down to pick up her granddaughter in her arms and swing her around. She wondered if Faiza would scream like last time, but apparently she did remember her and put her arms around Mariam's neck, kissing her face soundly before falling asleep.

Aasim's eyes met hers and Mariam smiled tremulously. Right now, this moment, this very moment, Mariam felt so happy, she could freeze it and store it in her memory forever. Aasim took Faiza from Mariam's arms and took her to the main bedroom where he stopped in surprise. The bed was covered with a magnificent crocheted bedspread.

'You made it?' he asked, his voice taking on a sense of wonder even as he lowered Faiza on to it gingerly. Mariam nodded, unable to talk.

'It's beautiful,' he breathed as she smoothed one end down. He picked up her hand and kissed her fingers lightly. 'How come it's for Faiza? And not for us?' he asked.

Mariam's face closed slightly. It was hard for her to explain it to him but Aasim, having loved her so unconditionally for all these years, understood without her having to give any explanation.

He nodded and then pulled her to him.

Later that night, Mariam voiced a doubt that had been plaguing her for a few days before his arrival.

'Faiza is a very bright child. She'll know about us,' she told him as he trailed his hand lightly down her arm. He didn't speak.

'And when she grows up, how will we keep it a secret from her? How old is she now? Nearly three? And so talkative! How will we… ' Mariam couldn't complete her sentence because Aasim had placed his finger over her mouth.

'That's why we shouldn't keep our marriage a secret,' he insisted and Mariam looked around uncertainly. This secret was all she had. How could she give it away?

chapter 45

In the summer of 1994, Mariam was preparing the house for Aasim and Faiza's arrival when the phone rang. Knowing that it would be him, she smiled and picked up the receiver and he let Faiza talk to her. Faiza was almost five now and knew very well that Mariam was her dadi. Her situation with Aasim still made her uneasy but she pushed it to the back of her mind when he took the phone from Faiza. Immediately Mariam knew that something was wrong. His tone was off and he sounded subdued.

'What is it?' she asked, feeling the first tentacles of fear clutch her heart.

'My wife found out about us, Mariam,' he sighed. Guilt and embarrassment started playing havoc within Mariam. She didn't want to know how or when but unaware of her turmoil, he continued talking.

'I explained the whole thing to her and... and she thinks it's best if I move back to India and live with you. She wants to continue living here with the children. She wants a divorce.'

The words echoed and boomed in her head and Mariam sat down, clutching the receiver, still unable to think of what this meant.

'Are you divorcing her?' she asked quietly, not knowing what she wanted him to do. The sound of his breathing from the other end was not reassuring.

'I... I haven't decided yet. I have a life here, Mariam. I have children and... ' he stopped.

'What about Faiza?' she asked, her voice ringing in the silence.

'She... she says that she wants to keep Faiza with her,' he sounded almost apologetic. The old anger against him resurfaced and before she could tame it, control it, she let it out.

'You know what? I think it's better if you stay with her and divorce me. Stay there and live the life you made there, Aasim. With your children. Just give me back my Faiza.' Mariam's voice trembled. Why had she agreed to marrying him? Why couldn't she have been content with the annual visits? Now everything was going to be taken away from her.

'You mean it?' he asked, his voice low and hurt. 'You want only Faiza? Not me?'

Mariam shut her eyes against the image that her mind formed of him.

'Tell me, Mariam!' his voice sounded in her ear, urgent and angry and she jumped.

'I don't know, Aasim. I only know that... we shouldn't have given in. We should have remained what we were—Faiza's grandparents. Now... '

'Now, you'll have me but not Faiza and you don't want that,' he completed.

Mariam swallowed, wishing there was some way in which she would know what was right and what was wrong. She straightened up after a moment's hesitation.

'I'm serious, Aasim. Tell her that you'll divorce me. Tell

her that she's more important to you. She is the mother of your children after all. I… I'm no one,' Mariam said, her eyes filling up with tears.

'Right. You're no one. Just like I'm no one to you,' he sounded bitter. Mariam placed her hand on her chest, wondering why emotional pain had such a physical presence, blocking, pushing and holding her down.

'Don't divorce her, Aasim. Please. Just return Faiza to me,' Mariam pleaded, her voice cracking.

'I can't promise anything, Mariam.' With that he ended the call.

If Mariam had known that it was the last time she would be talking to Aasim, would she have said the same things? No. She would have agreed to everything he said, even if it meant forsaking Faiza. But she hadn't known and after that phone call, she got up and went to Faiza's room and yanked the bedspread that she had put out for her. She bunched it in her fist and inhaled its fragrance, the fragrance of her grandchild which she knew was locked in somewhere within the knots and chains of the bedspread.

When a week went by and there was no call from Aasim, Mariam got worried. He normally called her every day or every other day. This was a first. He was probably angry with her she thought, because she had said she wanted Faiza and not him. But was it true? How could anyone even expect her to make a choice? Her anger against him, for putting her in a position where she had to choose, once again became her dominant emotion, but with it was a faint sense of worry and unease.

When he hadn't called by that evening, she did something she had never done before. Taking a deep breath, she dialled his number. It rang and rang and then she remembered that it was probably early morning there. But he always called her at that time. She wondered if he preferred this time slot because everyone else was usually asleep.

Feeling a bit squeamish, she waited and finally the phone was answered by a man who sounded sleepy.

'Yes?' he asked. This must be Aasim's son. Aasim had two sons and only one daughter, the girl who had become her daughter-in-law for a brief period of time.

'Is… ' Mariam faltered. Should she ask for Aasim by name? What would this boy think?

'Is Aasim there?' she asked finally, clearing her throat.

'Who's this?' he asked, his voice sounding more alert. Mariam felt sick to her stomach. Had Aasim's wife told her children about Mariam? Did they hate her too?

'I'm Faiza's grandmother,' she said finally.

'Oh! Aunty! I know Abba calls you to update you about Faiza but… it never occurred to me to call you now,' he said, his voice sounding strained. Mariam murmured a silent prayer of thanks because he had called her aunty and also because he sounded like he didn't know about the two of them.

'Why?' she asked, mentally preparing what she would tell Aasim when he came on the phone.

'Abba had a stroke last week, aunty. He's in the hospital. We don't know what will happen… ' his voice broke and he sobbed.

Shock and pain crowded for space inside her as she clutched her stomach and felt the tears begin to sting her eyes. 'No!' she whispered.

'We don't know what exactly happened, Abba seemed fine one minute and the next… ' he broke off.

'How's he now?' she asked, hoping her voice would not betray her emotions.

'The doctors say there's very little chance of him recovering. They're asking us to decide whether we want to remove the life support he's on.'

Mariam replaced the receiver without even saying goodbye as she crumpled to the floor, her trembling hands covering her mouth.

He was as good as gone. Her vibrant, funny, wonderful storyteller. Her Aasim. He was lying in a hospital bed somewhere in the other end of the world and she couldn't do a thing about it. At first the tears wouldn't stop but when they did abate, she remembered her last conversation with him and the tears started pouring out of her eyes afresh.

For two days Mariam sat by the phone, suspended in pain and grief, encased in the wall of accusations that she had hurled at him. She didn't know if she wanted the phone to ring or not.

When the phone rang finally, it had been ten days since she had spoken to Aasim. Fearfully she picked it up, wondering if some miracle had taken place. If it had, she would agree to everything he said, she thought fervently. She would even go and live with him there. Anything. Just let him live, she prayed.

It was the voice of a woman. She sounded tired and immediately Mariam knew who it was. The conversation lasted for exactly two minutes.

'He's gone. No one knows about you here. I want it to remain that way. I know he cared for you. But he's gone. Do you get it?' she asked.

Mariam didn't know how she could possibly counter those words. He's gone. Feeling as though her heart was being trampled upon, she sniffled and nodded and then realising that Aasim's wife couldn't see the nod, she said, 'Okay.'

'I don't want to hear from you ever again. I cannot give Faiza to you. I don't want to even remember that you exist but that's hardly likely, is it?' she asked.

Mariam stayed silent, letting the other woman talk, knowing that she deserved everything that she was saying to her. But, Faiza! Not Faiza!

'I want my children to remember their father for the man he was here. Not what he became when he went to India to you,' she said and ended the call.

Mariam held the receiver for nearly ten minutes after the call before she replaced it on the phone. There were all kinds of conflicting emotions inside her. She knew that Aasim's wife was entitled to her anger but… the way she depicted Aasim like he were some sleazy character… angered her. After all, he had wanted to come clean to his wife before marrying her. She was the one who had opted for secrecy, giving their relationship a clandestineness that had erased all the beauty from it.

She cried and mourned for Aasim alone. Once again, in less than five years, she was in iddat, although no one knew about it. Her daughter, who called her once every few months, asked her to come to Madras for a few days. It was an invitation that she issued periodically knowing that her mother wouldn't accept. Every single time, Mariam would tell her, 'I don't want to. Maybe some other time.'

This time, however, Mariam wasn't thinking straight. 'I can't' were the two words she told her daughter.

'What do you mean you can't?' Asma asked, startled.

Mariam paused for a moment. Years and years ago, she had

accused Aasim of being a coward. But he hadn't been one. All these years later he had wanted to come clean, to tell everyone that she was his wife and she had stopped him. And what had it cost her? Both Aasim and Faiza were gone from her life now.

'I married Aasim four years ago, Asma. He… passed away last week in San Francisco. I'm in iddat,' she said, surprised that the words tripped out so easily. Vaguely she registered the outraged gasp from the other end and wondered if word would reach Aasim's wife or her children. Even if it did, there was nothing to do now, she thought miserably as she listened to Asma rail against her. She shrugged and dropped the receiver into its cradle.

chapter 46

The room was quiet except for Shaista's laboured breathing. All eyes were trained on Mariam who sat on the bed, lost in her reminiscences, clutching the old bedspread to her chest. No one knew what to say except that each in their own way had been profoundly touched by her story.

From being harried and forever in haste, Arifa had metamorphosed almost overnight after talking to her husband. Her hands moved slower and with more deliberation, although every now and then there was a flash of the impatient person she had been. She bit her lower lip and got up to sit next to Mariam. Demonstrating physical affection had never been easy for her but she hugged Mariam awkwardly and then squeezed her hand, looking rueful. Taking her cue, all the others got up and crowded around Mariam until she shook her head and asked them to step back.

'Let me breathe, girls!' she said, pushing them back gently. She looked around at their faces, remembering how they had been when they first came and what they had become now. Timid Nimra had shocked her family by refusing to 'be shown' to another family and according to her, the situation at home was war-like. She had also taken the initiative to call her uncle and ask him to take her to Malaysia. Mariam looked at her fondly, thinking of how unalike she was from her own self. But who we are largely depends upon who shapes us from the time we are children and Mariam was thankful to her parents for imbuing her with a strong personality. Nimra was just taking baby steps now, but they were in the right direction.

Mariam glanced at Shaista uneasily knowing that life had been most unfair to this child. All of them had been shocked when they learnt that Shaista was barely fifteen. In fact, Amreen had lost her competitive edge and her poorly veiled animosity towards her had disappeared completely. Shaista had tentatively told them of how she planned to stay back in her own village once she goes back for the delivery.

'But won't your parents send you back here? What about your husband? Won't he get angry?' the questions had flown at her thick and fast, but she surprised everyone by telling them that if anyone forced her to come back, she would take the matter to the police.

'What about the baby?' Amreen had asked and Shaista smiled.

'He can take it. I don't want the baby,' she said and Amreen felt a jolt of unease.

'How? Why? You're a *mother*!' she had told Shaista, feeling angry at the injustice in the world. 'Think of how he will bring up the child! Think of the child!' she had urged her.

'I have thought of the child but I cannot come back and live with my husband. I am suffocating here. I need to go back to my village. Where there is sunlight,' Shaista said, unmoved by Amreen's remonstrations. 'And he will not let me keep the child. I know I have to let it go.'

Mariam had listened to her quietly, marvelling at how calm

she sounded. In fact, she sounded too calm and composed.

'We should be finished with this bedspread by tomorrow,' Amreen spoke and everyone looked at her, a little surprised because they had almost forgotten about it.

Mariam nodded and randomly picked up a corner to compare it with the one she had done all those years ago. It was almost similar, except of course her stitches had been smoother and neater. Never mind, she thought, quelling the urge for perfection, and smiled at them.

'What will we talk about?' Nimra asked, looking around as everyone sat down once again and resumed.

'Why don't you tell us what you'll do when you go to Malaysia?' Arifa asked her slyly and Nimra blushed.

'Oh, I don't know. I don't want to think about it yet,' she said, looking down at her lap.

'Why?'

'First let it happen. Then I'll think.' Nimra was glad that the others didn't know about her crush on Rocky or they would have ribbed her endlessly.

Their easy banter soothed Mariam who leaned back into her pillow and shut her eyes, knowing that they would go in a few minutes, leaving her alone with her thoughts. A far more alarming thought was of what she would do when the girls actually went their own ways. She was used to loneliness, but these girls with their stories and their hearts on their sleeves had affected her too and she knew she would miss them. She saw a little of Faiza in each of them and it had temporarily allayed her ache, as she imagined what Faiza was up to.

All those months ago, the phone call that had prompted Mariam to start the bedspread had again come from Aasim's wife who curtly informed her that Faiza was getting married. Her Faiza, she thought, clutching the phone hard, thinking of how many years had passed since she had seen her or heard her voice. Aasim's wife had called her once every few years to pass on a nugget of information about Faiza which she had clutched to her heart until the next nugget arrived.

'Who is she getting married to?' Mariam asked cautiously, aware that even after all these years, Aasim's wife harboured animosity towards her. Her own sense of guilt, however, had disappeared. It was all too long ago and she knew now that the happiness that she and Aasim had shared was special and she had been right in marrying him, however disastrously it may have ended.

'She's getting married to a Muslim boy from here. I am not making the same mistake of sending her to India like my husband did with her mother,' she said and ended the call.

Mariam hoped that if they finished the bedspread in time, she would be able to courier it to Faiza, and she really wished that Aasim's wife would let her have it.

When she opened her eyes, all the girls except Amreen were gone. Deepa looked sullen. She had probably been hoping to sleep for some time and was annoyed that Amreen was lingering in the house.

'What is it, Amreen?' Mariam asked, exhaling as she got up.

'Do you have any of his books, Amma?' Amreen asked. Mariam stared at her, remembering a time all those years ago when she had married Aasim. He had got her the whole set of his novels and given them to her. 'They'll be with you when I'm not there,' he had said, kissing her forehead and brushing away her protests.

She nodded and then walked to her cupboard slowly and opened it. In one corner, neatly arranged in a pile, were all his novels. Mariam took them out sometimes, looked at the yellowing brittle pages, and touched his name that appeared on the top of each page. Carefully she pulled out a few and handed them to Amreen who took them from her eagerly.

'So many?' she asked as she sat down on the bed nearby and flipped through them. Mariam looked at her and wished she had got herself a pair of glasses. At least, she could have read his books, revived him and remembered him. Words looked blurry to her.

'I'm so excited!' Amreen said, looking up at Mariam, her eyes shining. 'I'm positive he wrote all the female characters with you in mind!'

Mariam shook her head and laughed, something she hadn't done in a long time, and realised it felt wonderful. Of all the four girls, only Amreen was going to stay back in Vellore. The rest had dissipated like words in the air. She was glad for them but she also found herself wishing she could make things better for Amreen and then she laughed at the idea. As if *she* had done anything for the others!

She looked sideways at Amreen who was engrossed in the book that she had handed to her and smiled, feeling inordinately happy that Aasim's words, penned decades ago, could still captivate the imagination of a reader.

When the doorbell rang, Amreen jumped guiltily and smiled at Mariam before carefully keeping the books in her bag. She donned her burkha and hesitated before stepping up and kissing Mariam on her cheek.

'Thank you, Amma!' she beamed.

'For what?' Mariam was a bit shocked. It had been years and years since anyone had kissed her and the feelings it evoked threatened to choke her.

'For telling us your story. For somehow making me feel that it's not the end of the world if I don't have a baby. My husband's right, you know. He says we'll have a baby if we're destined to have one. Until then, there's no reason I should drive myself crazy, right?'

With that amazing insight, Amreen literally skipped out of the room and Mariam stared at her back and let out another sigh.

An hour later when the doorbell rang again, Mariam looked up surprised. Had one of the girls come back? She looked around for Deepa and realised that she was probably sleeping, so she shuffled towards the door herself, clutching her tasbih in her hands, and opened the door.

Tell me this is a vision. Tell me this is not real. The litany in her head was louder than the sound of her heartbeat because standing in front of her in a blue tunic that reminded Mariam of a bright sunny sky, white jeans, a blue scarf that covered her hair and large dark glasses that rested on top of the scarf, was Faiza. And she was holding a suitcase.

'Hello, Dadi!' she said simply, a dazzling smile on her face. 'Won't you let me come inside?'

chapter 47

She was spirited, this girl. Laughter boomed in the house and stunned Mariam with its mere presence. No one had laughed like that in her house for years. Mariam was reminded of that time when Aasim had brought a talkative little girl, because Faiza didn't seem to have changed at all. She kept up a constant chatter, lapsing from Urdu to English to Urdu again as she unpacked her suitcase.

Mariam learnt from her that the weather in Pacifica (which was actually where Aasim's family lived, a fact that Mariam had never known all these years) was terrible at the moment. The fog was depressing and there was hardly any sun, so Faiza was a bit awed by the scorching heat in Vellore. Finally, Mariam raised her hand and stopped her. Faiza, who had just snapped shut her suitcase and was looking for a place to deposit it, looked at her surprised.

'What is happening here?' Mariam asked, surprise and excitement churning inside her chest.

'What?' Faiza asked, tucking a strand of hair behind her ear and smiling up at her. She was on her haunches as she pushed the suitcase below the bed. Finally, she brushed her hands, got up and sat down next to her, and suddenly gave Mariam an impromptu hug.

'How come… ' Mariam started, unsure if she would be able to even get the words out, her throat was so tight with tears.

'Oh, Dadi,' Faiza said, leaning into her neck. 'I'm so happy to be here!'

Mariam raised a hand and let it rest on Faiza's soft hair, allowing herself a smile.

'What brings you here?' she asked finally. Faiza sat back. Mariam looked at her and was amazed at how pretty this girl, who had both their genes, really was. She was stunning.

Faiza sighed and then looked down at the floor and then back up at Mariam sideways in a gesture that reminded her so much of Aasim, that she wondered if she would break down crying.

'They told me you were dead,' she started. Mariam's heart sank.

'They?' she asked.

'My nani, actually. My uncles, I never really asked them and we didn't end up discussing you of course.'

Mariam nodded, as guilt climbed up behind her back and mocked her. Faiza continued.

'See, I'm supposed to be getting married soon,' Faiza smiled at Mariam. How much this girl smiled! It was like having sunshine in the house, Mariam thought, responding with one of her own.

'We hadn't fixed the date yet but during one of those numerous meetings, one of my uncles asked my nani if they planned on calling you. That's how I got to know you're alive and live here in Vellore. And you know, I've done my Masters in History. Reading between the lines, looking at things that aren't there or are there is something that comes naturally to me. So,

I started digging around a bit and found out more about you.'

Mariam listened silently, wondering just how much she knew.

'I remember Nana and I remembered coming to India with him. It was all very vague and foggy and I don't know but for some reason, I felt something, here, in my chest, and I knew it wouldn't go away unless I came here, met and talked to you.' Faiza pointed a finger at her chest as she spoke and Mariam's breath almost stopped. Was this some sort of cosmic joke? This girl… was she real? Was she a dream, a figment of her most fervent desires? 'Of course, Nani thought I was mad. She insisted there was nothing left for me in India but I didn't believe her. I locked myself in Nana's study, went through his books and everything… in fact, I read all his books in one go and I'm stunned to know we had someone like him in our family.'

'You read the Urdu books he'd written?' Mariam asked, surprised.

Faiza shook her head. 'No, but I read the translations and the ones he'd written in English. 'If he'd lived, Nana would have given Jeffrey Archer a run for his money,' she grinned. Mariam had no idea who she was talking about, but she nodded.

'Anyway, so I went through everything he had written. I found out about you of course. That you are not just my Dadi, but also the great love of his life,' Faiza said simply. Mariam swallowed audibly and found that she couldn't meet Faiza's eyes.

'How?' Mariam asked, and Faiza snorted.

'Funny you should ask. I found this short story of his in an ancient magazine but it was in Urdu so I took it to my uncle to see if he could translate it for me. My uncle's Urdu was shaky so he sent me to a friend of his who read it out to me.

He mentions you by name, Dadi,' Faiza said and Mariam shut her eyes. That infamous story.

'So, I told Sam that if he wanted to marry me, he would have to wait until I went to India and saw you for myself.'

'You are just like your grandfather. And who is Sam?' Mariam asked.

'Sameer. The boy I'm marrying,' Faiza said with a smile that veered more towards sly than shy. Mariam wanted to know so much more and of course Faiza willingly obliged.

'He agreed of course. He's been in love with me since we were in sixth grade so there's no way he was going to refuse,' Faiza said with a laugh and Mariam stared at her, open mouthed.

'What did your nani say when you found out... '

'Oh, she was pissed. She was really, really mad at me. She didn't talk to me for days and for the first time in my life, I decided that it was okay. You are important to me too. And I'm almost twenty-four. I'm old enough to make my own decisions.'

'No, I meant, what did she say when she found that you had told Sameer to wait?' Mariam couldn't believe this girl had the temerity or courage to say such things. Faiza shrugged and scowled.

'I didn't want to get married until I knew everything about my own life. I loved my nana. And if he loved you, so naturally you are important to me too. But that's secondary. You're my grandmother!' Faiza ended with a shriek and hugged Mariam again.

'But... you're not judging him because he loved me?' Mariam asked, feeling uncomfortable.

'It's love. It's a feeling. How could he have helped it? And he was in love with you since the time you were kids!' Faiza responded and Mariam smiled ruefully.

'You children are very idealistic. That's not how things work out in real life,' she quipped.

'No, no! I'm not at all idealistic!' Faiza protested. 'In fact, I'm more cynical than idealistic, but finding out about you and nana helped me discover that there is your kind of love as well.'

'What kind is that?' Mariam asked, surprised.

'Eternal,' Faiza smiled, hugging her knees. 'To be honest I felt bad for Nani at first. I mean any woman in her position would be… it's just a sad thing to be caught up in.'

'Now what?' Mariam asked, still feeling as though she were living in a dream.

'Now you make me something to eat while I shower and change into something comfortable. And then you can tell me,' Faiza said, getting up.

'Tell you what?' Mariam asked, surprised.

'Everything!' Faiza winked.

Faiza made friends with Deepa within minutes and Deepa couldn't stop gushing about this newest entrant to their house. There wasn't a single moment of silence, of course, as Faiza helped Mariam and Deepa make dinner that evening. She talked about her college, her fiancé, her friends and then went on to talk about her secret ambition.

'What is this secret ambition?' Mariam asked as she stirred the contents of the pressure cooker. It had been so many days since she made a proper dinner that she wondered if she had forgotten how to cook. Deepa was kneading the atta for rotis and Faiza was shelling peas, sitting crosslegged on the floor, next to Deepa.

'I want to become a writer!' Faiza announced in a loud stage whisper, and Mariam turned around and laughed.

'Like *that's* a secret!' she said, as she added the masalas to the kheema she was cooking.

'Oh yes, it is. No one knows that I want to write. They all think that since I talk so much I'm going to host a show on TV some day,' Faiza said, making a face.

'Oh!'

'TV?' Deepa asked, fascinated, her eyes growing round.

'No, no! I'm not doing any TV shows. The only thing is that everyone thinks I can't keep my mouth shut long enough to write a book. But I'm going to show it to them!' Faiza announced, looking determined.

Mariam laughed again, amazed at how easy it was for this sound to emerge from her chest within a few hours of meeting this wonderful girl.

They had dinner together, the three of them sitting in the hall, watching TV, although Faiza's non-stop commentary drowned out everything. Finally, Deepa, annoyed that she couldn't watch her favourite Tamil soap in peace, switched off the TV. She instantly forgave Faiza though, not because she was so pretty, smelled so wonderful and had the most beautiful eyes Deepa had ever seen, but because she was Faiza, the girl whom Amma had told them about.

'I've got you gifts!' Faiza remembered when dinner was over and Deepa had cleared away their plates. Back in the room, Mariam sat down and watched with a bemused expression as Faiza pulled out an expensive-looking cream sweater from a thick plastic cover and handed it to her.

'For me?' she breathed although she didn't have the heart

to tell Faiza that the heat in Vellore would never allow an opportunity to wear it. But Faiza seemed to have realised that herself as she sat fanning her flushed face with a magazine.

'Fat lot of good a sweater would do you,' she muttered in English before pulling out a scarf from the cupboard where she had kept all her things.

'Here, try this scarf,' she suggested to Mariam, draping a rust-orange scarf on her head.

'I look like a fool,' Mariam protested as she pulled it off but Faiza insisted she try out some of the others she had. It seemed she had at least fifteen different ones, which she used to cover her head.

'No, no! I'll keep the sweater. I don't want your scarves!' Mariam said taking back the sweater from Faiza and hugging it close to her chest.

'Dadi, I didn't know about Deepa. I didn't get anything for her. Is it okay if I give her one of my perfumes?' Faiza asked, getting up to rummage in the cupboard.

'That girl is already worshipping you, ma! Why do you want to spoil her by giving her a perfume?'

'No, no! It's okay. I have too many as it is!' Faiza insisted and called out to Deepa to give her a bottle of Givenchy that was as good as new. Deepa was stunned, overjoyed, and touched beyond words.

Later when they had settled down for the night, Faiza mumbled something and Mariam rolled her eyes in the darkness. This girl can't keep quiet even when she's half asleep she thought, reaching out to gently push her hair away from her face.

'What did you say?' Mariam asked when she realised that Faiza was still awake and speaking to her.

'I said, I want to hear the full story tomorrow,' she mumbled before turning over and falling asleep promptly. We'll see, Mariam thought, happiness so predominant in her heart that she thought she'd combust.

chapter 48

Faiza walked into the room cradling a cup of tea in her hands. She stopped short on seeing an assortment of women sitting on the floor, busily crocheting what looked like a large bedspread. Mariam hadn't told her that there would be people in the house and she looked around, surprised.

'Wow!' she breathed. 'Dadi, do you run some cottage industry? I've read about those, you know, how women in India run these embroidery and handicraft units and how successful they are!'

The others looked up at her, their eyes round with shock. Who was this beautiful girl, tall and so confident that every word from her mouth dripped with self-assurance? Nimra looked at Mariam.

'Did she just call you Dadi?' she asked, her eyes widening again when Mariam nodded.

'This is Faiza?' Amreen asked, covering her mouth with her hand. Faiza looked at her in surprise.

'Heyy! You know me? Do I know you? I mean, am I supposed to know you? You know this happens to me a lot. I'm accosted by a lot of people at weddings and family gatherings asking me if they remember who they are when… '

'Faiza,' Mariam started, as the others stared at her amazed.

'God, she really does talk a lot,' Arifa muttered, unable to move her gaze from this girl who had now sat down cross-legged on the floor with them. Everything about her was larger than life. It was like having a film star in the house.

'So, what are you guys doing? Can I help? Oh I'd love to! Please? Let me try?' she said, as she leaned across and tried to see the bedspread better.

'No, Faiza, wait!' Mariam stopped her not sure how to explain to her or to the others why she was here. But Faiza had already launched into one of her talkathons describing her flight and how hot it had been in Chennai when she landed. She pronounced it 'Chinnayi', and Nimra started laughing.

'So, when did you come?' Shaista asked, smiling shyly at her.

'Last evening and boy! was it difficult to find this house. But thank god Nana had the address written down in one of his diaries and I brought it along with me or the auto driver who brought me from Katpadi to Dadi's house would have been spinning in circles. I didn't want to call Dadi and tell her I was coming. This was supposed to be a surprise, you see!'

'But aren't you getting married?' Nimra asked as Faiza paused for breath.

'Oh yes… wait a sec… how do you know that?' Faiza asked and for once, waited for the others to answer.

'We're making this for you!' Amreen said, pointing to the bedspread. 'It is Amma's wedding gift for you.'

Faiza turned and looked at Mariam in surprise. 'You mean, you knew I was getting married?' she asked.

Mariam nodded, feeling the first tinge of unease.

'Yes, your nani called up and told Amma about your marriage,' Arifa said and Faiza's head turned back to her.

'*Nani* called you? And how come these girls know everything?' Faiza asked Mariam, placing her tea cup carefully on the ground. Mariam was a little upset that Faiza hadn't even bothered to see the gift that the girls were making for her, but before she could tell her anything, Arifa spoke again.

'Your dadi told us everything.'

'She what? She told *you* guys everything?' Faiza asked, getting angry and Mariam looked around helplessly wondering why she looked so mutinous.

'Faiza,' Mariam began, looking around for help but was a little distracted because the girls and Faiza were not getting along as well as she had thought they would. If she'd known that Faiza would take offence, she would have told the others not to mention anything but they would have been just as annoyed.

'How much do you guys even know?' Faiza asked, pouting.

'Why are you so upset?' Amreen asked and Faiza shrugged.

'I don't know. It's a part of my life. *My* history. And you guys have heard it all, straight from her, while I'm yet to find out,' Faiza grumbled.

'Well, I can tell you in minutes what your dadi took two months to tell us,' Arifa said, putting down her crochet hook and looking at Faiza with a set expression. Mariam felt a gnawing fear begin to claw on her insides once again. Hadn't Faiza said that she knew everything? So why was she looking so angry?

'Your dadi and Aasim were childhood friends, they fell in love and realised it only on the day of your dadi's engagement to your dada. She got married and went her way while he got married and went his way. Oh, and before he got married, he left messages for her in crochet magazines, telling her how much he loved her and then he was the one who suggested they get their children married. Then, when your parents died, he brought you here and he asked her to marry him. She agreed and they were married for four years after which he died. End of story,' Arifa said, looking around smugly, glad that she too could compete with Faiza in the non-stop talking game. She didn't realise that Faiza's face had turned ashen.

'What?' she whispered, looking at Mariam, shocked. 'You *married* him?' Mariam knew then that the idyllic few hours that she had spent with Faiza were too good to be true.

'Tell me it's not true!' Faiza asked, getting up and sitting next to Mariam and shaking her thin wrist.

'Oh, it's true alright,' Arifa continued, unaware of the turmoil her words had caused, oblivious to the apparent discomfort of the rest.

Faiza covered her face with her hands and she shook her head. 'I… Nani told me I wouldn't like the truth. I… thought she was just dissuading me from coming to India!' Mariam could barely make out her broken words.

'I… thought you knew everything,' Mariam said, awkwardly patting Faiza's back. Faiza moved away her hand, almost cringing at her touch.

'Yes! I knew that Nana loved you. But not that he went to the extent of *marrying* you! Not while he was still married to Nani. God, that's sick! How could you?' she said, getting up and running away from the room.

Everyone turned to Mariam, who looked stricken. Just yesterday, Faiza had told her that she didn't judge Aasim, but apparently her compassion and understanding didn't extend to Mariam. Mariam didn't know what to think. She had long passed the age where she felt the need to defend herself.

'Why do you always have to be so blunt?' Shaista asked Arifa much to everyone's surprise. Arifa narrowed her eyes.

'What do you mean?' she asked.

'Couldn't you have explained it to her more gently?' Amreen asked.

'So, I'm always the one who gets it wrong, is it?' Arifa asked her angrily.

Mariam got up, her knees feeling wobbly as she made her way out of the room. She could hear the girls arguing with each other and she shook her head. Great. Now the girls, too, had developed animosity for one another. This wasn't how she had envisioned their last class would end. But she had to find Faiza first.

chapter 49

Mariam found Faiza on the dusty terrace, sitting in a corner, her head bent over her crossed knees. Mariam's knees ached from having walked up the steep steps and she looked around bemused, noticing that Deepa hadn't swept the terrace in months.

How different this terrace was from their terrace in Vellore, she thought. And yet there were those very mountains in the distance. She shuffled towards Faiza and wondered if she should sit down next to her before she carefully lowered herself to the ground. Her sari would be unrecognisable when she got up, she rued.

As a rule, Mariam avoided terraces because of the memories they evoked. She didn't know what she could possibly say to Faiza that would make things better.

'Your nana and I used to play on the terrace of my house in Vellore from the time his brother got married to my sister,' Mariam started. She looked at Faiza who gave no indication of having heard her. Stoically she continued.

'We were kids, Faiza. We didn't know it was love. We would have carried on not knowing it for the rest of our lives but like Arifa said, we discovered it on the day of my engagement.'

Silence.

'When I got married, I put him out of my mind completely. I was angry with him. See, I had asked him to run away with me before I got married, but he disagreed then. So, I decided it was easier to hate him than to love him.'

More silence.

With a sigh, Mariam told her about Raheema bu, about crochet and how those strands of yarn had tenuously kept her connected to Aasim over the years. Decades even. She could see that she had Faiza's interest by then because the girl had lifted her head fractionally.

'What was that about messages in the magazines?' she asked finally. Mariam bit her lower lip wondering if she should give her the details. Faiza had said that she loved her nana, but going by her reaction she was going to hate both him and her by the time the story was done.

'Shall we go downstairs?' Mariam asked, regretting the question immediately because Faiza put her head down on her knees again. So, she told her about how she had come across the magazines after her parents died, and how her nana had suggested that they could get their children married when they were old enough.

'Why? Why on *earth* would he suggest such a thing and *why* did you listen to him?' Faiza asked, looking up and glaring at her in a manner that reminded Mariam painfully of Aasim.

'I wish I knew. I don't know why, but at that time he probably thought it would be an ideal way to stay connected, I guess,' Mariam said.

'And poor Nani? She knew all this?' Faiza demanded. Mariam shrugged.

'I really don't know. I hadn't expected Aasim to actually follow through with the plan so I was just surprised when it happened,' Mariam said, looking at the sky, which seemed to be turning as dark as Faiza's mood. She could smell rain in the wind.

'Then why wasn't it enough? Why did you have to get *married* to him?' Faiza shouted, flinging her hands in the air. 'How could you do such a thing? How could you marry a man who has a wife and children? Where was your sense of self-respect? Just because Dada died conveniently?'

Mariam felt as though someone had punched her in the chest. Words eluded her and although she opened her mouth to speak nothing came out. It hurt. It hurt so badly to hear it from Faiza, for her to acknowledge that what they had done was wrong.

They sat in silence and Mariam looked at the sky a little in alarm because fat drops of rain had begun to fall.

'It's raining,' she said and Faiza looked at her and scowled.

Where has my beautiful, sunshiny granddaughter gone, Mariam wondered, feeling her lips tremble and her mouth form a grimace.

'I loved him, Faiza. But I had no intention of doing anything. Believe me. I refused him when he asked me at first,' Mariam spoke with difficulty. This was beginning to sound like she was laying the blame entirely on Aasim when it wasn't true.

'It's easy to get over someone when they're not in your field of vision. But when you keep seeing them, you wonder about what attracted you to that person in the first place,' Mariam began, hoping that Faiza would understand.

Faiza shook her head vehemently.

'He was married,' she enunciated and Mariam blinked.

'So, you mean to say that it was alright for us to love each other, but it was wrong for us to look for fulfillment of that love?' Mariam asked and Faiza nodded.

Her eyes welled up to match the rain and she got to her feet with great difficulty.

'Come down when you want to,' she said and made her way down carefully. Her sari was wet and the dust on the terrace floor had made ungainly patterns on it. She was surprised to see that the girls were still there, but it was probably because of the rain. She sighed unhappily when she saw that they all looked put out with each other.

'You girls are still fighting?' she asked as she walked to her cupboard and pulled out a fresh sari to change into. She changed her sari behind the cupboard door and emerged, feeling a bit like a butterfly escaping its chrysalis. She called out to Deepa to take her sodden clothes away and sternly told her to wash the terrace when the rain stopped.

'Why? The rain already washed it na?' Deepa shot back and Mariam shook her head.

'You will be ashamed when you see how dirty Faiza's clothes are after sitting on that terrace,' she said and the words had the desired effect. Deepa lowered her head and stared at the floor before taking away Mariam's sari.

'Is she okay?' Amreen asked Mariam who sat down on the bed once again. Mariam shrugged. She had already lived her life, made her mistakes and regretted them. 'Maybe we should talk to her,' Amreen suggested and Mariam couldn't help but smile wryly.

'Really?' she asked and Amreen's face flushed. She noted how the girls weren't looking at each other. The rain outside pounded harder and Mariam suppressed a flash of irritation at that stubborn girl. What if she fell sick?

'Here, show me what you've done,' she said to Nimra who was sitting the closest.

'Saira's mother said that I can't leave the house today,' she said and the others fell silent.

'And? How did you manage to come?' Mariam asked as she inspected the stitches closely.

'I told her that she could try and stop me,' Nimra shared the information coolly. Mariam looked up at her surprised. 'She told me that if I left, I won't be allowed to come back in.'

'And still you came?' Mariam asked, thinking of how different Nimra and Faiza were. Nimra, who used to be scared of her own shadow, had stood up to her stepmother and had decided to take charge of her own life. And she had been truly happy for Mariam when she heard her story. But Faiza, with all her confidence and attitude, seemed hypocritical. Mariam curbed the thought immediately. For Nimra it was just a story, but Faiza was involved in it in many ways. Also, she had lived with her nani all these years, and would naturally feel greater affinity and sympathy for her. Nimra nodded. 'I called Abba when I came here. He wasn't happy at all and he thinks I should listen to *her*. So, if I'm not allowed back there, can I stay with you here for some time?'

Mariam's eyes grew wide. 'Your father won't allow that. And how can you stay here? Where are your clothes and other things?' she asked.

'It's just till my uncle arranges my visa and everything. I brought my things,' Nimra said. Everyone looked around. There was no sign of a suitcase or bag.

'Where?' Arifa couldn't stop herself from asking.

'My bag with some clothes and my passport is near the main door. And I just took this and came,' Nimra said, showing a pretty butterfly-shaped brooch in pink stones.

'You foolish, foolish girl!' Mariam said laughing, feeling some of the pain ease from her chest.

At that moment Faiza chose to come inside. She looked like a chicken that had been doused with water and just as miserable. She slouched towards the cupboard from where she pulled out some clothes and went to the adjoining room to change.

'Why is she still angry?' Shaista asked into the silence.

'It was the shock,' Mariam said, looking in the direction in which Faiza had left.

'These second wives, they're always shocking people,' Arifa said with a sly look and immediately Amreen pounced upon her.

'Shut up! Just shut up!'

'Listen, she doesn't know the story of the bedspread,' Nimra said, looking at everyone, trying to rouse their interest.

'So? We did tell her we were making this bedspread for her, that ungrateful girl!' Arifa spoke.

'No, but she doesn't know about the old one. Maybe Amma should tell her about it,' Nimra suggested, looking at Mariam who shook her head.

'I'm tired of defending myself to her, Nimra. I didn't ask her to come here with the expectations of a beautiful but unfulfilled love story. Those few months with Aasim were the most wonderful ones of my life and I won't let guilt or regret take them away from me. No matter what she says. No matter what anyone thinks. I can't *undo* it now just to make her feel better,' Mariam said firmly. Only then did she look up to see

Faiza standing in the doorway, looking at her squarely, and Mariam steeled herself.

But instead of addressing her, Faiza sat down next to the girls and asked, 'What's the story of this bedspread?'

chapter 50

She never could resist a good story.

Whether it was the fairy tales that her uncles read out from hardbound books in ice-cream colours or the ones that she seemed to conjure in her head whenever she was bored, the promise of a good story could make her change her mind. Eventually.

Right now, she was upset and angry and couldn't fathom anything that could change the way she saw things. She knew she had led an uncomplicated life, thanks to her nani and her uncles and aunts who had provided her with everything she had needed, especially love. Her thoughts quickly jumped across to Sameer, the boy with whom *she* had been in love since sixth grade and not the other way around, as she'd told her dadi. For a moment, she visualised his golden-brown face, his crinkly eyes, his smile and his delightful laughter and wondered what it would have been like to not see him for decades.

The thought was too painful to harbour for long and she immediately abandoned it. But as she looked at her dadi, this woman who had existed between her grandparents, metaphorically and then literally, she didn't know what to think any more. She felt betrayed for some reason by everyone. First by her nani for lying to her, but then she also marvelled at how her nani had loved her, despite knowing that she was at least one quarter Mariam's. The anger shifted its focus to her nana, the man who had built a life for himself in Pacifica and then squandered it away because of his love for Mariam. And lastly Mariam.

From the time Faiza was a little girl, she'd known she was different. For one, she didn't have parents. She also didn't have any relatives on her paternal side and it used to annoy her, sadden her, and pull at her for some reason. Now years later when her dreams were about to be realised, she had discovered the existence of her grandmother in India. It had suddenly seemed vital that she come down and see her, talk to her before getting married.

Faiza backed into the wall, listening to the girls over the sound of the rain, and thought of how happy she would have been if she'd remained ignorant. Everything that she knew had changed in the past month. From her discovery of her dadi's existence to learning that her nana had loved her, it had taken time for her to come to terms with everything. But she'd tried to look at the situation from a historical and romantic perspective.

When she read her nana's books, and gleaned all the information from them, especially that short story, she had felt as though she had stepped back in time to a period when love had been whole and unblemished. The idea of her nana and her dadi being in love had boggled her at first. She'd even been amazed at the coincidence that her parents were who they were—children of these two lovers separated by time and distance. But now, after learning the rest of the story from Mariam, she knew that it had not been a mere coincidence but a meticulous plan.

She glanced at her dadi, wondering how much Mariam had contributed to *her* mental make-up and the kind of person she had become now. She chewed her lower lip, telling herself she was an easy-going person who always looked at the bright side of things. But it was no mean feat listening to the past and keeping a straight face, especially if the players in the story were intimately connected to her.

She looked around at the motley group of girls whose names she didn't know. There was a heavily pregnant girl sitting across from her, looking uncomfortable as she massaged her lower back. There was a dusky, pretty girl who kept throwing shy glances her way. Then there was that woman who had succinctly summarised her nana and dadi's love story. She couldn't make up her mind about the other woman who smiled at her every now and then. She was plump and had a pleasant face and looked friendly. She had no idea what they were talking about so she cleared her throat (it was one of the longest periods she'd gone without speaking) and they stopped.

'I'm sorry I was rude earlier,' she said, looking down at the colourful woven mat on which they were all sitting. 'I didn't even ask your names and you seem to know so much about me,' she murmured still looking down.

One by one they introduced themselves to her and she nodded, storing their names and faces in her memory. She wasn't yet comfortable facing her grandmother so she looked at what the girls were working on, for the first time, with some real interest.

'This is so pretty!' she exclaimed, feeling a little butterfly take flight inside her chest while sadness threatened to stomp on it with its dirty feet.

'This is nothing. You should see the one Amma had made for you when you were a child!' Amreen said.

'Can I see it?' Faiza asked slowly. Hadn't the girls said that this bedspread was Mariam's wedding present to her?

'Amreen, you know where I keep it in the cupboard. Take it out and bring it here,' Amma said and Amreen got up, a little surprised. When she unwrapped the cotton sari a little while later, Faiza got up and came closer to inspect it and although she didn't remember it, there was something remarkable about it. It was yellowing along the sides but there was a beauty and elegance to the stitches that spoke of painstaking labour and love that was hard to miss.

'It's beautiful,' she breathed as she ran her hands over the firm stitches, still finding that she was unable to meet Mariam's gaze. She looked at the girl nearest to her and smiled. It was Nimra.

'What we are doing is nothing compared to what Amma has done. But she can't see so well now and she taught us crochet so we could make this for you,' Nimra said with a smile. Faiza turned away trying to process the quickly churning thoughts in her head. Her grandmother had always known about her. Why hadn't she made an effort to contact her then?

Until an hour ago, Faiza had found it so easy to fling her arms around this woman who had technically been a stranger to her and yet, connected on so many levels. Now, she wasn't so sure. Her gaze still on the ground, Faiza asked her the question that had popped in her head.

'Why didn't you get in touch with me?' she asked the intricate pattern on the woven mat. The girls fell silent and she knew all eyes were on her, including Mariam's.

'After your nana died, your nani called Amma and told her not to contact you and to forget that you existed,' Arifa promptly blurted, and Faiza looked at her impatiently. The others too clucked their tongues.

'Is that the truth?' Faiza asked Mariam, finally looking up at her. Her dadi's face was wrinkled, mottled, old, but there seemed to be something that glowed in her very core and lit her face. It was love for her, Faiza realised belatedly, but she kept quiet.

'No matter what happened, I was going to lose you, Faiza. Your nani asked Aasim to divorce her and go live with me, but she wasn't going to let go of you. I told him to divorce me and give you to me. In the end, I lost both of you. She told me not to contact you and so I didn't,' Mariam ended, simply.

'What's so special about this bedspread?' Faiza asked, changing the topic because Mariam's words implied that her nani had deliberately cut off Mariam from her life.

She looked up at Mariam who had curled her lips inside her mouth and then swallowed audibly. She opened her mouth to say something but then she stopped. She sighed and then nodded to Amreen, saying, 'You tell her.'

Arifa looked put out but before she could talk, Faiza spoke quickly. She liked the look of this Amreen.

'Tell me,' she said, placing her hand on her arm.

'Remember those crochet magazines with the messages?' Amreen asked Faiza who nodded, feeling a little foolish that these girls had a better understanding of her past than she did. She continued listening as Amreen told her about what her nana had done, about how the magazine had never reached Mariam and how Mariam had recreated the bedspread by just listening to Aasim's description of it.

'She made it for you. When you were not even five years old,' Amreen ended, gently. Faiza sat in silence, having listened to the story, wishing she had not been a major player in it.

Nimra spoke in the silence, 'Put yourself in her place, Faiza, and tell me what you would have done?'

'She loved you and she loved Aasim. But I think she always loved you more. Why else would she have asked him to divorce her and give you to her?' Nimra wondered aloud.

They were two different things, Faiza understood. The love for her and the love for her nana. She had overheard what Mariam had said when she came in from the terrace, that she couldn't undo anything just to make her feel better, and reluctantly, Faiza agreed that she was right. It would take time but slowly and steadily, she would school herself to accept the facts that had been thrust on her so unpleasantly today. She wondered what Sameer would make of it when she told him and if he, too, would be as judgemental as she had been, but the idea of someone else judging her grandparents was not acceptable to her, she realised.

Her options were clear. She could either leave right away, catch the next flight to San Francisco and rush into Sameer's arms to tell him not to delay their marriage plans, or she could linger here for a few days, learn more about this intriguing woman who was her dadi and maybe even pick up some crochet skills along the way and *then* rush into Sameer's arms.

Knowing that Sameer was there, waiting for her no matter which decision she made, gave her strength. She thought of Mariam who had loved Aasim without expecting anything in return. Without any knowledge that there would ever be a happy ending for them. Without even hoping for one. So, who was *she* to tell her that she'd been wrong when Mariam had been given a chance with him?

She smiled at Mariam hesitantly, and it seemed as though everyone else around her let out a pent-up breath.

'I brought that magazine back with me,' she said, feeling all the unspoken words clog in her throat. Forgiving was not an option because she realised there was nothing to forgive. *She* was not the wronged party, and it would be a good thing if she remembered that every now and then.

To Faiza's continued bemusement, everyone gasped. They all knew which magazine she was referring to.

'The one which has story the Aasim wrote for Amma?' Arifa asked unnecessarily. Faiza nodded and all eyes turned to Mariam, wondering how she would react.

'It's been a little more than half a century. How could you have not read it even now, dadi?' Faiza asked, getting up. She pulled out her suitcase from under the bed and she could feel the hushed silence grow behind her, magnify into something that was large and awe-inspiring.

She picked up the yellowed magazine from the bottom of the suitcase and handed it to Mariam, only then looking at her face properly. Mariam took the magazine and turned the pages slowly. Faiza was getting impatient. Her hands itched to quickly open the page where the story began, but she waited.

'Every word that he wrote feels like a love letter to me,' Mariam said slowly. Faiza winced a little, but stayed silent. 'So what difference does one more story make?' she asked.

Faiza knew that Mariam didn't mean to sound flippant. She could sense it in the way Mariam's hand shook—the story was indeed very important to her. To her surprise, she handed the magazine to Amreen and asked her to read it out, aloud.

Amreen's face flushed. She took the magazine from her, opened it to the right page and cleared her throat.

'Remind me to buy a pair of glasses,' Mariam said, to no one in particular, as she held Faiza's hand and gave it a gentle squeeze.

Acknowledgments

The Sum of All My Parts is technically the fifth book I wrote. It's very close to my heart because of the various themes and because of Mariam, the woman at the centre of it all. Writing this book made me miss my grandmother all over again because she was the one who lovingly wielded her crochet hook to create beautiful doilies for us. Some thank yous are in order:

My family, for supporting me through my consistently crazy bouts of writing.

My brother, Junaid, for making me laugh because he thought Mariam wanted to make the girls into spies for a top secret save-the-world kind of project. (He was so disappointed on learning that it was not the case.)

My editor, Rashmi Menon, for sticking with this book and not letting it go.

Pooja Premnath, whom I reduced to a puddle of tears when I gave her the manuscript to read, and for saying it was one of my best books.

Smita Khanna Bajaj, for painstakingly editing this book.

Mishta Roy, for sweetly working and reworking the cover a million times until it was perfect.

Rupa Gulab, Madhulika Liddle, and Natasha Badhwar, for reading the book and giving such wonderful quotes.

Andaleeb Wajid has published sixteen novels in less than ten years. She writes in diverse genres—romance, YA, horror and recently, even children's fiction. Her novel *When She Went Away* was shortlisted for The Hindu Young World Goodbooks Award 2017, and also shortlisted at the MAMI Word to Screen, 2017. Andaleeb is a compulsive writer, constantly writing the next book either on her laptop or in her head.

The Sum of All My Parts is her seventeenth novel.